Murder in the Nudist Colony

An anthology of the best naturist crime stories

Murder In The Nudist Colony

Published by

Retired Eagle Books

Edited by Ted Bun and Will Forest

This is a work of fiction, and as a work of fiction, any resemblance to people, places or objects is entirely accidental. The creation of certain buildings and locations is entirely the work of the authors to avoid conflict and comparison with existing structures.

General notice.

This work of fiction deals with nudism and will mention nudity. It's sad that this has to be mentioned, as nudity should not be the shocking state that a person can be in, that's it considered these days. Note that this means nudity, not sex.

Cover Art Work

Retired Eagle Books

ISBN: 978-1-989019-22-1

Murder
in the
Nudist
Colony

An anthology of the best naturist crime stories

Murder In The Nudist Colony

Retired Eagle Books

Foreword

Early in 2020, naturist fiction author P. Z. Walker had the idea for a collection of mystery stories to be called "Murder in the Nudist Colony," deliberately using the antiquated term "nudist colony" for a slightly retro, humorous touch. On social media platforms, mostly Twitter, other folks associated with the fine network of naturist authors chimed in. Ted Bun put together the call for submissions, Robert Longpré set up the page to share documents as well as the ISBN, Fabien Barabé designed the cover… and we've ended up with fifteen submissions within a relatively quick timeframe. Ted and I volunteered to edit. The project has been a strong example of an online community working together!

The nudist "colony" as a setting for a murder mystery endures from at least the 1930s–with Peter Hunt's 1934 Murder Among the Nudists–if not earlier. What seems to fascinate is the peculiar juxtaposition of innocence and guilt: the innocence represented by nudity, and the guilt behind such a heinous crime. I know that my local nudist park, for instance, has hosted from time to time those mystery dinner parties where everyone assumes an identity and tries to solve a murder. In any case, this collection looks to be the first multi-author anthology featuring this particular focus.

And, this collection has it all! Stories set all over Europe and the Americas and beyond? Check. Naked murder victims? Check. Oddly clothed murder victims? Check. Victims murdered at the nudist resort? Check. Victims murdered elsewhere and then brought to the nudist resort? Check. Nudist murderers? Check. Non-nudist murderers? Check. Gendarmes, constables, cops and miscellaneous support folks who have to get naked to do their jobs at the nudist resort? Check. Same, but who choose to get naked at the nudist park? Check. And a long list of etceteras – you get the idea: theme and variations. It all makes for a very entertaining read!

And of course, like any good collection of mysteries, there are red herrings, bizarre details, spectacular suspense, gruesome finds, intriguing characters, oddly plausible motives, and much, much more! Get ready to be knocked off your bare bottom by some stellar stories!

Will Forest - Co-Editor and author

Charity

When the idea was being discussed, we had no idea which charity was going to benefit. Slowly we realised that to reflect the authors and the readership, we needed at charity that was:

- International in scope
- Unaligned to a belief system
- Unaligned politically
- Humanitarian
- Recognisable to the general readership

We selected Médecins Sans Frontières from the many good causes.

Médecins Sans Frontières/Doctors Without Borders (MSF) is an independent international humanitarian organisation that delivers emergency medical aid to people affected by armed conflict, epidemics, natural and man-made disasters or exclusion from health care in more than 60 countries around the world.

We are sure they would be delighted to receive any further donations to support their work.

Ted Bun - Co-Editor and author

Table of contents

Murder in the Nudist Colony

P.Z. Walker

"Isn't that weird?" Jeannie pointed at the floor near the toilet building. "Shoe prints." She and her friend Carla were there to clean the building that day, as per the roster they had set up with all the other nudists.

"Maybe someone had to go to the loo last night," Carla said, not really seeing a problem.

"Maybe, but… with proper shoes on?" Jeannie didn't understand it but since Carla didn't make a big deal of it, she decided to let it go as well.

The two made sure the toilet building was spic and span, and then they joined all the other naked people who were here at the Bare Tan Nudist Colony.

***

It was 1954, and everyone at Bare Tan was enjoying a wonderful summer's day. Bartholomew Sanders, Bart for friends, was strolling around to see if everything was in order in 'his' place. He had sort of inherited the nudist colony from his parents after they had deemed themselves too old to maintain it, and he was ever so grateful that he had done so. It was a joy to his heart to see so many happy people all around, carefree and enjoying themselves without the burden of clothing. In three years this place would be ten years old and Lucy, his wife, and he were already making plans for some kind of celebration.

"And still it's something that bothers me," he heard someone say. Bart looked around and saw Jeannie Smith talking to some friends. Jeannie's husband was on the chaise next to her and seemed to be asleep.

"What bothers you?" Bart asked. 'Bother' meant something was wrong and he was here to take care of that. Jeannie explained about the shoe prints she and Carla had seen that morning. "That is odd. I'll go and have a look. Thank you for telling me. Have a good day, folks!"

Bart sauntered along the neatly looked-after paths to the toilet building and started looking around, and indeed, despite the many sandal-wearers and barefoot-going people, he detected some deep footprints made by outside shoes.

"Is there a problem, Bart?" The man asking was Joe Rollins, somewhat of a friend of Bart's. Bart explained what he had heard and found and pointed at the proof. "Now that's crazy." Joe and Bart walked around the building, finding even more prints there.

"I think they go down there, Joe," Bart said, pointing over the lawn and to the fence that was almost fully covered in high-growing, crawling plants. Bart crouched down and found a few prints in the thin grass near the building. Towards the fence the tracks vanished but near the fence itself they found scrape-marks.

"Yep, they climbed up here," Joe agreed. "Couple of weirdos perhaps. Should we keep watch tonight?"

"Nah. They probably won't come back and if they want to go through all that trouble just to take a leak..." Bart shrugged. "Let's get back to business."

"Sure," Joe said. "For me that's doing nothing. For you that's work!" He clapped Bart on the shoulder.

***

Bart was a light sleeper. Therefore, it didn't surprise him that he woke up in the middle of the night. His wife was used to it and didn't even react to it. Bart checked his alarm clock. 2:19am. Not a good time to wake up, he thought to himself. Experience had taught him he should do something for half an hour and return to bed. Otherwise he'd be staring at the ceiling for hours and he would feel horrible the next day.

It wasn't his favorite thing to do but he got up, found his slippers and made his way out the bedroom without waking up Lucy. He paused at the bedroom door where his two sons were sleeping. All quiet. That was good.

Bart went outside. This was the time of the year to be outside no matter the time of day. It was a shame Lucy never warmed to the idea of sleeping outside. That would be wonderful, he thought, as he started walking along one of the paths.

That was when the shot rang out.

"What the hell?" Bart immediately was on full alert. Guns weren't allowed on the property, so this was a severe violation of camp rules. As he got his bearings as to where the shot had come from, lights came on in several cabins, and people came crawling from their tents, asking what had happened.

"I have no idea, folks," Bart said as he pointed, "but I think the shot came from that-away."

"Let's go there and see what's up," one of the woken-up guests said. Everyone agreed, so a group of over a dozen strong started walking to where Bart was sure the shot had come from.

As they progressed, Bart had the uncanny feeling they would end up at the toilet building. His feeling was right. The sole light over the door was on as usual. The door was wide open and the lights inside were on as well. "That's not right… Stay back, folks, let me have a look first."

He walked into the building and almost stumbled over a pair of legs sticking out from under the door of one of the toilets. He opened the door and saw a man lying there. The man wore a grey suit. His hat had fallen on the ground next to him. A large red stain spread out over the white shirt in the chest area.

***

"Yes sir, I am quite convinced he's dead," Bart said to the police officer on the telephone. "No, I didn't see who did it. I just heard the shot as I couldn't sleep. Very well, sir, I'll wait for them at the gate. Yes, sir, it's the Bare Tan Nudist Camp." He understood the hesitance in the voice of the police officer; it wasn't often they had to come out here. He hung up and looked at Lucy, who was holding their two boys. "The police are on their way. We're not to touch anything. I'm going to the gate to wait for them."

"Maybe you should put something on," Lucy said. "Because, you know."

"I know, but this is a nudist camp and they know it. They'll have to deal with it. Should I make everybody else put clothes on too? That would be something." With that, Bart walked out the door, carrying a flashlight, just in case.

He didn't have to wait long for the squad car to arrive. As soon as he spotted the vehicle, he opened the gate and waved them in. The car passed by. Bart frowned. Was that a woman police officer in the passenger seat?

The officers left the car and indeed, one of them was female.

"Mr Sanders?" the male officer asked, shining the light of his flashlight on Bart's naked body. "You're, ehm, not dressed."

"I am indeed Bart Sanders, officer. And this IS a nudist colony." Bart didn't feel he had to offer an apology for his appearance.

"Right…" The female officer nodded. "Can you show us to the crime scene?"

"Certainly. Follow me." Bart took the lead and walked to the toilet building. He heard the police officers whisper behind him but he didn't care. This was his terrain. "Here it is. We didn't touch anything, just like you asked."

A large group of curious spectators had assembled near the building by then. Bart hoped they hadn't gotten too close. There would be footprints of the dead man and probably of the killer too. As he thought that, he shook his head. A murder in a nudist colony. What was the world coming to?

Bart tried to make the crowd disperse so the officers could do their job, but his efforts were in vain. It seemed that the more people arrived, the harder he tried.

"Mr Sanders?" It was the female police officer. "Maybe you should, ehm, do something. There are children here." She nodded towards the crowd where Bart had also seen some of the teenagers. "NAKED children."

"I don't see your problem, officer," Bart said, keeping his composure. "They are here for their holidays."

"But they are not wearing clothes," the officer said, keeping her voice down, "and they see all those naked people."

"Jones, come over here," the male officer said. The female officer huffed and returned inside.

"Bart." Lucy, his wife, pushed through the throng. "What is all this?"

"Calm down, woman. We have a dead man in the toilet."

"We have WHAT?" She was loud enough to wake up the rest of the camp.

"Hush, Lucy. It's all under control."

"Bart! It isn't! Who died there? What happened?"

Bart had no other option than to wrap an arm around her and usher her away from the crime scene, while he explained what had happened. "And we don't know who the dead guy is," he ended his account. "I just hope they take him with them. It's not good publicity to have a dead man lying around."

"Mr Sanders?" The female officer walked up to them. "Can we use your telephone? We need to alert the County Coroner to collect the body. And can you make sure no one comes near the building until we have come back tomorrow to check for tracks and potential evidence? It's too dark for that now."

"Oh, sure. Lucy will show you to the telephone. But what do you mean by NO ONE GOING TO THE BATHROOM? We're just a small nudist colony. We only have one toilet building. I can't ask the guests to just not go until tomorrow!"

"I don't know. Can 't you dig a hole or something? Now I really need to make that call."

Bart looked at the woman as she walked off with Lucy. "Can you believe that?" He returned to the crime scene where the male police officer was talking to some of the guests, asking if they had heard or seen anything. No one knew more than what he already had heard though. There had been a shot. And a dead man. In the toilet.

The County Coroner was less surprised by all the naked people who were there. The man was all business as he and his assistant carried the stretcher over to pick up the murdered man. "Strange place to get shot," was all he said after going over some paperwork with the police officers.

Bart wasn't certain if the man referred to the toilet building or the camp but didn't ask. He just wanted all this behind him and perhaps to go back to bed for a few more hours. It was almost 5:30 in the morning and he'd been up for over three hours.

Most of the guests had returned to their beds already by the time Bart closed the gate. The police officers had been the last to leave. He guessed that others would come back in a couple of hours, to look for their precious evidence. They had a dead guy. What more evidence did they need?

He slipped into bed next to Lucy, who was still awake.

"Are you going to try to sleep?" she asked.

"That's the plan," he replied. "I'm still worried about people having TO GO."

***

Bart didn't fall asleep until it was time to wake up. He envied Lucy for being able to fall asleep so easily as he dragged himself out of bed and had a shower to wake up. As they were having breakfast, it occurred to him that more people were up already - and probably paying visits to the toilets.

"Drat," he muttered and conveyed his thoughts to his wife. "I should have put up a sign or something."

"Well, too late now," Lucy said. "I wouldn't worry about it. We can't tell people to do their business somewhere else. We don't have a somewhere else."

"Yeah. Maybe we should get another one. A combination of showers and toilets. We have more people coming in lately, so that would be good." That, however, was long-term planning.

After breakfast, Bart went to have a look at the crime scene, while he wracked his mind over what could have happened there that night.

Why had two people come here? What had been so bad that one of them had gotten shot?

People were waiting in line at the small building. Bart frowned. Hopefully they weren't there to see the blood splatters on the floor. He wished he could have that cleaned as soon as possible, but the police still had to show up. The camp owner was relieved to find that the guests were avoiding the crime scene. How fortunate that there were toilets on both sides of the building!

Around 9 am, two police detectives announced themselves at the gate. Lucy had warned Bart; they had called ahead, so he was there in time to let them in. These two also seemed surprised about Bart's lack of clothing, and again he didn't care.

"Mr Sanders?"

"That's me."

"Detectives Vogelberg and Mortimer. You had an incident last night."

"Well, that's one way to describe it. A guy got shot in a restroom." Bart showed them to the now deserted building. "Is there anything I can help with?"

"Not for now, thank you." The detectives got to work.

After almost an hour they were still at it. Bart wondered what took them so long when one of the detectives called out in surprise, "I got something."

"What's that?"

"A piece of paper." The detective seemed quite happy with his find.

Bart shook his head. That was all? A piece of paper? Cleaning the place would have made that show up much faster - and the toilet area would look good again too. "And what's on it?"

"It's rather cryptic," the detective said, holding up the paper. Bart glanced at it and read a few words. He saw a year, 1935, and GENERAL UNITED BANK. General United? He had heard of that, but that bank had gone under about a decade earlier. Not many people had suffered from that, as the bank hardly had had customers. Why would people be interested in that?

After another half hour, the detectives gave up their search and told Bart they had seen enough. "If we need more information, we'll come back, sir."

"Of course. I'll see you to the gate so you can leave."

***

"Lucy? We can go and mop up."

"Finally." Lucy was sitting outside, reading a newspaper. "Did they find anything?" she asked as she got up.

Bart told her about the paper and the few handwritten words on it and followed her inside.

"That's strange."

They got buckets with hot water and soap, and mops, and with those attributes they made their way to the toilet building.

"Wasn't there a bank robbery at General United in 1935?" Lucy said as they were busy cleaning away the blood and other residues.

"Was there?" Bart couldn't remember. "Oh, right." At least the bank robbery came back to him. How on earth did she remember that year?

"My dad had an account there back then," she explained, "and he feared everything was gone. After that robbery, he took all his money from the account and kept it at home."

"So much for trust in banks," Bart said as he carried out the bucket. The water in it was too red for his taste. "Do we need more water?"

"Don't think so. This is almost done…"

Bart emptied the bucket into the toilet and flushed the stuff away. With that job done, he made his way home.

After Lucy had returned, they made coffee and talked a little more about the strange writing on the paper. Why would two men from OUTSIDE come here, get into the toilet building and then one of them got shot?

"Maybe they knew something about that robbery," Lucy suggested.

"In the toilet of our nudist camp? There are better places to talk about that, honey." Bart shrugged. "I've got some more things to do."

"Okay dear. Don't find more dead people, please. It's so much extra work."

***

A few days later they got a call from the police station asking if two detectives could come over once more.

"Sure, no problem," Bart said. He would be at the gate to see them in. He hoped it would be the same two who had been here before. They seemed okay people. They also hadn't appeared too upset around nudists. "Did you discover something interesting?" He was told that this was police business and therefore the person on the other end couldn't give him more details.

"We'll see about that," Bart told the phone after hanging up. There was some time before the cops would show up, so Bart went outside and enjoyed the wonderful weather as he made a round to check on things. Lots of folks were around and in the pool. ALL THOSE ADAMS AND EVES, he thought to himself, appreciating how well his little nudist camp was occupied. Maybe they should expand. More and more membership applications were in and there simply wasn't enough space. If they were to expand, they would definitely need another washroom and toilet building. Bart rubbed his chin. One where people wouldn't get killed.

The detectives - they were the same ones - arrived late. Bart felt a bit silly, waiting there at the gate, but when they arrived and explained about the flat tyre, it was clear what had caused their delay.

"As we were fixing the tyre, we talked about this place," one of the men said. "It's intriguing."

"If you say so," Bart responded. "For the people here it's just relaxing."

"Yeah, obviously," the other detective said. "So I was wondering if it would be okay for us to take off our clothes while we do our job here. And I do ask this in confidence. We don't want people at the police station to know about this. If we do it at all."

"Ehm. Joe." The first detective looked worried. "Are you really going to do this?"

"Matt, we talked about this." The detective called Joe looked at Bart. "So, would it be okay?"

"Of course," Bart said. "The less you wear, the more you will blend in. With that garb on you stick out like a sore thumb."

"I hope I'm not gonna regret this," said Joe, as his partner looked in horror how he started taking off his clothes. He tossed them in the back of their car.

Detective Matt shook his head but remained silent. Joe grabbed a small case and with that they walked off to the toilet building.

"I had it cleaned," Bart said as they arrived there. "Because, you know..."

"Of course," said Matt. "No one likes to use the facilities when there's blood all over."

"Exactly."

"We have done some investigating as to what the words on the paper meant. The bank, the date."

Bart nodded and told the two what Lucy and he had come up with so far.

"That's entirely right, sir," Joe said. Matt had fallen silent. Bart had a quick thought that the man's clothes seemed to stifle him. "The money taken from that bank has never been found. We discovered who the murdered man was, and he proved to be connected to the bank robbery."

"What? He didn't look old enough for that," Bart said.

"Indeed, but one of his uncles was, and that man was not a stranger to the police in his days." Joe explained how easy it had been for them to find this man. "We don't have much evidence yet, but we suspect that these two men were here for the stolen money."

"Here? In a toilet?" Bart had heard many weird things in his life but this was way at the top of the list.

"Not in it, sir." Matt finally broke his silence. "We think it's beneath it. Somewhere under or close to this very building. It's the only explanation we can come up with for why they were here."

Joe took over. "Somehow they must have found some paperwork from their uncles or fathers which led them to believe the stolen money was hidden here."

"Right." Bart frowned. What was all this? And what if they were right? Were they going to tear up the only toilet building of the camp to find that money? Could they actually do that? "And that means what?"

"Actually we are here to ask your permission to dig under the building, sir. It's a difficult situation, we understand that, since it's on your property."

"And then there's the..." Joe shut up as Matt shot him a look, but Bart insisted on knowing what Joe had started to say. "There's the fact that by today's standards, the amount of money stolen isn't that high. Our experts aren't sure if tearing down and rebuilding the, ehm, facilities would justify what money will be recovered, if there is indeed any. Records from the insurance companies show that it wasn't a fortune, and everyone was reimbursed the year after the robbery."

"I see," Bart said. "Well, nothing's going to be ripped open now. We're in full season, there are guests everywhere and this is the only toilet building available."

"Of course. We understand. We just wanted to come over and tell you. Ask your viewpoint. If you don't want this particular operation to continue, we will tell our supervisor." Joe, the naked detective, nodded at Bart, then turned to his partner. "I told you so. Let's go back and finish the report."

Bart escorted the two men to their car and watched them drive off after Joe had dressed again.

***

In the autumn all guests had left.

At the nudist camp there was a lot of activity; a company was building two new toilet buildings, with modern showers and all kinds of amenities to make nudist life even better.

Where the old toilet building had been, was now a statue of a nude family. Their marble presence was a beautiful sign of their lifestyle.

Bart and Lucy were waiting for their new car to be delivered.

A question of sex

A short story by James Gault

'The law is a profession for men. Judges, *notaires*, advocates; they do not like to have lady lawyers. And the *juges d'instruction*, the examining magistrates, they too are misogynists.'

Sophie Rousseau, newly qualified French *juge d'instruction,* believed this passionately. She was convinced it was why she had been banished from her home city of Paris and deposited in the middle of an unfriendly forgotten corner of southwestern France. Either that, or it was the revenge of her ex-boss and self-appointed protector: a lecherous senior judge who leered incessantly and at the slightest excuse placed uninvited hands on her leg.

"You have good fortune, Sophie. It is a small jurisdiction, yes, but it is for you alone. You will investigate all the cases in your area. It is quite an opportunity for one so young," he had assured her.

He hadn't told her that her area had the lowest crime rate in the country; that there were no cases to investigate; that the gendarmes knew all the criminals, who invariably confessed when challenged. She found herself doing nothing more demanding than filling in forms all day. So her heart leapt when she read the slip of paper she had just been given.

'Suspicious drowning at Freedom Holiday Centre, please attend and meet Lieutenant Beaumont. Montpellier Tribunal.'

At last! A long–awaited chance to prove herself. 'Please God,' she hoped, 'it wouldn't turn out to be just a simple accident.' The Satnav app on her phone located the place for her; it was fifteen minutes away.

***

The Freedom Holiday Centre looked more like a prison than a palace of pleasure to Sophie. Located on the edge of a *lotissement* just outside the village, the property was surrounded by a high wall and protected with large security gates and a heavy entrance door of solid wood. Sophie wondered what the inmates were supposed to be 'free' from. She was soon to find out.

The door opened by itself when she pushed the bell. The woman in the reception area stopped tapping on her computer to welcome her, in English.

"Hello, welcome to the Freedom Centre. How can I help you, my dear?"

Sophie was taken aback. Not so much by the English - she should have expected that from the name of the place. What was really troubling her was the woman's clothing: a towelling bathrobe. The way it hung on her body made Sophie think she had nothing on underneath. It seemed an odd way to dress for a lady of around sixty in some sort of receptionist role.

"I'm sorry, don't you speak English? *Je peux parler Français.*" the bathrobed lady asked, misinterpreting her hesitation.

"No, it is not a problem. I speak English well. My name is Sophie Rousseau and I am a *juge d'instruction.*" Sophie showed her warrant card. "You have had an incident, I am told. I have to meet a gendarme lieutenant here."

"Ah, yes. What a to-do, I must say. Your colleague is at the swimming pool, with goodness knows who else. The whole world has descended here this morning, it seems. Not that I would know much about it; no one ever tells me anything. My husband is dealing with it, I'll call him." She lifted her mobile, pressed a key and announced, "Jeffrey, there is a young lady here to talk to you. It's about the … unfortunate event." Then she turned to Sophie. "He'll be with you in a second, my dear."

The husband appeared almost instantaneously. Sophie watched wide-eyed as he came in. He was totally naked. He pulled up a chair in front of her and introduced himself. "Jeffrey Whyte. My wife and I run this little naturist centre."

Sophie took out a notebook and tried as hard as she could to keep her eyes focussed on his face. "Could you tell me what happened, please?"

Whyte frowned. "I have a business to run. I already gave all the details to your colleague."

"I am the one in charge of the enquiry, sir. As for my colleague, he will be helping under my supervision."

"She!" Whyte corrected her.

"Excuse me?"

"She. Your colleague is a woman."

Sophie was angry with herself. She had automatically assumed anyone with the rank of lieutenant in the Gendarmerie would be a man. She had the feeling that she had betrayed her gender, but put it down to the distraction of having a naked man sitting across from her. "In any case, I'm afraid you must give me all the information again," she insisted.

Whyte exhaled his exasperation, and began to retell his story in a pained voice. "I went to the pool at seven this morning and saw a body floating in the middle of the water. It wasn't what I expected to see."

"You don't expect people to go swimming so early in the morning?"

"No, it's not that. The man was wearing a business suit. Here, people don't wear anything when swimming."

"Did you recognise this man?"

"No, he was floating face down. I called the gendarmes immediately."

"And you did not try to take him from the water to see if he was alive?"

"He wasn't moving. He was just floating. I was sure he had drowned."

Sophie frowned, it seemed too calm a reaction to her. "Anything more you can tell me?"

"No, sorry. I waited here for the police to come, and then they took over. So you'll need to ask them."

"I will. Thank you. Can you take me to the gendarmes?"

He took her through the back door of the reception room into the complex. On the left was a car park, and on the right the other wing of the building she had just left. There was a *terrasse* with chairs and tables, probably where the guests ate. The swimming pool in front of her had a line of chalets down each side, but the pool itself was screened off. A euphemistic sign said: 'Closed for Cleaning'.

An elderly man and woman appeared from one of the chalets, dressed in nothing but suntans to die for. The man hailed Whyte. "Jeffrey, what's this nonsense with the pool being closed? Not that I mind for myself, but poor Di didn't get her usual morning dip. Did you, dear?"

The woman smiled obediently and looked at the ground. Sophie hated to see women behave so submissively. Why couldn't this woman speak for herself?

Whyte made his excuses. "Sorry for the inconvenience, Jonathon. I found something in the pool this morning so I thought it best to get it cleaned, just in case. Can't be too careful when the wellbeing of our guests is at stake, I'm sure you'll agree."

"Hmmph! I trust you'll have it all up and running soon," Jonathon grumbled, and led his wife off to the *terrasse*.

"That's them all now," Whyte said to himself.

"Them all?"

"Our guests. We only have six at the moment and they're all at breakfast now. Whoever it was in the pool, it wasn't one of them. Look, your colleagues are behind the screens there, I need to go and serve my guests. Can you find your own way?"

Sophie nodded and passed through the screens. There was a hive of activity round the pool. A forensic team was lifting fingerprints, and over in a corner a doctor and a gendarme were examining something under a sheet. The gendarme saw Sophie and walked over to her. Sophie remembered seeing the lieutenant around the office. A tall dark-haired woman about her own age; a whiff of Chanel among the testosterone. Sophie recalled wondering if they could be sisters-in-arms: two females fighting it out in a man's world. Perhaps they would now.

"Hi, I'm Laure Beaumont. You'll be..."

Sophie interrupted. "Sophie Rousseau, I am your judge on this case. I'm so relieved to meet someone wearing clothes."

Laure smiled. "Don't worry, you get used to it."

Sophie looked puzzled. "What do you mean?"

"I used to feel the same when I first started going swimming at the naturist beach at Cap d'Agde. But now I don't notice any more."

It struck Sophie that perhaps Laure wasn't quite what she had imagined. But they had a job to do. "I understand the victim was found drowned at 7 a.m., floating face-down in the pool. He was wearing a business suit."

"She!"

"Excuse me?"

"She, not he. The victim is a young woman. And when you say 'wearing a business suit' it is a little... exaggerated. She was wearing only a shirt, a jacket and trousers, all far too big for her. Nothing else. No underwear, no shoes or socks. And there are some signs of bruising around her neck."

"What does the doctor say?"

"As usual, nothing for certain. She probably died yesterday, in the morning; she may have been strangled; perhaps she did not drown. He cannot be sure, you know. He has to do tests."

"She is dead, though?"

"Oh yes. He did confirm that."

"Any identification?"

"Nothing in the clothes, and she was naked underneath them."

"Oh my God. Do you think it was some weird sexual act?"

"Could be."

Sophie thought for a moment. "We need to find out if anyone here knows her. We'll bring the staff and guests in one by one and show them the body. After that, you and I will interview each of them in turn. Agreed?"

***

After the forensic team had gone off with their samples and the doctor had gone back to the morgue with the body, Sophie and Laure finished interviewing the staff and guests. They had all gone to bed after their evening swim. No one had heard or seen anything during the night. And none of them had recognised the victim. So now Sophie and Laure were discussing where they were with the enquiry and what they should do next.

Sophie summed up the case so far. "We have an unidentified female victim, around twenty, perhaps strangled yesterday morning. She was then dressed in a man's clothes and thrown into the pool during the night, where she was discovered at seven this morning by the owner."

"We cannot even be sure where she was murdered. She was maybe killed here and hidden until night time; or else she could have been murdered somewhere else and her body brought here and dumped," Laure added.

"If the murderer was someone who is staying here, one of our witnesses is lying. What do you think?"

"One can never be sure, of course. But I just had a feeling they were all telling the truth."

"Yes, I did too. But two of them might have been in it together and they made up a story for us. Anyone who is capable of murder will be good at lying too, no?"

"Well, we'll know a bit more once we have the report from forensics. They've taken fingerprints and DNA samples," Laure informed her.

"Yes, that might get the residents here off the hook. Now, let's consider the second possibility: that she was killed somewhere else and the body brought here."

"It doesn't make sense, I think, Sophie. For two reasons. Why would the murderer bring her body here, where it will certainly be found? And who would know about this place? The high walls hide everything inside the complex."

"You're right. It couldn't have been a stranger. It must be someone who had already been inside and knew the layout. Ask Whyte for a list of all the people who have ever holidayed here."

Laure had another suggestion. "I saw a security camera on the gate. It may have a recording facility. It's possible?"

"We'll ask. And perhaps the village has some CCTV coverage for parking and speeding. We might find something useful there too."

***

It was only twenty-four hours since she had been called to the Freedom Holiday Centre and Sophie was feeling very pleased with herself. In Laure, she had found someone it was a pleasure to work with and she'd made a breakthrough on her first big case. The forensic and doctor's reports were on her desk, and she was waiting for Laure to bring what she claimed was exciting news from the CCTV footage.

Her office door opened and Laure strolled in, a big file in her hand and an even bigger smile on her face.

"I think we have our man, Sophie. Did you see the post-mortem and the forensic reports?"

"Yes. The unidentified girl was killed between 9 a.m. and noon on Tuesday, the day before she was found in the pool. She was strangled, and the marks on her neck were caused by a rope. There were no traces of any sexual activity, but there was one perhaps significant piece of news: she was ten weeks pregnant. Also, there were no fingerprints or DNA of the people at the centre on her body or on her clothes. So someone else probably killed her."

"I agree. And I believe we may know who that someone else is. We've been very lucky with the CCTV. The village cameras caught a large Mercedes driving into the village at two ten a.m. and back out at two thirty. The pictures were very dark, but we used image enhancement and this allowed us to just make out the number plate. It was a vehicle from Burgundy."

"But we don't know where this car went in the village, or that it had any connection with the holiday centre," Sophie pointed out.

"Well, we have two further clues. The security camera footage Mr Hyde gave us shows a large car stopping outside the gate of the complex. The gate opens and the driver takes something large and heavy from the car and carries it inside. He comes out again ten minutes later, empty-handed, and drives off."

"Can we be sure it's the same car?"

"No, the recording is very fuzzy. But it looks very similar to the car in the other video, and the times match: two fifteen to two twenty-five."

"It's not conclusive, though, is it? And how could the driver of the car open the gate, unless someone was waiting for him?"

"I'm afraid Whyte's not very security-minded, he gives all his guests the code to the gate. And we traced the owner of the car and checked it against Whyte's list of guests. The owner stayed at the centre in June this year."

"Did he come to the centre on his own?" Sophie asked.

"No, with his wife."

"What is this man's name, Laure?"

"He is called Maitre Alain Verdier, and he's a *notaire* in Dijon."

"I think we'd better speak to him as soon as possible," she announced. "It'll take about eight hours to drive up there. We'll interview him this evening and come back tomorrow. I'll need to call the Dijon authorities and arrange for a couple of their policemen to come with us to the interview. It's a pain, but rules are rules."

"You're too tied up by rules, Sophie. You should try breaking some, and come nude bathing with me this weekend."

Sophie's face broke out in a noncommittal smile. "Thanks, but swimming with no clothes on is not for me, I think."

***

That evening, Sophie and Laure, with their two local minders from the Dijon police beside them, rang the doorbell of the Verdier home.

They were rewarded by a shuffling noise and an unseen woman's voice. "Who is it?"

"Police, we need to talk to you," one of the two Dijon police officers shouted.

The voice behind the door whimpered, "My husband's not in."

"We'll wait for him. May we come in?"

"He doesn't like people in the house when he's not here. Can you come back later?"

Sophie sighed. "Look, we've come a long way. Will you open the door or will we need to bring a warrant?"

The door creaked and, through the narrow opening that was created, a middle-aged face appeared and inspected its visitors. Mme Verdier must have been reassured by the police uniforms, because she pushed the door wide. "I suppose you'd better come in, but he won't like it."

She showed them to a large living room and they spread themselves around the sofas. Mme Verdier sat in a chair in the corner, as if she was trying to disappear.

"When do you expect your husband back?" Sophie asked her.

"I don't know. It could be anytime. He comes and goes as he pleases, and he tells me nothing."

"Was he at home two days ago, on Tuesday?" Sophie was trying to establish if Verdier had an alibi. The three police officers produced their notebooks in unison, and waited with pens poised.

"He left for work very early, around seven. He didn't come home that night at all. I didn't see him again until last night."

"Didn't that seem unusual?"

"No, he does it all the time. My husband considers himself a very busy and an important man in the community. He tells me I am here to serve him, to cook and clean and be there whenever he needs me."

Sophie wasn't sure whether she was exasperated or sorry for this woman. She glanced over at Laure who had an eyebrow raised.

Sophie carried on. "Mme Verdier, do you know the Freedom Holiday Centre in Azillanet, in the Herault department?"

"Why would I know anywhere so far away from anything?"

"You weren't on holiday there last June with your husband?"

"I never go on holiday. My husband doesn't like to travel; he has to be away so much with his work. And every June, he goes to his law convention."

Sophie noted that Laure's eyebrow was raised again. They must both be thinking the same thing. Whyte's list showed M and Mme Verdier had stayed there. Had someone else been impersonating the couple? If so, were they on a wild goose chase? Sophie needed to know if the Verdiers really had any connection with the case. She made up her mind. What she was going to do was risky, but they had to know. Taking out her phone, she pulled up the picture of the dead girl's face and showed it to the witness.

"Do you recognise this woman?" she asked.

Mme Verdier's face paled, and when she finally spoke it was in a strained whisper. "It's Nathalie, my daughter. Where is she?"

This was awkward. Now they would have to tell the woman that her daughter had been killed. Sophie played for time.

"So her name is… Nathalie… Verdier." She was writing it down.

"No, Nathalie Collier. She's my daughter by my first husband. Where is she?"

Still stalling, Sophie asked, "When did you last see her?"

"Over a year ago. There was a family quarrel. My husband and Nathalie didn't get on, and she left home. She was at university here in Dijon, it was a stupid decision. Living here was very convenient for her. Why do you have her photo?"

Sophie continued to ignore her questions. "Do you have her new address?"

"No. Has she done something bad?"

"You never tried to find her?"

"He would not allow it. He said she could come back here if she wanted, but we would not go looking for her. She had made her decision. If there was to be a reconciliation, she would have to make the first move. Please, tell me where she is. I miss her so much."

Sophie swallowed hard. She shouldn't have shown Mme Verdier the photo, and now she couldn't avoid passing on the bad news any longer. "Mme Verdier, please prepare yourself." Sophie saw the woman's eyes widen with fear, and wished she didn't have to say what she had to say. "I am sorry to have to tell you your daughter has been murdered."

The woman broke down in tears. Sophie had got herself into a bit of a mess. Good practice demanded that Mme Verdier be consoled, but for the sake of the investigation it was also important that she did not speak to her husband before he had been interrogated. Sophie whispered to the Dijon policewoman who had come with them. "Take her into the other room and look after her. We'll stay here and talk to the husband."

Verdier turned up at the house some ten minutes later. They heard the car draw up in the drive and the door slam, but they waited until he came into the living room.

When he saw them, he began to shout. "What are you people doing here in my house? Where's my wife? I've told her so many times never to let strangers in here when I'm out. Carole!"

"Please sit down," Sophie spoke very calmly. "Your wife is with one of my colleagues."

"Who are you? What right do you have to come into my home?"

"My name is Sophie Rousseau, I'm a *juge d'instruction*, and I'm investigating a case. We think you have some important information that might help us."

Verdier began to bluster. "You have no right. I have nothing to say to you."

"As you wish, M. Verdier. We can talk here, or my friends here will arrest you and we can all talk at police headquarters. In either case, you will help us."

Verdier sat down, scowling.

"Where were you two days ago, on Tuesday?" Sophie began.

"I was at work, as normal." His tone was defiant.

"When did you leave home?"

"The usual time. No, a little bit early, around seven. I had a lot of work to catch up on."

"You went straight to your office? You did not go somewhere else first?"

Verdier reddened. "What are you trying to suggest? Of course I went straight to the office. I had just begun to work when one of my friends from another practice called me. He was going to a conference in Lyon with a business partner, but the partner had called in to say he was ill. My friend knew that I very much wanted to go to this conference, so he asked me to take his colleague's place. We drove in my car to Lyon. After the conference we drove straight back."

"Who was this man you went to Lyon with?"

"Maitre Martin. I have his card here." Verdier pulled out his wallet, withdrew a business card and handed it to Sophie, perhaps a little too eagerly.

"Can anyone else confirm you made this trip?"

"My partner Jules. I told him I was going, as he had to take an appointment for me. He waved us off from his office window. He can confirm that." At this point, he lost patience again. "Why are you quizzing me like this? I'm a person of some standing in this community, I'd have you know."

"So your wife told us. Nevertheless, we have reason to believe you have information relevant to our enquiry and we need to question you. When did you get home?"

"I don't like late nights, I'm a pillar of the community. Eight, eight-thirty."

"That's strange, M Verdier. That is not what your wife said, is it, Lieutenant Beaumont?" Laure nodded.

"You shouldn't listen to anything my wife says. She's a bit, shall we say, forgetful. She's not really part of our world at all. I do my best to protect her, but..." Verdier shrugged his shoulders.

Sophie found this man's attitude to his wife was upsetting her in spite of her professional training. But she pressed on; time to change the topic and throw the suspect off guard.

"Do you have any children?" she asked.

The question seemed to surprise Verdier. "No," he replied, after a second or too.

Sophie frowned. Strictly speaking he was right, but she felt sure he was trying to hide something.

"Stepchildren, then?"

"No."

"What about Nathalie?"

Verdier didn't say anything at first, and when he did, his voice was condescending. "I do not consider her part of my family any longer. She was bringing disgrace to our good name."

"So you don't know where she lives now?"

"No."

Time for Sophie to change tack again. "I see. And you came home around eight on Tuesday evening. Did you go back out that night?"

"No."

"Hmmm. That's strange. Could you explain how your car came to be seen in the village of Azillanet in Herault Department at 2 a.m. the next morning?"

Verdier started to bluster again. "It wasn't me. I was at home at that time. Someone must have made a mistake. And I don't know this Azillanet place; I've never been there in my life."

Sophie looked at Laure and nodded.

Laure took this as a signal to play 'hard cop'. "M. Verdier, we have CCTV footage of your car in the village. We have a video of you carrying your stepdaughter's body, dressed in a man's suit, into the Freedom Holiday Centre there. It would be better for you if you stopped making up fairy stories and told us the truth."

She had perhaps exaggerated the quality of the evidence, but the ploy paid off. The colour drained from Verdier's face and he sat for a long time looking at the floor. Eventually, he seemed to regain some of his composure, and he became more cooperative and contrite in his attitude. "I've been very stupid. I ask you to forgive me, but with the stress and worry I wasn't able to think straight. I'll tell you truthfully what happened.

"My stepdaughter is like her mother, very disturbed. It's been a trial, but I've been trying to look after them both, and keep them apart. They are not good for each other. On Tuesday morning, I went to check up on Nathalie at her flat. I found her hanging from a rope tied to the chandelier. She was dead. I panicked. I couldn't let her mother find out, and there was the family reputation to consider. I had to cover up this tragedy. So I disguised her in a man's suit and drove her to Azillanet. I was sure nobody would know her there and it would all be forgotten about."

"My God. Why did you not call the authorities? How could you possibly have known she was dead?"

"There was a suicide note."

"Where is it?"

"I destroyed it."

Sophie was speechless. Could she really believe that a qualified lawyer could act like this?

"Where did you get the man's suit?"

"I went to a nearby hypermarket and bought it."

"Do you have a receipt? Did you use your bank card?"

"I paid cash and threw the receipt away."

This was too much for Sophie, who turned to Laure. "Do you believe this story?" Laure shook her head. "What about you?" she asked the Dijon policemen who had been listening and talking notes the whole time. He too shook his head.

"Nor do I. M. Verdier, you will need to come with us. We will be investigating your story further, but in the meantime we are taking you into custody."

***

It took until the next morning to extricate Nathalie's address from her evasive stepfather, and then to organise the forensic team. Sophie and Laure went with them to the house, which Verdier claimed to be a let shared by Nathalie and three other female students. There was no one there when the police team arrived. Sophie and Laure followed the scientists around, making sure not to get in their way. It wasn't the tiny student apartment they had expected, but a large mansion set in its own grounds. There were four bedrooms upstairs above two public rooms and a kitchen. Sophie wished she could have had the use of a place like it when she was a student.

On closer inspection, the house revealed secrets that made it appear less of a paradise than it had seemed at first sight. For one thing, there were the contents of the cupboards in the living rooms. The two girls watched the forensic team pull out a variety of objects and lay them carefully on the floor. There were about a dozen ropes, of various thicknesses, one of which could have been the murder weapon. Then came two pairs of heavy ankle irons and handcuffs. This esoteric collection was rounded off by a large goblet and two long daggers, all in pure silver, each one engraved with a strange insignia: a black eagle in a starry sky carrying a pair of swords. None of them knew what it could mean.

The wardrobes in the bedrooms too were a revelation. The police teams found girls' clothes in each, exactly the kind of items you would expect in rooms occupied by young female students. But they also discovered two or three men's business suits and shirts of various sizes in each room. The suits were all an exact match for the one found on Nathalie's body. Like some sort of uniform. But the most disturbing finds were the hooded cloaks. There was one set of these for each suit and an extra one, which Sophie guessed belonged to the suit found on Nathalie's body. The cloaks were made of a fine black silk that reminded Sophie of judge's robes, and they were all adorned with the same mysterious insignia engraved on the chalice and the daggers: the eagle bringing retribution?

When these items were shown to her, Laure whistled. "What's been going on here?"

"I don't even want to imagine," Sophie replied.

"I think we'd better find out who owns the property," Laure said, taking out her mobile. She called the police office and asked them to check it out.

"Let's find out if the neighbours know anything," Sophie suggested.

They left Forensics working hard and walked round to the next house. Luckily, a woman answered the door. They showed their warrant cards.

"Good morning. I wonder if you could help us, Madame?" Sophie asked. "Could you tell us anything about the house next door?"

The woman shrugged. "I have never been there. I believe that it is let to four girls. We see them go in and out from time to time, with their books in their hands. Maybe they are students. We do not ask; they do not say."

"Are they noisy? I know what students are like," Sophie prompted.

"No, for us, they are good neighbours. They do not make much noise; there are no wild parties and loud music at night. They seem to be very serious young women."

"Do they get many visitors?"

"Now and then, some older men come. Perhaps the owners to ask for the rent? Or perhaps their fathers, making sure they are all right? We do not ask; they do not say." The neighbour shrugged again, emphasising her ignorance.

"No young men of their own age?"

"The boy friends, you mean? We have not seen any. They seem very good girls."

"Have you seen the girls in the last two days?"

"No. But perhaps it is the end of term? Perhaps they have gone home to their families? We do not ask; they do not say."

Sophie and Laure said their farewells. "Thank you, Madame. You have been very helpful."

They left before the woman could ask any awkward questions they wouldn't want to answer.

As they walked back to the other house, Laure's phone rang. Sophie watched her colleague listening and nodding, and eventually breaking into a knowing grin.

"That was interesting," she told Sophie. "Our mysterious house is owned by an anonymous company called Burgundy Student Houses, and my team will try to trace the real owners. But they did manage to find out that the property is managed by a *notaire*. You may recognise the name: Maitre Martin. Verdier's alibi. I think we need to ask him a few questions."

***

When Sophie and Laure appeared at Martin's office, he appeared very surprised to see them. What could they possibly want to speak to him about? He was no more than a simple *notaire*, going about his boring business of inheritances and property sales. What would he have to say to the police? 'Another blustering man trying to hide something,' Sophie thought.

She began by trying to find out if the *notaire* would lie to confirm his friend's false alibi. "Can you tell us your movements on Tuesday of this week?"

Martin's answer was like a well-rehearsed speech. "That was the day of the conference in Lyon. My colleague phoned to say he was not well, so I got in touch with Maitre Verdier and we arranged to go together in his car. We left Dijon around 10.30 am, had a drink after the conference ended and then we drove back. Maitre Verdrier dropped me back at the office at 8 pm. I collected my car and drove home."

"That's very interesting, Monsieur Martin."

"Maitre Martin," the *notaire* insisted.

Sophie ignored the correction. "Unfortunately, Monsieur Verdier cannot confirm your story. It appears he was in a village in the Herault department that night."

Martin swallowed hard, but he recovered quickly. "He must have gone there after he dropped me off."

"He was seen there at two am, he could not possibly have driven that far in six hours."

Martin shrugged, "He's a fast driver."

Sophie and Laure both smiled to themselves. He was clutching at straws.

Laure now turned to the question of the student house. "I understand you manage the property where M. Verdier's stepdaughter lodges?"

Martin's answer was evasive. "I didn't know he had a stepdaughter."

Laure wasn't going to be put off so easily. "The house is owned by a company called Burgundy Student Houses, and you are registered as their agent."

Martin continued to prevaricate. "Not me personally. Perhaps it is one of the minor interests of the practice. We do a lot of things, I am not aware of everything."

Sophie had had enough of this self-important upstart. She handed him her business card. "M. Martin, this is an official investigation, and you are required to provide me with the information we seek. You will send me full details of the relations between Burgundy Student Houses and your practice in the next few days. Do I make myself clear?"

"Of course." Martin accompanied his answer with a mock bow that, to Sophie, exactly summed up his arrogance.

***

It was one week later and a self-satisfied Sophie Rousseau was re-reading her report for the final time. Her first major case, investigated and resolved within a week. Not a bad achievement for a young judge, and a female one as well. That would be a lesson for those chauvinists who controlled her profession.

As she had expected, Verdier's story had been discredited. The coroner had laughed at the idea that the victim had hanged herself, pointing out the marks on her neck were consistent with someone putting a rope round her neck and pulling it hard. Verdier's DNA was all over her body and the clothes she had been wearing. The suit and shirt had not been cheap hypermarket brands, but from an expensive tailor with whom Verdier had an account. And a blood test had shown that Verdier was the father of the pregnant girl's child. The evidence that he was lying about the suicide was circumstantial, but it was convincing, perhaps even overwhelming. Verdier, and Sophie, would have their day in court and to Sophie the outcome looked very certain.

Her phone rang and she picked it up.

"Judge Rousseau?" the voice said.

"Yes?"

"It's the prosecutor's office at Montpellier here. It's about the Collier case. The actual murder took place outside of our jurisdiction. We have to transfer the case. So you must send all the information to Maitre Georges Dupont at the Dijon prosecutor's office. He will take the necessary next steps. This is in accordance with our rules and conventions, so please see to it right away. We don't want to upset any of our colleagues. Thank you."

The caller hung up. Sophie was flabbergasted, then furious. All that work, so well done, and all the kudos and credit would go to some male judge from Burgundy who had done nothing. Their rules and conventions, they could stick them. She had enough of rules and conventions, she wanted to break free and enjoy a bit of freedom. And she knew exactly how. She lifted her phone and dialled.

"Laure, it's me, Sophie. Are you going skinny dipping up at Cap d'Agde this weekend? Can I come with you?"

"Of course, Sophie. I'll look forward to it. Actually, I was just going to call you. We've found out who's behind Burgundy Student Houses, the company that owns the suspect student mansion where Nathalie Collier was killed. It's a group of about a dozen lawyers and judges based in and around Dijon. But there are three major shareholders: Verdier, Martin and the chief prosecutor in Dijon, a Maitre Dupont."

"Georges Dupont?"

"Yes, have you heard of him?"

“I’m afraid I have,” Sophie replied.

Death on the treadmill

By Andreas Nudetzki
Kindly translated from German by Paul Z. Walker

The flashlight lit up the eyes one more time. Nothing stirred in them. No pulse, no breath. The emergency doctor who had been called over could only confirm the victim's death. The male body was leaning with his head against the wooden wall of the small fitness room and seemed to stare at the treadmill that was still running, its engine letting out a nerve-racking whining.

The man was naked except for a pair of sports shoes. As he did a quick examination of the body, the doctor detected scratch wounds on the man's back. Even though he couldn't make any official statements, for the doctor it was clear what had happened: an accident. The man had probably been running on the treadmill, hadn't activated the emergency stop nor connected the safety clip, went too fast and then had been thrown off the belt against the wall behind him. That was the most reasonable cause of death.

Crime commissioner Melcher entered the room at this late hour and had the local police force inform him about the facts that so far had been determined.

"Does anyone know who the dead man is?"

"We're going over the premises as we speak, and we talk to the people present if they can be of help in identifying him," one of the policemen answered.

Melcher had a quick look around and then focussed on the treadmill, his lack of appreciation apparent. "Can someone switch that bloody thing off? We know it was running. Having to hear that noise this late in the evening gets on my nerves!"

To him it also looked as if this was an accident where the victim had fallen from the treadmill. However, the first proper facts would be brought up by crime scene investigators, and during the autopsy of the body.

"Who found the deceased?" he asked.

"A local guest. He wanted to leave the premises. As the fitness room is on the way to the exit, he had a look inside and he wondered why there was still a light on inside at this time. So he checked and found the body," one of the policemen said.

“And this guest couldn't identify him?" Melcher asked.

"No, apparently not. He probably wasn't a regular, just a one-time visitor or so. At least he called the police immediately. Which was a bit problematic as the cell reception here in the forest is pretty dismal. The good thing was that he knew the code to open the entrance gate so we could get in straight away."

"So what kind of place is this? It looks like a campground but something's off here. I didn't see a reception or similar…" Melcher wanted to know.

"No. As far as we know this is a nudist resort. They have this huge area in the forest, since over a hundred years ago. You'll find campers, trailer, tent spots and sports facilities all over. It's an old FKK sports group. That also explains the fitness room."

"Okay, that explains why the deceased is naked. I get it. Right. Doing sports naked isn't my thing, but to each their own."

Behind the two men, a door opened. Crime Scene Investigation came in. Outside, the coroner's car was already waiting. In the meantime, a group of guests had assembled near the cabin. They had been attracted by the blue flashing lights of the police cars and the unrest that wasn't typical for this time of day. At least they're all dressed, Melcher thought as he stepped into the door opening. Clearly it was now too cold, even for nudists, although the night was quite mild for this time of year.

"Would someone be able and willing to identify the body? It won't be a pretty view but unfortunately, we need this information. It's important."

The group outside remained depressingly quiet until a young man stepped forward. As he and Melcher went into the fitness room, CSI was already at work. The young man paled as he saw the body. He stared at the face of the dead man.

"Yes," he said, hesitantly, "I know who that is. He's the caretaker of the resort. Helmut Dreyer. He lives here with his family, across the road. How terrible..."

After that, the young man closed up and didn't want to say more. Melcher ordered two officers to go to the deceased's house and inform the family. Mrs Dreyer had woken up because of all the noise already and was standing outside the house, wearing a bathrobe. When she heard the news, she started trembling uncontrollably. She nodded, barely visibly, when asked if she was willing to come with the officers and identify the body.

Inside the fitness room, it was quickly obvious that this was indeed her husband. She burst out in tears and it was close to impossible to calm her down. She was taken outside quickly, where a female officer stayed with her. She used her cell phone to call someone who specialised in mental emergency care.

After two more hours, work in the fitness room had ended. Melcher's boss, who had been informed of the incident, had ordered that a special committee should be set up first thing in the morning.

***

After a night that was far too short, Melcher and his colleagues got together for the first committee meeting. It was a good thing that the police station coffee was very strong. They all knew this day would present them with a lot of work.

Melcher first presented the initial findings of his crew.

"First we need to determine if this was an accident or an actual murder case," he ended his presentation.

The plan was to go to the club grounds and chat with the chairman – and possibly some of the guests – before the results of the autopsy were announced. He also wanted to find out as much as possible about life at the club.

He turned to his colleague. "Schneider, I'd like you to drive straight to the pathology lab and let us know the initial results of the examination."

***

The chairman of the FKK group still looked shocked. It was all over his face. His deputy, the secretary of the group and several other members who had gathered in the small meeting room, shared his expression and feelings. The sky was bright blue, but even the trees outside looked sad.

Melcher was relieved these people were at least dressed. He had counted on the worst scenario. Investigations and talks with nude people had already haunted his dreams that night. Slowly daily life started at the resort. Some of the guests were on their way to the washrooms, either wearing bathrobes or nude. *I guess I will have to get used to that view*, the commissioner thought.

No one was greeting others as abundantly as usual that day. Most of them formed small groups and debated the events that had transpired the previous night.

"Yes… Our Helmut," the chairman, Norbert Fuchs, sighed. "I don't know at all what I should say to all this. He lived here with his family. He was our… handyman, and more. Anything regarding maintenance of the area. He also acted as caretaker of all the buildings. Usually at night he would go into the fitness room and do some training."

Melcher said, "So far everything points to an accident. He probably slipped or tripped on the treadmill, fell backwards and there he hit the wall so badly that he got lethally hurt."

"How tragic," said the deputy chairman, Andrea Nauman.

"It was," Melcher agreed, "and usually this would be strange, finding the man naked. For us this all would point to a murder, but in this location, it isn't so surprising."

Everyone in the room looked at him in surprise.

"Naked? Helmut was naked?" the chairman asked.

"Yes," Melcher replied, "but seeing this is an FKK group… It would make sense that people work out in the nude, right? Or is that not the case?"

"No, no," Fuchs assured him, "but naked? Helmut? Never!"

Miss Nauman folded her hands over her chest. "Helmut lived here, that's true, but none of us have ever seen him naked. Never. No way he would undress and go around like that. Even in our lake he would be the only one with swimming trunks. Of course, he would usually go there only after the last naked guests had left."

The others present were speechless. Melcher grabbed his phone and called his colleagues. They might have a suspicious death on their hands.

***

"It looks like the victim got severe scrape marks on his back." The coroner informed Schneider about his preliminary findings in the meeting room. They both held on to their coffee during their talk. "This could, of course, have happened as he fell on the treadmill. But in that case, the wounds would have been far less pronounced. Normally he'd have been flung from the machine quite quickly, and maybe the carpet would have left some marks. But now it looks as if someone deliberately pushed him down on the treadmill. The rotating belt would have acted like sandpaper that way."

Schneider felt quite uncomfortable as he heard all this. He also wondered why the emergency brake had failed if everything had been according to regulations. Then he realised that there was no way the victim could have attached the emergency strap to his clothes since he hadn't worn any. Considering the fact this had happened in a nudist environment, that was quite probable. He tried to imagine at which part of the body the victim could have used the safety strap, when the coroner continued.

"Another interesting find I made: in almost every wound I discovered traces of fabric. So that might indicate the victim had been dressed on the treadmill, and the belt scraped his clothes away including the skin."

"Right, but that doesn't explain why the body was entirely naked in the end," Schneider said. "That's a question that still needs more investigation."

The coroner added, "The cause of death was, at any rate, a strike to the back of the head with a blunt object. At least when he hit his head against the wall of the fitness room. The strike must have been very powerful. Does anyone know how fast the belt was running when the body was found?"

Schneider added another mental note. That was something in need of clarification.

"Anyway," the coroner said, "the belt must have gone very fast, to create such a deadly impact and wound. Especially if the victim was found leaning against a wall that was over six feet behind him."

***

Melcher was sitting at a table in the FKK-club's canteen. That was the name this small bar and restaurant had gotten. It also was the club house. In front of him was a cup of coffee. From his seat at the table he saw many of the club's guests who were present. In the morning, all the guests had been asked not to leave the premises. Melcher had by then decided that the murder had to have been committed by one of the members of this group. It was, unfortunately, not clear if the perpetrator was still around, or if he had slipped away in the dark.

All the people in the room appeared to have dressed, Melcher saw with relief. He had already worried that he would have to face an unfamiliar flesh viewing during this meeting. At that moment, among the almost thirty people present, he noticed a woman who was, indeed, entirely naked. She sat on a chair, only having a towel beneath her. Damn, Melcher thought, that's just my luck. As he thought that, he did admire her athletic appearance. Okay, don't blush, he thought. Hardly surprising, that was the moment where his face turned entirely red. He quickly hid behind his cup of coffee. He was relieved that all attention was on Norbert Fuchs, the chairman of the club. He was informing all those present about what had happened. As agreed beforehand, he didn't go into the details.

Finally, it was Melcher's turn to speak. He asked questions about their way of life, and about the preferences and habits of the victim. Everyone had the same good things to say about the man. Not just that Dreyer kept the area in perfect order and how competent he was, but also how he had often supported and assisted the members in their efforts for gardening and tree care. He had also been liked for agreeing to get into a small rowboat and drag a group of screaming, naked children through the water.

Clearly there was no dispute that Dreyer, if only by living on the grounds, had a good life. It was clear that most people here would prefer to live here all the time. The only thing that surprised everyone was that the caretaker never was nude himself. This was odd because he lived and worked in an FKK club and therefore he had all the opportunities to be free of clothing.

After listening for a while, Melcher was impressed by the friendliness and almost intimacy of this group. It appeared as if all the people in this club, which was quite large with around eight hundred members, were one big family. Time and again his eyes were drawn to the nude woman as she stood out in this group of dressed people. Despite being naked, she looked open and friendly. Melcher wondered if he would have noticed her if the others had been naked as well. Maybe he would have felt awkward then, being the only dressed person in the room. He didn't have more time for questions regarding the wearing of clothes or being naked, however.

The meeting came to an end and Melcher watched the naked woman leave the room. Then he took his phone and called the murder squad. The person answering told him the first results of the autopsy. He also learnt that CSI had discovered remarkably many skin particles and bits of clothing on the treadmill. If the victim had tripped, there would have been only a few of those. Adding all this together, it looked as if the victim had been on the belt for a long time and that way his clothes and skin had been scraped off.

***

Melcher was back in the fitness room and had another look around. This time he took in everything more carefully. Also, his colleague Schneider had returned from the coroner's office and was ready to assist him. They had some questions that needed answers and they also tried to recreate the situation as it had been on that fateful evening. Melcher was standing on the treadmill and tried to figure out how one would have to fall in order to fall on the belt on one's back. That was because that was the only spot on the dead body where the scrape marks had been. He wasn't making much progress.

In order to look at this from all perspectives, they had even resorted to YouTube fails in the fitness rooms, and they found that people usually fell on their stomach or at times on their side, but usually they were only on their back after rolling off the machine and landing on the floor. But then the wounds couldn't have been this extensive nor all over the body.

Unfortunately, no one had remembered or seen how fast the treadmill had been running. Melcher recalled that he had been irked by its whining sound and he had ordered it to be shut off. But it was clear that, had the machine been at high speed, falling on one's back would have been extremely improbable.

Melcher's head was close to releasing smoke. "I really need a break now," he told Schneider, and so they both set off to the restaurant. From there they would view the world of the nude ones.

***

The sun was out and the restaurant's outside terrace was well occupied. Everywhere, guests sat under the large sun screens and enjoyed a beer and their food, which was remarkably affordable.

Again, Melcher and his colleague turned red in the face as they saw so many nude patrons, only having a towel with them - to sit on. The only garments in sight were hats or baseball caps, and that was all. Also, the naked woman from the meeting sat at one of the tables and sipped from a glass of Coke. She smiled at the commissioner, who was very happy he was wearing pants at that moment.

When he looked around, he noticed that this group of people represented a decent cross-section of society. Old and young, men and women, big and small, tall and large, every body type was present, and everyone acted like you'd expect in any ordinary restaurant. The waitress was, next to the two policemen, the only one dressed. That was probably because of hygiene. From the playground next to the restaurant, laughter drifted over. A group of children and youngsters had fun on a trampoline.

Some were dressed, some were naked, and they went about as if that was the most normal thing in the world. At the same time there was a scent coming from a nearby sauna which mixed with the smell of pizza and schnitzel.

Melcher and Schneider both ordered an alcohol-free beer and enjoyed the sun, the blue sky, the green nature, and slowly they began to appreciate this place. If only there hadn't been this awful murder last night…

"Yes, today everything is a bit quieter than usual. Luckily the kids seem not to be bothered. They probably didn't even hear about it. Good morning, dear colleague."

Melcher almost drowned in his beer as he was addressed that way by someone who suddenly appeared at his side. Next to him was a tall man in tennis clothes, who sweat from every pore.

"Gosh! Dirk! What are you doing here," Melcher asked.

Dirk Seiler was the chief commissioner for the corporate crime squad. He had a day off and regularly trained here at the tennis court of the nudist club. He was dressed when the sun was out too strong.

"I'll be right back," Seiler said and he walked off to have a shower.

He returned after mere minutes. Towel, sunglasses, sunscreen. That was all he had with him. He sat down on a chair next to the dressed policemen. "And now I need a good beer. Without clothes this is heaven, you know. Why are you two even still dressed? Oh, of course. Work. I don't even know if that's still valid when you're investigating something in a nudist resort. When you're naked, it's so much easier to investigate things around here."

"Being naked and being inconspicuous during investigations doesn't sound very probable," Schneider countered as he grinned. On the other hand, in clothes they stood out more here than wearing actual police uniforms at a teen-band concert.

***

"I had no idea you're a member of this nude people club," Melcher said.

"Yeah, well," Seiler said. "I can practice my sports here and at the same time I can let my soul roam. The feeling of air and sun on your skin. And you keep meeting nice people here. It's like one big family."

"And then when there are such nice women, like the one at that table..." Melcher nodded in the direction of the attractive lady at the next table.

"Ah, yes, that's Heidi. She's definitely someone to look at," Seiler laughed. "She's something special alright. I don't think I've ever seen her in clothes." Seiler then rose. "Come on, let me show you two around a bit."

As the three left, Melcher nodded at Heidi, who returned his greeting in a friendly way.

They leisurely walked over to the swimming-lake. Once there, the two policemen were the only ones wearing any kind of clothing. On a small island in the middle of the lake, a group of youths were having a battle with a group of adults who had remained young at heart. It clearly was about gaining 'control' over the island. The group had a lot of fun while performing their staged fight, and many of them risked falling into the cold water.

Small children were playing in a sandy area using buckets and small shovels, under the supervision of their parents. All around the lake were families, couples and also single guests on sun beds and picnic blankets. The mood here was one of peace. There were a few small groups sitting down who clearly were still processing everything that had happened the night before.

"This is our pretty swimming-lake," Seiler said. "It's the centre of our place. A few years ago we dug it out, with Helmut. It was quite an act of force to get it done. It's strictly clothes-free as long as the weather allows. In the water, swimwear isn't allowed. Ever since I joined this club, I haven't gone to a regular swimming pool any more. All that being careful not to be seen naked… Wrap a towel, try to get out of your stuff. Then trying to get into the swimming trunks. And always there's the risk of some idiots being around. Or the constant staring at women, to decide which one has the best bikini figure. No, Melcher. I don't need that."

"But aren't there peeping Toms here?" Melcher wanted to know.

"Oh, that probably happens a bit, but when everyone's naked, that gets boring quickly. At some point you don't notice it any more. And if there is someone who's here just for the staring, or who doesn't know how to behave, then we'll make sure he's on the other side of the fence very quickly. We had that happen a few times."

"And what kind of people visit this place?"

"We have people from all layers of society. Even some high-ranking managers. As you know I am in the police In addition we have members who are teachers, factory workers, and of course many pensioners who like to spend the last years of their life here in peace. The kids have a lot of fun too. When everyone's naked, no one has anything to hide. This way we're all equal, the same. And after a while it's the most normal thing in the world. Some of our guests call this place paradise."

Now Melcher became serious. "And last night there was the fall from grace. A murder probably has a huge shock-effect here. Maybe that's why so many people were dressed this morning?"

"Who knows," Seiler replied. "People were shocked, were scared. It's not the kind of thing you push aside just like that. Even when it looks a little like 'back to normality' at the moment."

Melcher nodded. "Apart from that young lady called Heidi. She seems to be naked all the time. And you? Where were you last night?"

That question shook Seiler's confident appearance. "Me? You don't think that I..."

"Why not? You were on the grounds, so you're one of the potential suspects."

Seiler looked at the ground and nodded. "You're right. And I have to admit that I didn't notice anything of what had happened overnight. My camper is on the other side of the area and I must have slept like a log. Alone, in case you need to know."

At that moment, a loud scream came from the centre of the lake. A boy held up a torn t-shirt that he had clearly found while going underwater.

***

Melcher handed the t-shirt over to the two officers in the police car, who would take it to the lab for examination. The piece of clothing was completely shredded on the backside, and judging from the size it would be a perfect fit for the victim. At the same time, he ordered for divers who had to search the waters of the lake for more pieces of clothing.

***

It had become afternoon by now. Members of the homicide squad went over the premises and gathered information about the guests. Their main focus was where they had been that night, and what their relationship had been with Helmut Dreyer.

Melcher and Schneider drove back to the precinct. They were there for an evening meeting about the situation. The lab had by then discovered that the t-shirt from the lake had belonged to Dreyer, and they had also found other DNA traces. There had also been fibres from the t-shirt on the belt of the treadmill. That made it clear that Dreyer had been dressed while working out and that he had lost his upper clothing either when lying down, or it had been torn away from him. They decided that the members from the FKK-group, who had been present that night, would all be submitted to a saliva test over the coming days.

***

The sun was as warm the next day as the day before. Once again, many guests had found their way to the lake. This time, however, none of them were in the water. Instead, the police diving team were doing their job at about five metres underwater, near the muddy floor of the lake.

At the same time, a long queue was forming near the restaurant, where everyone participated in having their saliva sample taken. Out of respect for the police technicians, almost no one was naked. While not dressed most people wore at least a bathrobe. Only Heidi was naked and sat in front of the restaurant, enjoying a cappuccino and watching the goings-on.

"Do you mind if I sit down with you?" Melcher asked the woman. It had taken him some inner strength to address the attractive, nude woman. But she had piqued his interest. "Melcher is my name. Commissioner Melcher."

"Heidi Luft," she replied.

"Now that is a great name for a naturist," he laughed. "It looks as if you never wear clothes, do you?"

She smiled at him, flashing her sparkling, blue eyes . "No, never. Even my dearly departed husband often had to run errands for me because I didn't want to wear clothes to go into a supermarket. Now I live here and I don't have to worry about trivial things like that anymore."

"I'm sorry to hear about your husband. How long have you been widowed?"

"For six years now. He died in an accident back then. But… I am trying to get over what happened and I focus on my life, here and now. Financially I'm safe, because his retirement money allows me to live comfortably."

"That is good to hear," Melcher agreed. "But this total freedom from fabric strikes me as quite radical."

She smiled, for a moment engrossed in thought. "Yes, perhaps. But I never felt good in clothes. You know, even skin sometimes is a bit too much for me. People who voluntarily wear clothes… No. I'm sorry." She looked over at the trampoline again, where the children were having fun again. Just like the day before: some were dressed, some were nude.

"You see," she continued. "Those children are here with their parents. They practically grew up here. I don't understand at all why they put on any clothes. It's just grotesque. Being dressed in a nudist resort!" As she talked, she got enraged and Melcher noticed that her eyes had gotten a different expression, changed so much from the kind appearance earlier. He even seemed to detect a bit of hate in them.

Now he noticed her well-trained body, but also a few scratch marks on her arms and legs. Normally, had she been dressed, he wouldn't have noticed them. So, people being naked did have some advantages. Melcher rose. "Excuse me, I need to find the bathroom, but please don't leave. I'm very interested in what you just told me."

On the way to the bathroom, he called the homicide squad and told them to run a check on Heidi Luft. He also requested the details concerning her husband's death.

He had just re-joined Mrs Luft when a police officer reported that, indeed, more articles of clothing had been found in the lake. It looked like they had belonged to Helmut Dreyer and they were taken to the lab at that very moment.

When Melcher turned back to his conversation partner, she looked him over top to bottom, and smiled as she said, "Why are you still dressed? You're on the premises all day long. Isn't it enough that there are so many people dressed already? Come on, take off those things. I can't believe you actually are able to stand that!"

Melcher nodded. "Did you ever invited Dreyer to take off all his clothes?"

"Not once but often. I don't even recall how often. It's rare to find someone who is so stubborn. Okay, he did a great job here, but to go around a place like this, fully dressed all the time… I couldn't wrap my mind around that. To live here, to get paid through FKK friends' money and still be dressed..." There was no more kindness left in her expression. "At least he died naked."

Melcher got a funny feeling in his stomach when his phone rang. He excused himself as Mrs Luft was catching her breath after her rant and walked off to answer the call.

"Hey Melcher. This is Schneider. We ran that check on this Mrs Luft. So far she hasn't been on the radar, although in the matter of her husband's death she was one of the suspects for a short while.

Those charges were dropped quickly though. It probably was an accident."

The commissioner thanked him and sat back at the table with Mrs Luft, thinking about what he'd just heard.

"Bad news?" she asked.

"No, not really. Just some investigation findings. We're trying to get all the pieces of the puzzle in place and see if they fit." He took a short break before he asked, "And your husband? How was his attitude towards you wanting to be nude all the time?"

She relaxed a little. "Oh, you know, at first he thought it was so great. He said it was sexy, the way I walked around in the nude for him, cooked, cleaned and… anything really. But he liked to keep his pants on. And after the first heat between us was over, he started to feel embarrassed about it. He always wanted to go out; to the movies, to bars, to the theatre. But I always refused to get mixed up in the world of textiles. Each time he went into town, I came here. I trained in the fitness room, swam in the lake. Yes, a totally different life. And one day he suffocated in his own clothes."

Melcher was surprised. "He did? How did that happen?"

"He got his tie caught during garden work. We had a wood chopping unit and… He wore a tie! In the garden! Can you imagine how low that man had sunk? I talked to him until I was blue in the face, but he didn't listen…"

Heidi Luft now had the same heated expression as when she had talked about Dreyer. And again Melcher's phone rang, so again he apologised and answered the call.

***

"Mrs Luft," Melcher said as he returned to the table. "I fear you do have to get dressed now."

Heidi Luft jumped out of her chair with so much energy that the chair shot back at least two metres.

"I beg your pardon? Are you out of your mind? I am not getting dressed. Not for all the money in the world!"

"I just got back the DNA results from the traces on the t-shirt and the treadmill. From the death of your husband we still had DNA values from you. They match the ones we found on Dreyer's clothes and the belt of the treadmill. Mrs Luft, you are under arrest for the murder of Helmut Dreyer, caretaker of this FKK resort."

Heidi Luft looked at him in disbelief. "But all I want is to be naked. Why doesn't anyone understand that?"

"And because of that you even had to scrape off his skin, because even skin can be too much?" Melcher wondered.

And then she ran off, naked as she was. Melcher immediately called for his colleagues and went in pursuit of Heidi Luft, who was hurrying towards the exit. There, a police car had been stationed since the early morning. The officers there were checking all the guests to the resort. They caught Heidi Luft and took her into custody.

***

It was late in the afternoon and still quite warm everywhere. Still, police officers were present. The divers had finished their job, the lake lay there peacefully and the first guests showed themselves again.

"Why did it have to be Heidi," commissioner Seiler said to Melcher who stood next to him. "She was such a role model for all of us. After all, she led the life that all of us just dream of. Naked all the time: work naked, do shopping that way. Whatever. But you can only look at people's heads, not inside them. It's one thing to take off your clothes in front of others, but what goes on inside you, even when you're nude, is impossible to tell." Seiler looked out over the lake. "What will happen to the ideals of nudism now?"

"At some point she must have become radical," Melcher added. "She couldn't stand it anymore when someone was dressed. And Dreyer, who lived here and was dressed all the time, was the person who pushed her provocation over the limit. So when he was alone in the fitness room, she took one of the dumbbells that were lying around, whacked him over the head and then pressed him onto the belt. She is strong enough for that, judging from her trained and athletic appearance."

Seiler was barely listening. "...and no one picked up what was going on inside her. We're one big family here! In paradise! Yes, it's obviously possible to end up on either side of the horse. But for a nudist to commit a murder because of that… That shows we need to look after each other more."

Melcher nodded. "Yes. We don't live in paradise, Seiler. We can only try to build part of it here. And the way it looks, you're doing quite a good job here at the resort. But you're right. We need to look after each other more so paradise doesn't turn into some kind of hell."

He took a moment to admire the lake, the wonderful weather, and slowly started to relax. "Case closed. Now I need two things. First one is a large, cold beer. And then, secondly, I'd love to take a dip in this lake. Too bad I don't have my swimming gear with me."

Seiler woke up from his thoughts and laughed. "Why that? You have everything you need to go swimming. Except a towel… I'll get you one!"

Epilogue

In a way it hurts me a little to basically set this story in the location where I went so often and that is so peaceful. It's hard to imagine a murder taking place there. But the location and also the people there were perfect hooks for this story:

The caretaker who really never undressed, even though he lived and worked there, really exists. And yes, he did cause a lot of head-shaking among the guests of the resort. But he did a great job and the place always looked amazing, so it was hard to stay annoyed.

Heidi Luft is, in reality, a nice, elderly lady, who did indeed once state that even wearing skin at times feels too much. She really doesn't understand how people, even the kids on the trampoline, don't want to be naked all day. I really doubt she would be able to commit a murder like this. I am truly sorry, my dear, that I put this crime on you!

Chief Commissioner Seiler is a real person as well. He doesn't just play tennis; he also likes to write exciting crime stories. His stories are amazing; my little story can't even stand in their shadows. Hat (and clothes) off to him! Perhaps he should place his next novel inside a nudist resort too.

Lovely Shade of Death

Jacob M. Drake

Annie Cleary opened her eyes and slowly breathed, enjoying the fresh scent of the country air just as she did every morning when she awoke at her favorite nudist club. It was so much better than her everyday life in the city, but at twenty-seven years old and still trying to carve her niche out of society, until she could afford to make the move to living fulltime at Natural Country Life, the club she had decided to make her home, spending weekends and holidays would have to suffice.

Throwing back the covers, she went to the door of her cabin and opened it. The morning was as beautiful to drink in with her eyes as it was to breathe through her nose. Turning back inside Annie picked up a small bag that contained the items necessary for her morning ritual: shower gel, shampoo, toothpaste, toothbrush, and dental floss. She selected a large, fluffy towel and washcloth and headed outside to the path that led a short distance to the clubhouse where she would make use of the showers and restroom.

Several cottages along and just around a slight curve in the path Annie noticed a small crowd of people standing about outside of Bob Miller's cottage. Bob was one of the oldest members of the club and had taken up fulltime residence more than twenty years previous. She slowed as she approached and looked to find Rita Jackson, one of the other long-time residents living fulltime on the grounds, glancing anxiously her way..

"Annie," Rita said in a hushed tone, as though trying not to disturb anyone else, "it's Bob. He's dead."

"What?" The news caught Annie by surprise. Bob was a likeable man who took great pleasure in making others laugh. "How did he die? I mean, he was so robust last night at dinner and around the campfire." Tears welled up within Annie's eyes and a slight blink caused them to release, rolling down her cheeks.

"I know, dear. I feel the same way." Rita drew the younger woman in with a hug and held her close. "No one knows how he died yet. The police have been called, but not yet arrived."

"Step aside, please," Elaine Wilkins, the manager of the club shouted out as she drew near to the ever-growing crowd. "Police are here. Let them inside so they can do their work, please."

The crowd parted like the Red Sea as a small cadre of police officers walked up. There were three in uniform and two, one man and one woman, in suits. Annie knew they were the detectives in charge of the case, especially since she knew the man, Detective Benjamin McLane, a friend of her father and the last officer her dad had trained as a detective, her dad having served on the job for thirty years before retiring. McLane glanced over at her, his face reddening in blush when he recognized the young woman he'd known much of her life. She smiled slightly, enjoying his embarrassment at discovering her in this setting where she was completely nude, other than the towel draped about her neck that didn't succeed in covering her small yet well-rounded breasts. Annie held a finger up against her lips, indicating silence. She didn't want to interfere with his investigation, if there was one to be made. She knew he'd be at the club long enough for them to speak later.

Detective McLane entered the cottage with his team. Annie continued to the clubhouse for her morning clean-up.

***

Nearly two hours later Detective McLane found Annie sitting on a blanket in the middle of a small clearing, surrounded by various trees and flowers. Birds were singing and squirrels were running up and down the trees as Annie tossed peanuts on the ground for them to snatch up and store for the winter. Annie caught sight of this friend who she knew was only six years older than she was and waved at him. Again, she caught sight of his blushing as he hesitated and then approached.

"Hi, Benny," she said, standing from her cross-legged position so she could greet him with a kiss on the cheek. "Or should I call you Detective McLane, since you're working?" His face turned an even darker shade of red at being so close to a completely naked woman as pretty as she.

"N-no, B-Benny's fine," he stammered, his voice barely audible.

"You know, it is getting too hot for clothes," she chided. "The least you could do is remove your jacket. I won't tell."

The detective pondered a moment and then removed his jacket and glanced around the opulent glade they were in. "This is a beautiful place," he said.

"Of course it is. Come. Sit down with me and tell me all about old Bob Miller – if you can. I don't want to interfere with an open investigation." Annie resumed her place on her blanket and patted the space next to her. McLane considered a moment, glancing at the smattering of others sitting or lying about the area, and then sat, making sure his leg didn't come into contact with her leg.

"There's really not much to tell," McLane began. "So far all we know is the deceased died in his sleep. Whether from natural causes or something else we won't know until the medical examiner finishes the autopsy. Did you know the deceased?"

"Bob? Of course. Everyone here knew him. He was the life of the party even when he was sober, which he usually was unless there was a party. So, it seems like natural causes?"

"So far. From all the deaths I've seen, if I had to guess I'd say it was by asphyxiation."

"You mean someone strangled him?"

"No, more like he rolled over in his sleep and smothered in his pillow. We'll have to wait for the coroner's report, but the signs are all there for asphyxia."

"Poor old Bob," Annie sighed quietly. "I'll miss his humor."

They sat silently long enough that the detective began to grow uncomfortable once more, so he stood to his feet. "Well, I need to get back and do my report on this. It was great, ah, seeing you, Annie." He pushed his right hand out to shake, but Annie once more hugged him, this time longer than before, then gave him another kiss and waved as he headed back toward the parking lot.

"Asphyxia," Annie mused to herself. I wonder…" She picked up her blanket and the bag of peanuts, then headed off toward the cottages and cabins.

***

Most of the cottages, which were reserved for full-time members living year-round at the club, had flowers planted around them, placed there long ago after the club first opened. Annie wasn't exactly a botanist, but she had studied horticulture and floriculture her first year of college and had always possessed a love for all things natural, hence her attraction to living nude as much as possible. Annie knew just enough about plants that could be considered poisonous to know they almost always had very beautiful flowers and often secreted poisonous fluids beneath the petals. As she moved from one cottage to another, scouring the various forms of flora, Annie thought about Bob Miller and how he had seemed the night before. He was a difficult one to label, since even when he was depressed or ill, he hid behind his natural geniality, telling jokes and humorous stories so no one knew how he truly felt inside. Last night Bob seemed jovial enough, but he had also seemed a bit stuffed up and had sniffled quite a bit. The indications were that he might have been catching a cold or dealing with allergies. Was it possible his sinus problems could have been a result of the pollen from a poisonous plant?

Nothing of a suspicious nature had turned up at Bob's cottage or the ones closest to his, but when Annie walked behind the fourth cottage in, the one inhabited by Mildred Jennings, a member who had been at the club almost as long as Bob had, she stopped short when she spied a small thatch of beautiful blue flowers growing back towards the trees behind the cottage.

"Monkshood," Annie barely breathed the name of the plant. It was also known as Wolf's-bane and several other names, but no matter what one called it, the plant and flowers it grew were highly poisonous, causing death within a few hours. One of the possible effects from Monkshood poisoning was asphyxia, but it was so bitter to the taste that anyone ingesting it would spit it out immediately. Still, the roots were the deadliest part of the plant and anyone touching the roots with their bare hands would experience an immediate tingling sensation. Washing one's hands quickly enough could alleviate the problem, but if someone didn't know what was happening the poison could be absorbed into the body causing paralysis and finally death.

"Annie?" A voice from behind her called out and Annie reacted, perhaps too quickly, by spinning around, she was sure with a guilty look on her face. It was Mildred, the inhabitant of this cottage for nearly twenty years. "Is there anything I can help you with, sweetie?" Mildred drew closer. The only thing she wore was her trademark floppy straw hat to keep the sun from burning her head when she was out gardening. Annie noticed the older woman was donning a worn pair of gardening gloves. Was that because she recognized the Monkshood and was concerned over what Annie might be thinking?

"I was just admiring these flowers," Annie said, turning back toward the poisonous plant as though she didn't know exactly what it was.

"Oh, yes, the Blue Rocket," Mildred said, using one of the less common names for the plant. "It is such a lovely shade of blue, isn't it? When I first moved into this cottage I noticed it right away, but there was so much of it that I trimmed it all back so that this," she waved her hand to indicate the small area the plant covered, "was all that was left."

"Is there a reason for cutting it back?" Annie asked, trying to seem ignorant.

"Only that I wanted to have space for all the other flowers I've planted. I like variety and try to keep any one plant from dominating too much soil."

"That makes sense," Annie said and reached out with one hand as though to touch the petals, wondering if the older woman would stop here.

"Oh, I wouldn't do that, dear," Mildred spoke up and Annie pulled her hand back. "The Blue Rocket may look pretty, but it will cause your skin to tingle if you touch it and even worse if you don't wash soon enough. If you want a cutting from this, I can pot one up for you."

"Could you? That would be so generous of you," Annie beamed, as though Mildred were doing her a great favor, and she was, since this would ensure Annie had something to show Arnold McLane, depending upon the toxicology report.

A few minutes later Annie held a small clay pot holding half-a-dozen flowering stalks, each one a vibrant bright blue. She took it back to her cabin and set it on the coffee table, then withdrew her iPhone from her purse and took several pictures. She then sent them all in a text to Detective McLane and a few minutes later she received a phone call from him.

"Hi, Annie, this is Detective, ah, this is Benny."

"Hi, Benny. Thanks for calling back."

"So, what's this flower you sent me pictures of?"

Annie proceeded to tell the detective all about the flower and how she had found it on the club grounds. "I'm sure you don't have the toxicology report yet, but I thought this might be something to suggest keeping a special eye out for."

"This flower?"

"Yes, it can cause asphyxia and death. I just thought the ME might want to screen specifically for this, just in case."

"I'm sure the report will show this, if it's in the body."

"Only if the exam is done within twenty-four hours. The poison from this plant will disappear in that time and any screening done too late won't show it."

"You seem to know an awful lot about this plant. Should I be worried?" Annie laughed at his concern and inference that she might have had a hand in Bill's death.

"I studied it my first year along with a lot of other flora before deciding to settle on forensic science as my major. Once I got it in my head, I went searching the grounds here until I found some of it."

"Hmm, ok, I'll ask the coroner if she can do the toxicology testing right away, stressing the urgency of the time already lapsed. Thanks for your help, Annie."

"Anytime I can." She ended the call and sat back, looking at the potted flowers and wondering if her suspicion might be right. She hoped not. She liked Mildred.

***

Annie was sunning out near the smaller of the club's two lakes when her phone beeped, letting her know she had a text. She glanced down to read the screen. "Where are you located?" She saw the text was from Benny, Detective McLane. "At the small lake. Are you here at the club?" "Yes," came the reply. "I'll get directions and be right there."

She sat up straight and crossed her legs. She didn't know why, but her heart was beating faster and she felt a bit flushed. She grabbed her towel and dabbed at her skin, drying the perspiration beads from lying in the sun. She heard a rustle of leaves and turned to look behind her just as Detective McLane pushed past the few minor branches that had begun to grow out into the pathway. He stopped when he saw her, and his expression indicated he felt flushed as well.

"Don't stand over there, silly," Annie said and caught herself just before she giggled. When did she become the type of girl who giggled? "Join me. That's what you're here for, isn't it?" Her words seemed to make Detective McLane flushed all over again, but he closed the distance and stood towering over her.

"I see you aren't wearing your jacket. When are you going to go native and undress? You are at a nudist club, you know."

"Ah, well, I am on official police business," he almost stuttered, making Annie smile at the emotion he was trying hard not to display.

"Sit," Annie said, patting the blanket. As dutifully as any pet dog he sat. "I assume there must be something important or you wouldn't have driven all the way out here twice in the same day."

"What? Oh, yes, right." McLane pulled a paper from his shirt pocket and unfolded it. "The toxicology report shows a high level of Monkshood poison in the deceased's system, specifically in his GI tract."

"You mean he actually ingested it?" Annie's eyes widened. "How could he possibly get past the bitterness?"

"I don't know, but that's where the highest concentration of it was, so yeah, he ate something that had the poison in it. Maybe that's how he was able to stand the bitter taste, because it was masked by something else." Neither one said anything for a moment, and then McLane asked, "Care to show me to whoever is growing this stuff?"

"Oh, oh, sure." Annie stood to her feet and leaving her blanket and other items where they were began walking toward the path leading away from the lake. Behind her she heard a stifled laugh and turned to look. McLane was shaking his head with his eyes closed. "What? Did I do something weird?" Annie turned about as though trying to look behind her for something that might be hanging off her body.

"It's not you. You began walking away and for a moment I was struck stupid by you being naked and well, I almost asked if you were going to get dressed first but caught myself before actually speaking the words."

Annie laughed with him at his faux pas. "That's ok, we all get brain farts at times. And by the way, we prefer using 'nude' to 'naked.' 'Naked' infers vulnerability. 'Nude' simply means lacking clothing. I may be nude, but I guarantee I'm never vulnerable." She threw her hip in a certain way as she turned away to walk down the path, causing the detective to fix his gaze securely on her backside. He agreed from the confidence of her gait that she was telling the truth.

"Right over here is Mildred Jennings' cottage. The Monkshood is in the back by the trees. You might want to be careful while talking to her. Mildred is one of the leading members of this club. She's, well with Bob gone," a tear welled up in one of her eyes and she brushed it away, "Mildred is probably the oldest member here. She has a lot of pull with everyone, but I just can't think of her as being a murderer."

"We don't know that she is," McLane looked toward the cottage and nodded. "For all we know it was an accidental poisoning. Let me talk to her and we'll take it from there, all right?"

"Sure." They finished the walk to Mildred's place and Detective McLane knocked on the door. No one answered, so he knocked again. When there still was no answer he leaned over and peered through a window with a hand shading his eyes.

"I don't see anyone," he almost mumbled. "Let's take a look out back."

"Mildred could be at the clubhouse or visiting another member," Annie offered as they rounded the house and the back yard came into view. She pointed with one hand toward the start of the trees and said, "The Monkshood flowers are right back…" She stopped, squinted her eyes and leaned forward slightly, as if that would help her to see better.

"What's the matter?" McLane asked.

"The blue flowers. I don't see them. That's odd." Annie pushed past the many other plants growing in the yard and came to where she had seen the Monkshood flowers. Instead of blue petals all she found was a hole where something had been dug up.

"Are you sure this is where the Monkshood flowers were?" McLane asked.

"Positive," Annie said, a sinking feeling forming in the pit of her stomach. She looked at the back wall of the cottage and scanned for a moment. "Mildred has a wheelbarrow she keeps back here. I don't see it."

"Which means that if she's the one who poisoned the deceased, she's disposed of the rest of the plants to deflect suspicion away from her. Is there somewhere you can think of that might be a good place to hide the plants?"

"Pretty much anywhere in the forest would be a good place," Annie said, opening her arms wide and indicating the vast spread of trees before them. Her gesture caught the detective's attention and his eyes momentarily flickered to her breasts, but he caught himself and turned his gaze toward the trees, where they rightfully should have been.

"Hmm, any way of narrowing it down? I really don't want to call in uniformed officers for a search party, especially since we don't know for certain yet that a murder has been committed."

Annie looked down at the ground and looked about. "It looks like something pushed through here recently, judging from the way the other plants have been pushed aside. Probably from Mildred's wheelbarrow. Let's see if we can follow this new path anywhere."

Once more Annie took the lead and the detective didn't at all mind taking up the rear.

As they walked deeper into the woods McLane thought about the setting they were in and how perfectly natural it all seemed for Annie to be outside completely naked, no, nude, he mentally corrected himself. There no longer seemed to be anything wrong with it at all, as he'd felt earlier when he'd first been called out to this place to investigate the death. The thought began forming in his mind that perhaps, just perhaps, he could give a try to being nude out here.

"Shhh, stop," Annie said in a hushed voice and held a hand back toward him. She motioned with her hand for him to take a look. He moved past her and stood looking down toward where a gentle creek burbled along across the land. A lone figure came into view of a nude body, one that was obviously female and much older than Annie, judging from the long, white tresses flowing along down her back. She didn't seem to be moving, but rather standing in one position as though looking down at something.

He turned slightly toward the girl next to him and started to ask what Mildred was staring at but realized she wouldn't know any more than he did. Instead he resumed walking toward the figure. As he closed the distance, he noticed the old woman's body begin to sag a bit, as though she might be getting ready to sit, but the way in which she was tilting seemed off. Suddenly Mildred slumped down and lay sprawled on the ground, showing that she had been leaning on a shovel in front of a large grouping of Monkshood flowers.

"Damn it!" McLane spat the words and sprinted forward, hoping his fears were wrong, but knowing they weren't. He arrived at the prone figure and knelt beside her. He checked her throat for a pulse, but didn't find one, so he lifted her wrist and tried there. "Nothing," he said more softly this time.

"She's dead?" Annie asked, kneeling beside the woman she'd gotten to know since joining this club.

"As far as I can tell." He withdrew his cell phone but couldn't find a signal. "Figures. No cell coverage out here."

"She's not wearing gloves," Annie pointed out.

"What?"

"Gloves. She's not wearing any. That means she dug up and replanted the Monkshood flowers without protection on her hands. I think she must have regretted what she'd done to Bob and decided to make amends in her own strange way. She couldn't have traveled this far as fast as we did, so from the moment she began digging up the flowers she'd begun absorbing the poison and by the time she'd gotten all the way out here and finished planting them the poison had been in her system long enough to stop her heart."

"What a waste of two lives," McLane shook his head. "I guess we'll never know why she did it."

Annie stood and looked about, searching for clues that might lead to answers. She cocked her head at something, then grabbed hold of the fallen shovel and walked about twenty feet away where she began digging.

McLane walked over and stood nearby, noticing that the ground Annie was digging up had already been recently overturned. She wasn't digging a hole, she was redigging one. Annie stopped digging and moved the last bit of dirt away with the shovel blade, exposing black, brown, and white fur.

"Is that an animal?" McLane asked, squatting and peering into the hole.

"Feisty," Annie said, and then since the detective was giving her an odd look she continued, "Feisty is – was – the name of Bob Miller's dog. He was a cute little terrier mix, but as you can guess, he had a feisty nature. Mildred complained a lot that Feisty was always digging up her flowers and got in Bob's face about it. With Bob's lackadaisical but jolly sort of nature he never did anything to stop his dog from his digging. My guess would be that Mildred had gotten fed up with it all and somehow poisoned Bob. Whether she actually meant to kill him or just thought it would give him a scare, I can't say, but once he was dead, she must've gotten rid of Feisty, too, burying him down here. He liked coming down to this area to play in the water."

For several seconds neither of them said anything, and then Annie said, "Oh," and ran to the creek. McLane stood and watched as she first squatted in the creek and rubbed her hands vigorously for several minutes and then began splashing copious amounts of water all over her body, scrubbing at something he was unable to see. For the first time since coming out to this nudist club the detective was glad he still was clothed, or he'd be embarrassed beyond measure at what Annie's antics in the creek had elicited from a portion of his anatomy.

Once Annie had finished her impromptu bathing ritual, she came up out of the creek, sluicing water down along her flesh. McLane turned away, mentally doing mathematical calculations to distract his mind and emotions.

"My hands started tingling," Annie offered as she walked back near him. "Guess there was enough Monkshood residue on the shovel to give me a thrill." She looked over at the expression on her friend's face and knew he'd had his own thrill recently. She smiled, happy he was having that reaction over her.

***

It took a few hours for the ambulance and emergency crew to get to the club and retrieve Mildred's body. By the time they had departed, and everything began getting back to normal, the sun was dipping low over the treetops. McLane had been busy explaining what he and Annie had surmised and filling out reports. Annie had drifted away somewhere, though he had no idea to where. Slowly the detective looked about, but not seeing who he wanted to see, began ambling his way toward the parking lot.

"You plan on leaving without saying goodbye?" McLane turned and found Annie walking his way. His heart once more leapt at the sight of her and he knew it wasn't only because he liked how she looked without clothes.

"I figured you must've headed off to bed," he shrugged.

"Nope, just waiting for you to finish up with work. I didn't want to get in the way. Hey, it's been a long day for you, all the driving and dealing with two deaths. I know you haven't eaten anything the whole time you've been out here, so I whipped something up for you. C'mon, it's just inside the clubhouse kitchen."

"You didn't have to go through the trouble of cooking for me."

"If it was any trouble, I wouldn't have done it. It was a pleasure, oh, but only one stipulation." She stopped facing him and he cocked his head to one side.

"What's that?" he asked, afraid he already knew what her answer would be.

"If you're going to spend the night here you can't wear clothes."

"I don't think I cou…" His eyes grew large and then squinted. "Did you say, 'spend the night'?"

"You know I did," she said, closing the gap between them, his clothes the only barrier between their bodies. "We can eat dinner, soak in the hot tub, or go for a swim in the pool if you'd like, and after that, well, we'll see, ok?"

"But I didn't bring…"

"There is nothing you didn't bring out here that is going to be necessary. I have extra towels and blankets and for everything else, well, the suit you were born in will do just fine."

For once McLane's face didn't show signs of embarrassment. He smiled, nodded his head, and then began unbuttoning his shirt.

Murder at Sunny Green Acres

Robert Longpré

The sky was dark, threatening another day of rain. I slipped out of our bed in the camper to cross the lane in order to use the toilet facilities. Our camper is small, a seventeen - foot 2009 rPod. It is so small, that a couple has to be comfortable with the cramped interior. Luckily, I had bought an add-a-room for the camper which more than doubled our living space, though technically the add-a-room was really more of a tent shelter than camper. Once back from the closet campground toilet, I put on the coffee. We had arrived at Sunny Green Acres three days ago and had another three days left before we had to return to our home and our jobs. I'm an investigative journalist for our city newspaper, and my wife is a Licensed Practical Nurse.

When we arrived a few days ago, it was sunny with the promise of warm temperatures and sunshine for the full six days of our visit to Sunny Green Acres. We had been members of the club for the past five years and enjoyed at least two visits each year since then. We had made friends quite easily. This club was different from the other naturist clubs as it had a core of members who lived on the property year round. Of course, come the Canadian prairie winters, there were no outdoor naturist activities to be had though monthly swims at a pool in the city which was a half hour away did allow us to keep in contact with our naturist friends. We have visited other naturist clubs in western Canada, and even a few in Europe. In our mind, Sunny Green Acres suited us the best. Sauna, swimming pool, hiking trails, sports grounds, a huge clubhouse – and best of all, people who are authentic, welcoming, and great people to have as friends.

Yesterday afternoon, the sunshine disappeared, and with it, the forecast for sunshine during the rest of our stay. We'd been here in the past when the weather turned inclement. And, when that happened, life in the clubhouse became more active. We knew we could also expect a camper crawl, the naturists' version of a pub crawl. Rain and blustery weather didn't mean that our vacation would be cut short.

"Is the coffee ready?"

My wife finally emerged from the camper to join me in the netted enclosure. And, almost on cue, a single male, Josh, as well as the neighbouring couple, Amy and Doug, were visible walking over to our site. We were enjoying a second cup, when we saw Josette rushing towards us. She never came over in the morning, so we were surprised to see her approaching with a serious look on her face.

"Help! Rejean isn't moving. And, there's blood!"

People always came to our campsite when there was any health issue whenever we were at that campsite because Denise is an LPN, the closest thing to a doctor within twenty kilometres of the campgrounds. "I'm coming Josette," she called out. "Rick and Doug, you two come as well. I might need some help lifting him."

Rejean was a big man. His health was poor with high blood pressure and cholesterol, as well as diabetes. Rejean and Josette were one of the seven families that lived full-time on the grounds. Rejean was club president and Josette the club secretary.

Denise entered the house trailer which was the second in the row from the club house. She saw Rejean laying on the floor, face down. There was no movement, no indication that he was breathing. She saw the small pool of blood beside his head and wondered what had happened. She placed two fingers on Rejaean's neck to check for a pulse. There was none. She also noticed that the body had already begun to cool, indicating that Rejean's death occurred at least a few hours ago. Not wanting to compromise the scene for the coroner who would likely have to come, she gave instructions.

"Doug, call the coroner, then come here and do your thing as a cop. Rick, go back to the camper and get your camera." Rejean was dead, and it looked suspicious in her opinion. She backed away from the body and went to comfort Josette who was crying, giving a shake of her head.

"He's gone, Josette. I'm sorry there is nothing I can do for him."

"What am I going to do? If only I had woken up earlier, I might have been able to do something," Josette spoke with self-blame. "It's my fault."

I returned with the camera and began taking photos of the scene following Doug's instructions. I wouldn't be able to use any of these photos for a news article, nor would I if I could. A suspicious death in the campgrounds would make for a sensational story, feeding into all sorts of readers' fantasies. And that was not going to happen if I had any say in the matter.

It was strange to see Doug acting like a professional cop while he was naked. Come to think of it, I was never naked when I was at work as a journalist gathering photos for a story either. Doug and Amy were our friends in the textile world as well as here at the campgrounds. We socialised in our homes as naturists at times, and often went out as couples to events that required us to wear clothes. Speaking quietly to me so as to not upset Josette, Doug suggested that this wasn't a medical death. There was something about the scene that told him Rejean had been murdered.

I could barely keep my voice from reaching Josette and Denise, "What? You have to be kidding. Murdered? Who in hell would murder Rejean?"

"Finding the answer to that depends on why would anyone *want* to murder him," Doug whispered back. "But let's not say anything to anyone else. We need to wait for a coroner's report to determine the real cause of death."

Two hours later, once Rejean's body was transported off the naturist grounds, the rumour mill began to speculate on all sorts of causes. The most popular reason was a heart attack. A fall would account for the small amount of blood at the scene. No one voiced the possibility that it was anything but a natural cause of death. After all, in the naturist world, the crass and violent outer world was held at bay. Naturists were good people, and good people didn't do these kinds of things.

Denise had gone with Josette into the city to deal with medical authorities and to make any necessary arrangements for the body. Doug had also returned to the city with his notes and print copies of the photos I had taken. If Doug's assumptions proved correct, he needed to make sure that the investigative team that would be sent to the naturist campgrounds, were prepared to do their work in a world where no one was wearing clothing. He would have to make sure they were sensitive enough to the protocols of naturist interactions and behaviours so that their interviews weren't compromised. I remained behind to give the residents and visitors at the campgrounds the best answers I could about Rejean's death.

It wasn't long before a group of the ladies from the club decided to organise the community to make sure that Josette would have the support she needed. An agreement was made to have potluck dinners at the clubhouse for the next while. Rejean's death had affected the whole community, and they needed each other now more than ever. Since the majority of them were seniors, their own mortality was amplified.

Josh decided that he needed to keep me company while Denise was in the city. He was a quiet man, the volunteer who mowed the extensive grounds, and served as the grounds keeper's assistant. He had moved into the community two years earlier when he retired as a truck driver. Often for most, he was an invisible man. I was one of the few who made time for him, asked him questions that let him know that he was seen and appreciated as a person. As a result, he was like a moth circling around a flame when I was at the campgrounds. I got used to his almost constant presence.

"Is Josette going to be alright?" Josh asked as we left the clubhouse where the majority of the women were establishing who would be doing what for Josette when she returned. No one wanted to have her left alone.

"I don't know, Josh. One never knows how grief will affect a person," I replied. It was rare that Josh asked questions about others here on the grounds.

Later in the afternoon, Denise returned without Josette who couldn't find the will to return to the house trailer, as she would feel Rejean's absence too much. She had plans to stay in the city at her sister's for the next few days. When Denise told the other ladies, there was a general level of distress. Without Josette being there, they had no way to help process their own grief. Doug came back about a half hour later. He was accompanied by a small team who were going to carry out an investigation. The evidence of foul play demanded that they question everyone who was on the grounds overnight prior to the suspected murder.

“Doug, do they have to be in uniform? You know that being confronted by people wearing clothing is stressful enough when one is naked.”

“Don’t worry,” Doug began as he went on the explain. “The team has agreed to wear shorts or bathing suits for the interviews. Their badges will be on lanyards so that they retain some symbol of their office. The captain wouldn’t agree to any other concessions. I’ve spent most of the time prepping the team on how to question people here. Look at those being interviewed with the focus on their faces being rigidly maintained. You know, the basic naturist etiquette for interactions.”

“I guess it’s the best to be expected considering the situation,” I admitted. “Do you want my help?”

“Yes. If you could be the one to introduce a pair of the investigating team to residents as they are called to be interviewed. I will take care of the second team. The interviews will be happening in the main hall. My team will use the kitchen as an interview room, and your team will use the library beside the hall as an interview room. We need to gather the campers in the hall to await their turns. Do you think Denise can help Amy get everyone into the hall?”

“If there is free food, it won’t be a problem,” I replied with a chuckle evident in my voice. “Besides their curiosity would be enough to have them be in the hall.”

“Great. Now, all I need is a list of everyone who was on the grounds overnight. I imagine that Tanya has all that information.”

Tanya was the person who took care of signing people in; all visitors had to register each time they came. The full-time residents were a different story. Still, Tanya would know who among the residents had been on site. Of course, a few of them would have gone to work in the city. They would be the last ones interviewed once they returned home.

For the next few hours, though there were a few resistors, things went smoothly. Tanya’s list had proven invaluable. She was the one who let Doug know who hadn’t shown up in the hall, who still needed to be interviewed. It was no surprise that those who were absent were mostly those who had jobs in the city. Only three others hadn't shown up. A couple who were occasional visitors had disappeared without letting anyone know where they were going or when they would be returning. The third person was Josh. His absence didn't surprise me as he felt real discomfort when in social conditions. I made a mental note to reach out to him later, when the rest of the interviews were completed.

Just as the missing couple returned and had their interviews completed, a number of the ladies, along with a few widowers, began to organise for the potluck meal. I had told Doug about Josh's continued absence and asked him to go with me. Doing his interview could be done in private, thus bringing a conclusion to the interviews. Well, that was with the exception of Josette. That interview would wait until the data from the interviews gave a clearer picture. Doug was a stickler for protocol. Even though the spouse is typically the one who ends up being guilty, Doug didn't want to interview her without first doing all of his homework.

I knocked on Josh's screen door. Josh's place was a ramshackle affair that had the appearance of being cobbled together using old windows, old panels, and mismatched wood. There was no answer though the wooden door was not closed. Whenever Josh left the campgrounds, he always closed his inner door and locked it. As Doug knocked again, I saw that Josh's old motorcycle was not parked in its usual spot.

"It looks like Josh is gone," I noted to Doug. "No wonder he isn't answering the door. Funny that he left without closing the door and locking up."

"Hm," was Doug's only response. Not hesitating, he opened the door and walked in while calling out Josh's name. No response was given. I walked in right behind Doug and was shocked with the sight of Josh's body laying crumpled on the kitchen floor. The pool of blood by his head was already drying up.

"Stay here," Doug commanded. "I'll go get the other officers. We need to get as much evidence as we can. Just don't touch anything."

I couldn't believe it. A second murder, and that's all it could be, a murder, in one day. To make matters worse, it meant that the murderer was still in the campgrounds. Would he strike again? I immediately had to correct myself. I had no reason to assume that the murderer was a man, though statistics would support my assumption.

While Doug and his team processed the crime scene, I was sent back to the clubhouse to give the news and notify everyone that no one was to leave the campgrounds without first being cleared to do so by the investigating team. The news was received with outrage and more than a bit of fear. I studied each person to see how they responded to the news. As an investigative reporter, I had developed a keen sense of honest versus feigned responses. As much as I studied their faces and body language, I couldn't even begin to suspect a single person in the clubhouse.

Doug reappeared a short while later.

"Well, what do your investigative skills and intuition tell you?" Doug asked, curious as to what my response would be. He had a lot of experience with my intuitive leaps that rarely proved wrong.

"If I was to hazard a guess, I'd say that the killer isn't here, and we have all present and accounted for that aren't on holidays somewhere."

"So, we have to look outside for the murderer. It has to be someone who knows Josh and Rejean, someone who is familiar with the club, perhaps a recent visitor?"

"Doug, I think you're right. Let's go and find out who has been a visitor so far this season. The answers will help us begin to ask better questions."

"Right as usual, Rick."

We soon got to see the visitor log. Most of the visitors were from out of province, folks who decided to make a stop at our campgrounds before heading west to Alberta and British Columbia. There were only three individuals, two single women, and a single man. The man was from Fort Qu'Appelle, a town not too far away beside a series of lakes, and the two women were from the city.

"Now, all I have to do," Doug stated, "is to find out as much about these three as visitors here, and how they connect with Josh and Rejean. Let's go back to the club house."

Doug announced that the threat of more deaths was gone. The evidence pointed to an outsider, or perhaps more than one as responsible for the murders. As the gathering gave a huge sigh of relief, they began to leave to return to their campsites, or their homes in the city. Doug found two regulars who lived on site, and a couple who were residents for the full five months of the late spring to early fall of the season. The four stayed back as the others left.

"So, what do any of you know about Martha, Joanne, and Dan, recent visitors to Sunny Green Acres?" Doug began.

"Martha is a frequent guest during the winter swims in the city," one of the four offered.

"I remember her," I remarked. "She's quite fit if I remember correctly."

"Joanne is a widow, you know, the petite woman in her late sixties," offered the wife of the couple.

"So what about Dan?" Doug prodded. "Anyone meet him and get to know him a bit?"

"Um," began the man who was married. "We'd had him to our place on two different occasions. What would you say, Grace? Would you characterise him as a bit of an odd bird? Personally, I didn't like him. We never invited him to our place after his second visit."

Grace confirmed her husband's statement, "He was weird, very weird. I was the one who told Pat that he wasn't to invite him over again. He gave me the creeps."

A few more general questions followed before Doug thanked them and had them leave.

"Well, what do you think, Doug? Is Dan our main suspect?"

"No. I think Grace and Pat would like Dan to be the main suspect."

"So now what?" I asked.

"Well, we got our wives waiting for us. Tomorrow, will be soon enough to solve the mystery. Let's go grab a beer and sit around the fire before our wives send out a search party for us."

Later that night, while laying in bed, Denise breathing softly in her sleep, my mind couldn't rest. I had the sense that the answer was there, in front of my nose. I knew better than to force it as that would only push it further into the background. So, I slipped out of bed to take a stroll around the sleeping campgrounds. I needed the exercise to still my head. All the lights were out in the rows of campers and trailers, all but one set. I didn't consciously register that fact as I continued my walk wearing only a pair of flip flops. I didn't go barefoot as there were too many stones on the path.

Returning back to my camper, I slipped into bed, trying hard not to disturb Denise. I had no sooner pulled her closer to me when a light bulb flashed on in my head. I had to talk to Doug, now.

"Don't go," Denise mumbled.

"I'll be right back," I promised.

Doug's trailer was the second one in our row. I soon found myself tapping softly on his door. The door opened and I could tell that Doug hadn't been able to fall asleep either.

"Well, Rick? What has your spidey sense come up with?"

"Pat and Grace."

"Motive?"

"I don't know, Doug. That is going to be up to you to figure out."

"Give me a second, I'll just make a call to the station," Doug said.

A few minutes later, Doug could be seen nodding his head. I hadn't heard the conversation as Doug had kept his voice low so as to not disturb anyone.

"Are your ready to come with me?" Doug asked. "If so, get some clothes on. Two officers are on their way and will be here in twenty minutes. We will be taking Pat and Grace in for questioning. I need you to let them know that their help is vital. Thanks to their information, we now have a prime suspect. I'm sure they will be very happy to cooperate with us."

"Sure, I better go let them know so that they will be ready to go the station in the city. We can't exactly appear while nude," I spoke with a grin on my face.

While Doug went back into his camper to get dressed before heading to the gate to meet his colleagues, I went to Grace and Pat's to inform them of the situation. As Doug had predicted, they were more than happy to help.

Three quarters of an hour later, we arrived at the station. The four of us went into the Suburban rather than take our separate cars. Just as we reached the front desk, handcuffs were produced and placed on both Pat and Grace.

"What?" screeched Grace. "What are you doing?"

While she was protesting, Pat made an attempt to run. He didn't get far.

"Pat and Grace," Doug stated, with a serious tone, "You are being arrested on suspicion of murdering Rejean and Josh. Anything you say can be used in court. You have the right to an attorney. The police will provide you with a phone to make a call to your lawyer, or anyone else. Now, please follow me to the interview room."

"The couple were placed in a room that had two video cameras, a two-way mirror, and a table with six chairs arranged, three on each side. No sooner had they been seated, when we left them in the room by themselves. The cameras were activated and the audio recorder had been turned on.

I had done my part and was shown to the lounge where I would wait while the interview took place. I was surprised when Doug reappeared less than an hour later.

"They confessed," he uttered in relief.

"Why did they do it?"

"Pat and Grace have been covertly photographing people at the campgrounds, especially the children. They were making good money selling the photos. Josh saw them taking photos yesterday – I mean the day before now that it's after midnight. He confronted them, and then told Rejean. Knowing they would end up in prison for child pornography, they decided to take out the only two who knew."

"What a dust up! There's going to be a lot of pissed off people. This isn't going to go well for the campground."

“I think you’ll be surprised, Rick. Having the nudists react so quickly to a child pornography scheme will earn them a ton of respect in the textile world.”

“But they didn’t!” I protested. “They don’t even know what’s going on.”

“Think about it, Rick. You are a nudist, I am a nudist ... we responded very, very quickly to the situation.”

“Yeah, you’re right,” I admitted.

“Now, it’s up to you Mr. Journalist, to make sure that the media has the right story to tell, how major crimes of murder and child pornography were solved, with the help of nudists, at Sunny Green Acres Nudist Resort.”

Murder in a Nudist Colony

Ted Bun

"How the hell has that happened?" He had only left the site office a few minutes earlier. Now the door was wedged shut, something soft and heavy. He pushed hard on the stout wooden door and it opened another few inches, just not enough.

“Are you locked out, Pete?” The imposing bulk of Jim the Gym, so-called because of his toned physique, appeared beside him.

“Not locked out, but something seems to have got wedged behind the door. It moves a little if I push hard enough!” Pete, the Club Secretary, explained to the bigger man.

“Let me have a go.” Jim flexed his toned muscles, set himself solidly on his feet and got low to the door, like the rugby forward he probably had been.

“A rugger player then, Jim?” Pete observed.

“Yeah!” Jim grunted as he balanced himself ready to apply his considerable strength to drive the door back.

It took all his might and a bit of extra help from Pete to open the door wide enough. Pete slipped through the gap to clear the obstruction and promptly wished he hadn’t.

The object behind the door was, or had been, a middle-aged man. A man who had recently signed up as a member of the club. He wouldn’t be getting value for money for his membership though. He was dead.

The clues were pretty clear, he wasn’t moving, there was a large dent in his skull and he was cold when Pete felt for his non-existent pulse.

***

Inspector Merton was actually quite happy to be called in for the murder. He hated Saturdays with nothing to do; ever since his wife Wendy had left him and gained a divorce citing his job as co-respondent. Murder was quite rare in rural Shropshire, it would mean he could pass all the tractor thefts off onto his colleagues. He had come to the conclusion that there was only one tractor and it was being passed around; all part of a giant insurance scam. Still, he had his murder, if he was careful and got everything tied down neatly, it could be his ticket to the Chief Inspector's post that would be open in September, when his boss retired.

"Good Morning, Sir." The uniformed Constable at the gate lent through the passenger window. "The Forensics Team are inside. Plus there is a team of my colleagues securing the scene. If you need any help taking statements, give me a call."

"I'll bear that in mind." Merton chuckled to himself at the double entendre. Bear, bare… well he was just driving through the gates of the Nudist Colony. As he drove on, guided by the signs to the office, he thought he glimpsed naked people on the periphery of his vision.

'Oh God!' A thought flashed into his mind. 'Suppose that is Gordon or Daphne!' His ex-in-laws were keen nudists, as had been Wendy when he first met and courted her. In fact, it had cropped up frequently in arguments towards the end of their marriage.

"I gave up so much to be with you!" Wendy would shout.

He would ask, "Like what?"

"Weekends in the country, with my parents! I had to stop going because of your precious job!"

He couldn't deny it. He was fine, stretched out naked on a beach in Spain, but it was the risk of someone local seeing him, "He's one of those pervert nudist-people!" The thought of being outed from the dock was just too awful to consider joining his in-laws, ever!

Merton climbed out of his car and flashed his warrant card at the PC who was more interested in the odd glimpse of movement at the nearby pool.

"Fancy going to take down names and addresses do you, Son?" Merton paused, as the Constable's face gave away his enthusiasm for the task. "Well, it ain't going to happen."

Pete came hurrying to meet the new arrival. "Good morning, I'm Peter, the Club Secretary, I found the body."

"Good Morning, Peter. Inspector Merton, CID. The first thing I need from you is a complete list of everyone who is here today. I know there are sensitivities, so I assure you that I will be the only person who sees that list. Secondly, I want you to go around and double-check that everybody on the list is present and that nobody else is." Merton paused, to allow Peter to come back with any objection. He didn't. "Good, I see you understand how awkward I could make this."

"It would be quicker if I could have my clipboard, it's on the desk, a blue one, with about four sheets of paper on it."

"Hang on a minute, I'll see if Forensics have finished with it." Merton went over to the doorway and spoke with the Senior Forensics man. He returned with the clipboard, which was thick with fingerprinting powder.

"I'll need to speak to you in a little while. So be quick."

"I'll be as quick as possible, Inspector. If I am not back, you might want to start with Jim there, he was with me when we found the body." Peter pointed towards the big man, who was still obviously distraught.

***

The Pathologist had arrived to do a preliminary exam, so Merton went to have a word with the Forensics Team.

"The victim died about midnight, maybe the early hours of this morning. I'll be able to be more definite when I get core temperatures."

"Thanks, Doc, Any idea of the cause of death yet?"

"Actually, I think he choked on his own vomit, there is a head injury, but I think that happened post-mortem." Merton must have looked confused; the Pathologist expanded on his observations. "The victim was bound and gagged and was originally hanging from the roof beams." He pointed to the frayed end of a rope that still hung from a crossbeam, high up in the open roof space, some five metres above them.

"Kinky sex?"

"Maybe, Inspector. I'll know more when I get the PM done." He turned to the men from the Coroner's Office, who were waiting to take the body away. "I think we are done here; you can take him now."

As the corpse was rolled into a black, body-bag, Merton caught his first view of the victim's face. He recognised a small-time, local criminal. "I didn't have 'Phil the Fence' down as being dangerously kinky!" He observed out loud. Merton had recognised the local Pawn Shop owner. He was a 'known' character; the force had been trying to convict him of handling stolen goods for years.

The Pathologist wasn't looking at the corpse, he was more interested in the small pool of bright pink urine that the body had lain in. "Get me some pictures of that puddle will you, and I want a sample in a sterile container, please. Send it straight off for a drug screen."

The Forensic Officers moved promptly, to comply with the Pathologist's requests.

"Oh, and I would go cautious with the 'Kinky Sex' story, there are several things that point away from that."

"Sorry, Doc. What are you saying? A naked man, bound and gagged and it might not involve a sexual motive?"

"I'd consider that there are none of the usual signs of those types of sex games, no signs of whip or cane marks. There is no evidence that he had been penetrated and his feet were over two metres off the ground while he was hanging." The Pathologist paused, before adding, "As for the victim being naked, it is the dress code hereabouts!"

***

"I was late arriving this morning." Pete the Club Secretary explained. "We, my wife and I, had to stop at the cash-and-carry to get some snacks, beer and soft drinks for the bar. Last night's barbeque had been well attended, as is often the case when we have a good weather forecast for the Bank Holiday weekend. The party was still going strong when we left, about half ten. It must have been then or thereabouts because we got home in time for me to catch the Ten O'Clock News headlines."

"Pardon?"

"On the 'plus one' service, Inspector. I seldom get in to watch the news at the proper time, not since I retired."

"That explains that; so last night, when was the last time you were in the office?" Merton was trying to get the sequence of events clear in his mind. His main witness was still slightly shocked from discovering the corpse and wandered around the timeline.

"I took most of the bar takings, bagged them up and brought it over to put it in the safe. Just like I always do. I checked the key-board to make sure the keys had all been returned. They were all in place. I turned off the light and shut the door, I gave it a push to make sure it was latched. I do that every time, I came in one morning a few years back and found the door open."

"Was your wife with you at this time?"

"She was getting dressed and fetching my clothes from our locker in the dressing room." Pete pointed towards the breeze block building near the pool.

"I see," Merton made a note. "Then you went straight home, and got back here this morning; at what time would that be?"

"A little after ten, I am supposed to unlock the pool at ten and there was already a queue at the gate as I was a little late. I dropped the shopping and my wife at the clubhouse." That would be the big brick building, surrounded by a sheltering terrace, Merton surmised. "Then I dashed in here, grabbed the pool keys and went to open the pool up. I must have slammed the door as I came out, I normally keep the office closed."

"OK, what happened next, did you come straight back?"

"There was a bit of a delay while I dealt with a few questions and teasing about being late. It was probably a quarter to eleven. I went to open the door and something was stopping it opening. Jim was passing, so he gave me a hand pushing the door wide enough to get in. You know the rest."

"Had you noticed anything untoward, unusual, out of place when you went into the office earlier?"

“Sorry Inspector, I just dived in, grabbed the keys and shot out again.”

“Thank you, Peter, now what can you tell me about the victim? Was he a member of the ‘Colony’?”

“Yes, he was a fairly new member of the ‘Club’. We really don’t like the word ‘colony’ but we are stuck with it because the post office won’t change our address. Just because the first Rates’ demand, (the old name for the Council Tax) was addressed to the ‘Nudist Colony, Long Lane,’ almost a hundred years ago!”

Pete had pulled a black ledger out of his desk. “Yes, Phillip Butler, joined The Lawn and Pool Club in May this year. He came for a day visit with his wife, Justine, and joined the following week. Nothing came back on his CRB, Criminal Record, check.”

“Is Justine at the col … sorry, The Club today?”

“Now you mention it, I haven’t seen Justine for a while.”

Merton didn’t let on that, as far as he was aware, Phil the Fence Butler, had been single, ever since that nasty incident with his ex-wife. Dianna Butler’s brothers had roughed him up, more than a little, over two years back. “Can you give me a description of Justine Butler?”

“I can do better than that, I have her membership card details on the system, with a copy of the photo we used for her membership card.”

It turned out that Justine Butler was actually Justine Harris and the closest thing Phil had to a regular partner. One to follow up later.

A quick inspection of the door revealed it was a single Yale lock. Which bore scratches and marks of having been opened without a key a number of times. Merton advised the Club Secretary to get deadlocks fitted to all the doors, as these old fashioned locks were not up to securing a door for more than a few minutes.

Merton had his list of names but nobody had come forward in response to his appeal for information that might shed some light on the events of the night before. Until a young girl, of maybe twelve years old, approached Merton to tell him how she had slipped out of the family’s caravan to go to the toilet. She had no idea what the time was, except the moon was still bright enough not to need to use her torch. On the way back, she had heard an argument, something about keys. It wasn't any of her business, so she had just let herself back into the caravan and gone back to sleep.

Merton was starting to get worried, a body but no motive for the killing, the means were unclear and so far everybody and their dog had an opportunity.

"Opportunity," that was the opening, whoever had done this had gotten into the nudist colony, either invited or covertly. Time to find Peter again.

"I would be lying if I said it was impossible to get into the grounds through the fence. We have to chase off kids who find gaps at least once a year. Everybody else would have to sign in, electronically, at the gate using their gate card. The computer access record would show everyone checking in and the number of people passing through with them from the car park. We used to have a problem if someone swiped to open the gate and let in a whole group. So, we put in the turnstile and count people in," Peter explained as he showed the gate system to Merton.

"On the other hand, if there is a gap in your fence anybody could sneak in?" Merton was overwhelmed again.

"Yes, but they would stick out like a sore thumb; unless they dressed the part!"

Merton's phone rang; it was the Pathologist. "Interesting case this one. The first time I have come across a case of phenolphthalein as a cause of death."

"Sorry, Doc, Phenol what?"

"Ex-Lax poisoning. Somebody had given the poor chap a huge amount of the laxative, then hung him up. The trouble was he vomited, choked and died."

"Why would someone shove a load of laxative down somebody's throat? Then hang them up?"

"I would hazard an opinion that they were trying to recover something from the victim's gut and didn't want to get too messy."

"Drugs I suppose?"

“No Inspector, a key, it looks like a locker key, with a yellow tag engraved ‘L&PC’.”

“Lawn and Pool Club, I don’t wonder. I’ll check that out. Anything else?”

“A partially digested pawn ticket for a ‘gold and diamond ring’ securing a loan of £500. He had swallowed the ticket at sometime after eating a beef burger.”

“Thanks a lot, Doc! That might explain the motive.”

“While we are on motive, there are absolutely no signs of sexual activity before or after death on the corpse.”

“Thanks for that Doc, I look forward to getting the full report next week. Enjoy what’s left of your weekend!”

Merton looked around; he had wandered into the grounds as he talked on his mobile. There were several tents and caravans arranged around the edge of a small paddock. ‘I wonder …’

He turned on his heel and walked purposely towards the clubhouse.

That had been a waste of effort, except it ruled out a few options. The check on all the Club members that had stayed overnight had revealed a speeding ticket and a couple of parking fines. Otherwise, there was no record of any of them on the police computers.

There was better news from the Uniforms. They had found a break in the fence separating the Club from an adjacent field. After he had finished going through the list, Merton set off on foot to find the gap from the inside of the Colo … the Club grounds. He still struggled with the Colony vs Club argument.

“Sid!” There was a pause. “Sidney!”

Only one person had called him ‘Sidney’ in the past five years. Merton stopped and turned. “Wendy! This is unexpected!” The sight that met his eyes was familiar and still attractive. “You aren’t on the list I was given this morning.”

“I wouldn’t be, I only arrived a little while ago. What’s going on, I mean something major has to have happened to get you into the Club grounds?”

"There has been a death, which we are treating as suspicious, overnight."

"Oh!"

"I was about to go and look at where we think the perpetrators got in. Walk with me and I'll fill you in on the details."

"Sid, are you sure you want to be seen walking with a naked woman?"

"That's not fair, I am here on duty, I'm free to question anybody I need to." He held out his hand "Come! I'll tell you all about it as we go." He smiled and they walked towards the reported hole in the fence.

They found the gap in the fence and an area of crushed grass. Several cigarette ends lay in the trampled grass alongside a couple of screwed up pieces of foil. Merton called for Forensics to come and check for other evidence.

There was a rustling sound in the hedge behind them. Merton whirled around, half expecting to see a uniformed officer drooling over his wife's naked body. OK, his ex-wife's naked body.

It was a relief to see the long face of a brown horse looking through the fence. They both laughed and started back towards the clubhouse.

"As I understand it," Wendy mused as they walked, if the killers were after what that pawn ticket represented; they didn't get what they wanted last night. However, they must suspect that whatever they want is here somewhere. I expect they will be back."

"I expect you are right," Merton had missed that, he had been so wound up in the immediate, he hadn't looked forward. "In fact, you are spot on. I think they are desperate enough to try again as soon as the coast is clear."

He formulated a plan. He would get the Uniforms pulled back. Just the one car, lurking about a mile away for back up. He would stake out the dressing room and see who came calling.

"Just two problems, Sid," Wendy observed, as the last of the squad cars left. "One, you are overdressed if you want to merge in."

"Now they have all left, I'll strip off. I just never wanted it all around the Station about us, me … the nude thing." He removed his tie and started to unbutton his shirt.

"Yes, that'll help. The second thing is, you know we don't allow single men as members. If you want, I am prepared to be your partner for tonight." A look flashed across Merton's face. Wendy raised her hand. "Work partner, that's all!"

"Thank you."

"Come on Sid, there are still a couple of hours of sunshine, let's go and make our observations from the poolside."

They sat by the pool chatting, then moved to the clubhouse terrace, where Wendy had a beer while Merton sipped at a can of coke. Wendy kept up a commentary about the people they could see. They were all regulars at the Club. About eleven o'clock, the clubhouse started to empty, soon there were too few people left to provide cover.

Wendy produced a key from her handbag, "My parents' caravan, we can keep warm and out of sight in there. Although you may need to be outside from time to time, because we can't see the dressing room from the caravan."

They sat together in the caravan and chatted about mutual friends. Once an hour or so Merton went out into the bright moonlit night for 'a walk to the toilet block' and to have a listen to what was happening outside.

It was on one of these walks, that he heard the screech of tearing metal. Someone was in the dressing room jemmying open at least one of the lockers. Merton hurried back to the caravan and asked Wendy to summon the back-up car. He was going to try to get a good look at the perpetrators.

From outside of the dressing room - actually, it was a block-built shed that housed the lockers where people could store the clothes they arrived in and other belongings while they were at the Club - he could see very little. The windows were too high to look through, just the movement of a flashlight and the noise revealed that there were people inside.

The noise stopped, then a few seconds later the door opened. Merton had to act.

“Stop Police!” He shouted. One figure, a female he guessed, stood still. Then raised her arms. Merton moved closer. A mistake, a large man barrelled out of the door, crashing into Merton knocking him down.

As he regained his feet, Merton could see the figures running in the direction of the hole in the fence. Knowing where they were heading, how far it was and his own level of fitness, he took off at a steady pace initially losing ground.

It didn’t take long though for the slighter figure to start stumbling and falling back. The big man had to slow down for her, briefly pulling her behind him, until she stumbled and fell. He looked around and saw Merton was alone and abandoned his partner and ran onwards.

Reaching the gap in the fence, less than twenty metres ahead of Merton, the man did not stop for his clothes as he dived through the opening.

There was the sound of galloping hooves, something falling and a stream of oaths.

Merton cautiously looked through the fence. In the moonlight, he could see the horse standing a short distance off, flicking its tail. Nearby, the figure of a man crawled out of a patch of stinging nettles, whimpering as each new frond of vegetation brushed against his naked skin. The horse snorted, neighed and ambled away to find somewhere quieter to spend the night.

“You are under arrest,” Merton realised that he had no handcuffs or any equipment with him as he finished reciting his captive’s rights.

“I thought you might need these!” Wendy was walking towards him with his handcuffs held out.

“Thank you, how did you know?”

“You always get your man, Sid.” Then under her breath, she added, “or woman.”

Merton did not hear the aside, he was too busy getting the cuffs on his prisoner. “Did you see his partner in crime on your way up?”

“Yes, Sid. I don’t think she is going to cause any trouble. I left her waving the torch to attract your back-up team.”

They escorted the prisoner back down the slope and handed him over to the two uniformed officers. Eventually, they bundled the two, wrapped in blankets, into the back of the squad car and it drove off, blue lights flashing.

The prisoners had talked; they had told Merton about the insurance scam. The fake break-in at their house. The report of the theft of a very valuable, antique ring. A ring that had been pawned for a hundredth of its real value at Phil-the-Fence’s shop. Phil had found out the true value of the ring and refused to return it to them. They had discovered he was hiding the ring at the Pool and Lawn Club. When they had challenged him, he had swallowed the key so they couldn’t take it from him.

They had driven off into town and bought the rope and laxatives and returned after dark. Phil had laughed at them again, snatching the pawn ticket from them and had swallowed it. Then he had threatened to start shouting, attracting other people ‘to the burglary he had interrupted’.

“I grabbed him and stuffed all the chocolate in his mouth, then I gagged him with a bit of cloth. That shut him up. Then we tied him up. It was going to take a while for the laxative to work and it would be messy, so, we decided to hoist him up off the ground. We would be able to see fairly easily as soon as we got the key back. Then we went outside to get a drink and a breath of fresh air. When we went back into the office, he wasn’t moving at all and didn’t respond. We panicked and ran.”

They had still needed to get the ring back, so they had returned with a crow-bar and searched through the lockers until they found it. Merton had removed it from the unresisting female prisoner’s finger and put it into an evidence bag.

“I’d better be off too, get them booked in and questioned. Thank you for your help Wendy, and for such a pleasant evening.”

"My pleasure Sid, it has been, well, different."

"I'll need to take a witness statement from you tomorrow."

"I'll be here, bring a towel we can go for a swim afterwards, you know the Dress Code!"

Merton leaned forward and gave his ex-wife a peck on the cheek. "Until tomorrow then."

"Yes, until tomorrow." Wendy paused, then, as he walked off towards his car, she called, "Sid!" He turned to look back. "Don't forget to put some clothes on!"

A Murder in Eden

Gregg B. White

Pam was staring at the pool trying to figure out why and how it had such a red hue to it. There was no brilliant sunrise that could reflect such color. Had someone gone swimming during the night wearing a swimsuit that left red die in the water? Normally a midnight dip would be a “skinny dip”. Here, at Eden 2, the pool rules forbid wearing clothes. Certainly, someone wouldn't “streak” a nudist resort by wearing clothing? How strange would that be?

She was still puzzling it out when she heard a woman scream from over by the toilet facility. As the camp co-manager she ran over immediately to see what had happened. The red pool could wait.

Pam found Helen kneeling on the ground totally panic-stricken. Pam tried to help her stand and calm her down. Then she looked for the reason Helen was so terrified.

Just a few feet away lay a man, covered in blood with an ax buried in his face. He was almost totally unrecognizable. Only his waist and legs were clearly visible. Although Pam had seen hundreds of penises, she couldn't recognize who it might be. She just stared at the body lost in thought for a moment.

Her husband Dan ran up and brought her back to reality, telling her to take Helen to the office and call 911, while he cordoned off the area. She blinked back to reality and hurried Helen off. She gave Helen a cup of coffee and called the police, then poured one for herself. While on the phone she heard a car leave but didn't see who it might be. She waited by the gate for the police.

Two police cars raced up not two minutes later with lights and sirens. Pam triggered the automatic gate then ran out to direct them. She wondered if she should have put on a dress or robe, but decided that they would see many more naked people today anyway. Dan came around the corner just then so she pointed them in his direction and went back to Helen. She figured there would be detectives and the coroner coming eventually, so she waited in the office.

"This looks like someone was copycatting Lizzy Borden, Lt. Szpicelski."

"What do you mean, Doctor?"

"Don't you know the poem:

Lizzy Bordon took an ax

Gave her mother 40 whacks.

When she saw what she had done,

Gave her father 41?"

"No. What does it have to do with this case?"

"Well, Lizzy was the prime suspect, but was found innocent of the crime. One theory of how she did it was that she stripped off all her clothes before she attacked her step-mother and father. Then she took a bath and washed off all the blood, dried off, dressed and then summoned the police. Back in 1892, there was nothing that could tie her to the crime.

"And look at this blood splatter on the ground. The killer must have hidden in these bushes and, stepping out, immediately buried the ax into the victim's chest. The perp would have been covered in blood. You can see exactly where he was standing. The victim fell backwards and was dead or dying when the ax shattered his face. I put time of death between 2 to 3 am."

"Lieutenant, Doctor" said Pam who had just walked up as the doctor was telling the story, "there is a red hue to the pool this morning. Could that have anything to do with this?"

"Lead me there, and thanks for the clue." said Lt. Szpicelski. "Doctor, you may just be right."

As they walked, the lieutenant was looking down at the ground and stopped suddenly.

"Officer Green, grab those evidence markers from my bag and put one by this bloody print."

He spotted and marked six more between the toilet facility and the pool.

"Officer Green, please tape this whole pool area off. It doesn't look like anyone has gone for a swim yet today. Can you turn the pump off, so the water isn't disturbed anymore?" He said to Pam.

"It appears the killer dove in the deep end, swam to the shallow end, got out, and immediately walked to a car." He said as much to himself as anyone. When Pam joined him at the shallow end of the pool he asked; "Do you have video cameras anywhere on the grounds?"

"We only have one on the front gate to record arrivals and departures. People get a bit sensitive about having their pictures taken on the grounds. Society is not very accepting of our chosen lifestyle." Once again Pam realized she was nude while the detective was fully dressed; she just let the idea pass.

"Do you log everyone into the park when they arrive?"

"We do for guests, but our members have the code for the keypad by the gate. They can just let themselves in. No one ever logs out."

"Please review your video from last night and this morning along with Officer Green, and see who came and went. I am especially interested between 1 and 3:30 am."

"Lieutenant," said Officer Green, "we have a classic Mustang entering just after 1:00am and leaving at about 2:45. The plate was somehow obscured. The driver had the sun visor down and an arm covering their face when they entered, so they clearly knew they were being filmed. No one else entered or left the park until just before we arrived. The camera angle is such that whoever left is completely unrecognizable."

"Thank you, Officer Green, I presume you have the video files for evidence?"

"Yes sir, Pam was nice enough to provide us with a thumb drive."

"Thank you, Pam. I hope you can help us figure out who the victim might be and who left just after the body was discovered."

"I think I might be able to do that. The little piece of the car I saw leaving may have belonged to Robert and Alice - we don't use last names here if we can help it. We can walk up to their trailer and see if they are here or not. I saw both of them yesterday and the victim is the right size for Robert. I'm sorry I can't provide a better identification from the body." Pam said that last sentence very hesitantly and almost in tears. She had manager to control her emotions pretty well until she once again looked toward the body. Even if it was covered by a sheet, she couldn't unsee the horrific sight of this morning.

Robert and Alice's car was definitely gone, the trailer was unlocked, and it looked like the bed had been slept in but unmade. There were no personal items or clothes for either Robert or Alice except robes, sweaters, and pool shoes, all in the closet.

"I will need to get their last name and address from your records," said Lieutenant Szpicelski. "Right now, I am presuming Robert is our victim and Alice may or may not be our suspect. Here is my card if you find anyone else from the park who might also be unaccounted for or if anyone indicates they saw something that they didn't mention to our officers. Thanks again, Pam, for your assistance."

It was just after noon when Lt. Szpicelski arrived at the home of Robert and Alice Carinos. There was one car parked in front of the garage but no one answered the door. The detective canvased the neighborhood and learned from the neighbor across the street that Alice had driven up just as he was out getting his Sunday paper. He was surprised when she got out of the car totally naked and ran to the door. She fumbled with the keys for a bit before she got inside. He knew they were nudists but had never seen them nude outside before. He figured she was just nervous because she hadn't seen him until she was on the porch fully exposed. Then about 15 minutes later he saw her come out again, this time dressed, and get into a car that had just pulled up. No one else on the block had seen anything that morning.

It wasn't until almost 5:45pm that Alice drove up in her white Prius and parked next to her husband's car. Before she got to the front door she was met by the detective.

"Mrs. Carinos, I am Lt. Szpicelski of the San Bernardino police department. We have reason to believe something has happened to your husband."

“Really? His car is here, are you sure he isn't home? Look, the door is unlocked, he must be here. Robert!” Alice called.

When she got no response, she walked through the whole house with the detective following, occasionally calling her husband's name. When she got to the bedroom she found his wallet, keys and cell phone on her night stand rather than on the dresser where he usually kept them. Only then did she start to worry.

“May I ask where you have been Mrs. Carinos?” asked Lt. Szpicelski.

“My company was working a convention in Palm Springs this weekend. I went out Friday to set up, then worked our booth Saturday all day and Sunday until about 2:00pm. Then we broke it all down and headed for home.”

“Can anyone verify your presence there?”

“Of course, I have a crew of seven other people. We go to a show somewhere every other weekend. We all do the set up and tear down, work the booth at various hours and have dinner and breakfast together. I can provide you with everyone's name and phone number if that is what you need. But why are you asking me, what exactly has happened to my husband that you need to know my whereabouts?”

“I am afraid your husband has been murdered, and we need you to verify that it was in fact him.”

“Where? When?” Suddenly Alice seemed to be in a panic, totally surprised and shocked by such news.

“The body was discovered this morning at Eden Two nudist park in San Bernardino. It was a very brutal murder and no one could provide a positive ID. I am sorry to have to ask you to do this but we need to have you either ID the body or discover your husband’s whereabouts.”

“I don't know what to do! What was Robert doing at the park without me? How come his car is outside? Why are you asking me when I was two hours away all day?”

“Your neighbor said he saw you came home at about nine this morning in the other car. He saw you get out totally naked and go into the house. Then about fifteen minutes later you came out dressed and got into a car that had just pulled up."

"That is nonsense! At nine this morning I was working the booth in Palm Springs with five of my colleagues. And I would never go running around my front yard in the nude. Some neighbors think they know we are nudists but we have never proven it to them. Well, except for the Johnstons who we took to the park one weekend."

"Can you please come with me tonight? I would like to resolve who the victim is as soon as possible in case it isn't Robert. I will drive you to San Bernardino and arrange for your ride home again. I know it is about an hour each way and in your excited state I do not want you to have to drive yourself."

Alice went with the detective but was silent the entire way except for the occasional sob or nose blowing. When she saw the body, she said it definitely was Robert and appeared on the edge of hysteria the whole time she was in the morgue. Lt Szpicelski offered her some dinner but she said she couldn't possibly eat in her state. He arranged for a female detective to drive Alice home, and it was reported that she said nothing on the drive.

The next day Lt. Szpicelski went to Alice's office and verified what she had said about the convention. Since none of her co-workers were expected in until Wednesday, he would have to come back then to get their statements.

He then went to Robert's office. The head of HR told him that Alice had called in the morning and, through her sobs, said that Robert had been murdered. He asked to speak with Robert's colleagues to see if any of them might have any idea who might have done this, or if anyone knew the owner of a classic Mustang. As a group they said they hadn't seen anyone angry with Robert ever and no one knew about any affairs. As far as they all knew Robert was totally devoted to his wife. None of them however had ever met her. There was one woman however, Ellie, who looked so much like Alice that she could have been her twin.

He asked for a conference room he could use to hold individual interviews and went one by one with some basic questions. He really wasn't interested in anyone but Ellie but he didn't want to tip her off.

When it was Ellie's turn he began with basic questions like how long had she worked there and how long had she known Robert. She didn't last more than a couple of questions before she totally broke down in sobs.

“I was with Robert over the weekend. I knew he was married but somehow we had started an affair. Since his wife was away every other weekend we would go to his trailer. We were very careful to never let anyone at work know about us and we didn't socialize at the camp.”

“What happened yesterday morning that you left the camp abruptly?”

“I was awakened that morning by a woman screaming nearby. I noticed Robert was already out of the bed, but he usually got up early and at least once during the night because he took blood pressure meds and a diuretic, so he went to the bathroom often. Once awake I got up and headed to the toilets - we always use the park’s bathroom facilities. As I approached the facilities, I saw the gruesome dead body and knew immediately it was Robert.”

“How did you recognize him when no one else there could?”

“His foreskin only covers two thirds of the head of his penis. I had seen it many times so it was instant recognition. Most nudists don't look at each other's privates even though they are easily seen, so I can understand them not noticing.”

“What did you do then?”

“Well first I almost peed right there I was so shocked. I ran into the Ladies’. I almost didn't make it. As soon as I was done I walked out as calmly as I could and went back to the trailer.”
“Did anyone see you?”

“Dan was just approaching with some barriers to place around the area but he didn't acknowledge me and I didn't say anything to him.”

“Then what did you do?”

“I was just on the edge of panic. I loved Robert and would never have hurt him. I knew he was married and I didn't want to spoil his good name by linking him to an affair.”

"So take me through exactly what you did."

"When I got back to the trailer, I grabbed a bag and put all of our clothes and personal items into it. Everything but Robert's keys. I got into the car and drove slowly out of the park, not trying to draw any attention. Just after I turned onto the main road I saw two police cars heading toward the camp with lights and sirens going. I felt a bit relieved to have gotten away before they shut the park down. But then I realized I had his car and no idea where he lived. Before I got to the freeway I pulled over and tried his GPS system. I found his home address. I followed the directions and tried to remain calm thinking of what to do next. When I got to his house, I parked in the driveway, grabbed the bag, and headed to the front door. As I was trying to find the right key to unlock the door, I suddenly realized that I was still naked and had been that way the entire drive. I almost dropped the keys when that realization hit me. I went inside, found the bedroom, put all his clothes in the hamper and his wallet, phone, and keys onto the nightstand closest to the bathroom. Then I got dressed myself, summoned a Lyft and waited inside the front door until it arrived. I rode home in silence, then totally lost it for over an hour once I was in my own bedroom."

"You realize that by your actions you have broken several laws."

"Yeah, I guess so. But at the time I just went into survival mode and hoped I wouldn't have been found out."

"Did you know that you look enough like Robert's wife to be her twin?"

"No! I never met her and no one at the office ever said anything. That does explain why at the park he told me that if anyone called me Alice I should just go with it."

"So tell me how this affair began."

"Well, I knew most of the LA crew from when I worked in the Texas office, but they were just voices on the phone. About eight months ago the firm consolidated our department and paid me to move from Texas. In my first or second week, Robert mentioned to me that since his wife was working the weekend he would be honored to show me around LA, since I had never been here before and was just settling in.

"I agreed, and that Saturday he took me to the zoo and then up to the observatory for a good overview of the city. It was purely platonic, no hand holding, no arm around my shoulder or waist, and certainly no kissing. I felt quite safe with him, like a big brother.

"On other weekends we went to Hollywood Blvd., or the Getty Museum, the Tar Pits, etc. Then, I think it was in July, he suggested we go to the beach. I thought it sounded great and he even promised to pack a picnic lunch. Luckily, he gave me a few days warning because I needed to go buy a bathing suit and cover up, etc.

"I bought a very skimpy bikini with a thong bottom and a mostly see through cover up. The sales girl told me everyone was wearing those now. So, when he picked me up on Saturday and gave me the once over, quite approvingly I might add, he asked me how daring I was. When I asked what he meant, he asked if I had ever been to a nude beach. I said I hadn't and I didn't think I would be too interested in trying it. He said the beach is actually clothing optional so if I wanted to stay dressed all day I could, but would I mind if he went nude. I asked why and he said he just preferred it, but we could go elsewhere if I wanted, no pressure. By this time, I trusted him completely to be a gentleman about it so I said why not.

"We ended up driving all the way to Black's Beach in San Diego. He assured me that no one would recognize me there so I had nothing to fear if I decided to join in.

"So once we are down on the beach I take off my cover up and he strips down to nothing. It shocked me, but the first thing he did was start putting on sun screen and offering it to me. It seemed quite normal when he asked me to do his back and offered to do mine. After I did his back I laid down on my stomach and he proceeded to do my back. In the process he untied my top and told me he would be glad to retie it when I was ready to turn over.

"I stayed on my stomach for about half an hour watching all the other people on the beach and seeing how normal they looked. All the men seemed to be nude and those women who weren't totally nude were at least topless. I decided, what the hell, and rolled over and grabbed the sun screen and did my breasts. I put the top away in my bag. Robert said nothing but looked approving.

"After about another half hour he suggested we go for a walk along the beach, just to stretch our legs. I decided to stay topless and see how it felt. I really enjoyed it. When we got back to our towels, he suggested a swim. I had never worn a thong before and after our walk it felt quite uncomfortable. So, I decided, when in Rome… and took off my bottoms and went in for a swim. It felt glorious! We played in the surf, rode a few waves, chatted with the other people there. I distinctly remember talking with another couple, all of us nude, for close to an hour on the beach, and feeling so totally normal that I wondered why I had never tried this before. By the end of the day I was totally sold.

"When it was time to climb up the hill I said I really didn't want to put that thong on again. Robert said just put on the cover up and keep the suit in my bag. So I did. I felt a bit naughty because anyone within five or ten feet could see I was nude underneath, but no one seemed to care. When we got to the car Robert asked if I wanted to be really daring and ride the whole way home naked. I said why not, pulled off my cover up and buckled in. He had his shirt and suit off almost as fast and we hit the road. He never touched me inappropriately but all the way home he would look over at me and smile."

"He appears to have been slowly preparing you for an affair. Do you see that now?"

"I knew that on our next weekend together, but by then I was totally on board with the idea."

"How is that?"

"He told me that he and his wife had a camping trailer at a nudist park and wondered If I would like to try a whole weekend there. He quickly said it had two beds so that I could sleep in the bedroom with the door locked while he slept on the pull-out couch. I half suspected what was coming next but went along with it never the less.

"We spent the day swimming and hiking, playing tennis and volleyball. All of this totally nude and I just loved every minute of it. We didn't exchange names with anyone else and except for the volleyball didn't even talk much with anyone, which was just fine with me. That night when we were ready for bed he asked me to help him with the pull-out bed and while we were making it I noticed he had placed a condom on the windowsill nearby. He said nothing about it.

“I went into the bedroom and closed the door but couldn't fall asleep. After about a half hour of tossing and turning I got up, walked out and climbed into bed with him. We didn't sleep much that night and by the morning I was totally hooked.”

“I suppose everything changed from there.”

“Yes, every other weekend we now spend at Eden Two. All day long we would play like children who cast off our clothes and enjoyed the nude life. The nights were a different story. I was very careful to tell no one about it. Anyone at the office might have expected he was still showing me around the city, but we hardly spoke at the office anymore outside of meetings and only about work topics.”

“So, do you think his wife found out?”

“I don't know how, and I certainly hope not. But now I don't know how it can't come out at some point. I just hope it wasn't her.”

“She appears to have a solid alibi for that weekend, so we are hunting for other suspects.”

“Oh good! I feel so sorry for her. And I feel terrible that she might find out. But I honestly think I will miss the nude time together more than I will miss the sex.”

“For now, I am not going to charge you with anything, that will keep the affair under wraps should we find that someone besides the wife is the murderer. Now you might want to clean your face and go back to work like all my questions and your answers were just routine.”

“Well Lt. Szpicelski, it’s been over a week, where are we with the Robert Carinos murder?”

“I'm afraid, Captain, that you are not going to like what I have to tell you.”

“And why is that?”

“Because I know the wife did it, I know how she did it, in fact I know every step she took in the process and I can't prove one bit of it in court.”

“A perfect crime? Do you really believe she was smart enough to pull that off?”

“First off, she is exceedingly detail-oriented. Every two weeks she and her team show up at a different venue, set up a booth with everything they wish to sell or display for that particular convention, and work the show. She runs the team and she sees to all the details of each weekend’s activities. She arranges transportation, rooms, meals, product delivery, booth signage. You name it, she sees to it. Not one item escapes her. If she doesn't think of it then her team does without it.”

“And I presume her team lacks for nothing?”

“The company has just two such teams. Every weekend they are somewhere. Alice's team is always far better prepared and turns in far better results, so says her boss. He would like to have a clone of her for the other team. Another interesting fact, she makes almost twice what her husband earned.”

“So, she really didn't like the fact that he was playing around behind her back.”

“From what I can tell he had never strayed one bit before this, but apparently one was her limit.”

“Any idea how she found out?”

“My guess is there was either something out of place in the trailer, or someone at the park said something to her about 'last weekend'”.

“Nothing more than that?”

“She probably verified by putting a hidden camera in the trailer. Of course, that is just my speculation. She would have had to purchase it with cash and it was not still in the trailer the weekend of the murder.”

“But why such a brutal, violent killing?”

“Means and opportunity as far as I can tell. For instance, the fire ax was in a locked case on the wall of the toilet facility, along with a fire hose and spigot. The management just left the key on top of the box in case an inspector came by. No need to break the glass."

"What else?"

"One member of her team owns a classic Mustang. He had it painted to match the one in an old Steve McQueen movie. He told me she had shown an interest in the car and knew a whole bunch about the movie. And he had an old Hide-a-Key box under the front fender. You know, those little metal pill boxes with the sliding top and a big magnet glued to the back of it? Wouldn't work with today's keys."

"But why that car in particular?"

"All today's cars have a computer that records by GPS where it has been. Nothing like that existed when that Mustang was built. And she made certain to leave her phone in the hotel room."

"Okay, take me through the entire crime as you see it."

"First, it is only about 50 miles from the convention center to Eden Two, so she would need just an hour to get there. Second, she always got a ground floor room wherever she went so she could store the shipping boxes, etc, without having to take them upstairs or in an elevator. Somehow, she found out about the Hide-a-Key on the Mustang and the door key for the fire box was open to public gaze.

"So, she has dinner with her crew and they stay in the bar socializing until 11 pm. That was normal for every trip. She gets back to her room, takes off her clothes and puts on the complimentary robe the hotel provides. She has no need to leave until midnight. The hotel has cameras on the lobby and all the exit doors but nothing watching the parking lot. There was a gas station by the freeway onramp that showed a similar Mustang going west at around midnight and coming back around 4 am. I cannot prove it is the same car, but what are the chances? We couldn't see the driver.

"So, at midnight she opens the window in her room and removes the screen. She is already wearing gloves, so no fingerprints. She places a towel on the windowsill and climbs out. No DNA on the sill. She picks up the towel and closes the window leaving just a crack so she can open it again later. She walks to the Mustang, gets the key, puts some kind of tape over the front license plate, climbs inside, and starts it up. Incidentally, this car has a very quiet exhaust. No possibility of being heard starting it and driving off, especially by its owner."

"Why the tape on the front plate?"

"The park entrance and exit camera can get a good view of the plate of a car entering, but it's aimed such that the rear plate is never seen. Not intentional, just luck. We found tape residue on only the front plate."

"She is thorough, isn't she?"

"Sure is. When she gets to the park, she puts down the sun visor and holds her right arm over her face as she works the code with her left hand. She parks the Mustang by the pool, takes off her robe and goes to the toilet facility."

"What if someone saw her there?"

"As far as anyone knew she had been there all day. Remember, the mistress looks exactly like her. And a naked lady walking around a nudist park would just be normal."

"Okay, so she goes to the toilets, gets the key and opens the firebox, takes out the ax and hides waiting for her husband to come. What is she wearing at this point?"

"Just the gloves as far as we can tell."

"No shoes, nothing else?"

"She might have had those shoes you wear under flippers for snorkeling or scuba diving. I believe she does own some because they had gone on vacations where that was an option. And we weren't able to get a decent footprint or any DNA from anywhere she went."

"So she is waiting, hiding in the shrubs and her husband approaches. She was expecting him because he always had to get up in the night to pee. What if he had already gone before she got there?"

"My bet is she knew his schedule well and wasn't concerned about that. Besides, if he had she could always call it off and go back to the hotel without killing him,figuring there would be a next time."

“So she steps out, hacks him in the chest...”

“She managed to cut through three ribs and put a gash in his aorta with one blow. There would have been instantaneous and massive blood loss. The splatter pattern on the ground showed that she took the majority of the first blast. He fell to the ground bleeding out quickly and probably didn't even have a chance to call out. She buried the ax in his face probably only a second or two later, left the ax there and walked calmly to the pool, his blood dripping off her all the way. She dove in the deep end, swam to the shallow end, got out, went to the Mustang, put on the robe, wrapped the towel around her hair, got in and drove off.”

“Didn't the Mustang owner notice some missing gas?”

“She even thought that. Before she got back on the freeway she stopped at a station and put $50 worth into the car.”

“And you don't have video of that or a credit card number? Did she pay cash? Can we ask a cashier?”

“No such luck. We do have video but she knew where that camera was too, so we cannot see her face, just a person in a bulky robe with a towel on their head. And to pay for the gas she used a gift card that had no record of who purchased it or when. I have seen them in supermarkets so it could have been purchased anywhere between West LA and Palm Springs.

“So, she drives back to the hotel, parks the car, puts the Hide-a-Key back, pulls the tape off the front plate, opens her room window, puts the towel from her hair onto the sill, and climbs in. She probably took a shower and left the towel and robe on the floor for the maids. They would have been washed long before we even knew to suspect her. She could have put the tape and her gloves into the trash in the room or dumped them anywhere else before or after she got home. There are just too many places to look.”

“Okay, so there is really nothing we can give the DA?”

“Heck, I can't even fault her acting. When I confronted her about her husband’s possible murder, she was textbook ‘the unbelieving then grieving wife.’ That night she had us all thinking we needed to look elsewhere for a killer. If we had found even a sliver of evidence to point to anyone else, we would have been on it."

"But nothing else showed up at all?"

"Nothing! I am afraid, Captain, that she pulled off a perfect crime."

"Not perfect, just damn good! Leave the case open and let's just hope that something, somewhere shows up."

What's Inside of People

Matthew McDermott

"Don't get your knickers in a twist," Marie said, lying back on her chaise, eyes closed.

"Humorous," Gary replied, lying back himself, still scowling.

I got as tired of the day visitors as they did, but I didn't like hanging around these two while they got snarky at each other like this. And Gary never, ever missed an opportunity to complain about the non-residents who came to Sunny Valley.

He was looking at me, probably hoping for some moral support. I didn't want to get roped into their spat, but I knew I would have to throw Gary a bone or he wouldn't shut up.

"They're annoying," I agreed. "But I guess they keep the place afloat."

I picked up my book and opened it again, hoping that it would signal the end of the conversation.

"Do you see that one?" he demanded, nodding towards the far end of the pool. Even with dozens of people on the deck, and a lively volleyball game going on in the water, I could tell who he was referring to.

A young mother was emerging from the shallow end of the pool with her toddler. As soon as the little boy was seated on the side of the pool, she reached over and pulled out a light sarong, throwing it around herself while she was still wet. She knotted it at her chest, the flowing wrap covering her from armpits to thighs.

"I guess she's not clothed, technically," I observed.

"She's been doing that all day," he snarled. "Doesn't take it off till she's already in the water, puts it on the second she gets out. Why come here if you're going to spend the day under a dress like that?"

"Husband probably forced her to come," Marie said. She hadn't even looked up to see who we were talking about, but she knew. Gary was that predictable, obviously.

"Young fools. And now look at this—"

I heard the commotion before I even turned my head to see what had caught Gary's attention now. A woman, wearing a t-shirt, was running full-tilt through the pool enclosure.

She was moving so quickly, it took a second to register that she was wearing a staff t-shirt. "That's Cindy, isn't it?" I asked.

The three of us all sat upright at once. My book fell down beside me, but I ignored it. Cindy was about forty years old, and was normally calm and composed. If she was running, there was probably a good reason for it.

The three of us got up immediately and followed her. Sunny Valley was usually a calm and serene place, and Gary, Marie, and I were all longtime members. It might sound a little entitled, but members like us usually assumed that if something big was happening, we deserved to know about it.

I was in the lead, and as I trotted in Cindy's wake, the pool deck seemed to fill up with a churning mass of humanity. As I dodged around laughing kids, chatting groups, and stretched-out sunbathers, I just caught a glimpse of Cindy disappearing into the clubhouse.

Once inside, I headed straight to Melanie's office. I liked Mel; she had been the club's general manager for a couple of years now, and the club ran well under her oversight. She seemed like a level-headed person in general. I rounded the corner and walked straight through her office door.

Cindy stood beside the desk, crying openly. Mel sat behind the desk, phone up to her ear. Her hair was a mess—she must have run in from somewhere.

"Ambulance," she said in her clipped, authoritative tone. "And—probably police, too."

What on earth had happened?

"Yes," she said. "Sunny Valley Naturist Resort. The gate will be open when you get here, and a staff member will wait in the parking lot to direct you to the site." She pointed to Cindy, who nodded.

Mel put down the phone and looked at me.

"Fred Howard's dead," she said.

***

The day Fred died was like being in another dimension. Most of the members were clothed, and instead of gathering around the big common table or the circle of couches around the TV, everyone broke up into little knots of three or four and muttered together, heads down.

I sat with Brenda and Mike, a couple in their twenties who showed up almost every weekend, year-round. They didn't seem to mind hanging out with me, a forty-something divorcé. "Funny to see everyone with clothes on," I remarked, as the conversation sagged for about the tenth time. "Even Gary and Marie."

"They are like ten times the nudists we are," Mike said. "I thought for sure they'd be right in front of the cops naked, saying *It's my god-given right*." His imitation of Gary was pretty good, and I had to chuckle.

"No joke, I heard them complaining about the reporters being clothed earlier," Brenda chimed in. "Like they were supposed to strip off as soon as they came in the door."

I rolled my eyes.

"I'd prefer this place to be mandatory nude," Mike said. "I hate when we come in in the winter and everyone's wrapped up and we are just hanging out. It's like we're outsiders and we're the ones who are doing what you're supposed to do here."

Brenda nodded in unison. "Yeah, they get undressed to go in the pool for ten minutes and then they dry off, get dressed, and come in again. Like, why even."

"It's the smokers," I said. "They don't like to get dressed every time they go out for a puff."

"Stupid."

"Mister McNeil," a loud, stern voice called from across the room.

Brenda and Mike looked at each other, unsure.

"You can go in together," I reassured them. "They'll be okay with it."

They got up, holding hands, and made their way towards the office. The cop who had called out to them was a petite blonde woman, looking almost lost in her bulky uniform. Amazing how commanding she could make her voice sound. You never knew what was inside people.

"What's up, Mark?"

I turned around in my seat and found Mel standing behind me. "How're you doing?" I asked. "Have a seat. You look terrible."

I was glad that it dug a little smile out of her—she truly did look exhausted. She looked in the direction of the office, though. "I should probably get back…"

"Seriously," I said. "You could probably use the break."

She shrugged, and I thought she was going to walk away, but then she dropped into the chair next to me. "It's been a day," she admitted.

"So what's been happening?" I asked. "Unless you don't want to talk about it."

"Cops asking the same questions a hundred different ways." She rested her hands on the table and stared at them. "Did you know Fred?"

"I helped him with his fence one time. Seemed like a harmless enough old guy, I guess."

"Huh."

Mel was still looking at her hands, but I could read the tension in her voice. "What am I missing?" I asked.

She shrugged. "Just the usual stuff. Most of the guys are great around here, don't get me wrong. Just sometimes…"

I nodded. "A bit handsy, or…"

"Liked to touch my tits," she said. I grinned; I liked how frank Mel was about stuff like this. Then I realized I was smiling like an idiot about sexual assault, and I forced myself to straighten my face out.

"So, an asshole," I confirmed.

"Definitely."

We sat there in an uncomfortable silence for a couple of minutes. "Still," she said at last, in a more cheerful tone of voice, "I don't think it was anything worth murdering him over."

"No, I suppose not," I answered. I could sense that she was forcing herself to sound cheerful, and I didn't want to make this any harder on her. "I…"

It finally occurred to me what she'd said.

"*Murdering?*" I exclaimed.

"Shh!" She waved her hand frantically at me. "The cops don't want that getting out until they've questioned everyone. You've already talked to them, right?"

"Yeah. I was one of the first."

"It seems someone was in his cabin last night, and they…" She shut her eyes and took a deep breath. "I don't know. Blunt force trauma, they say."

"Are you okay?" I asked. I was pretty squeamish about blood and that kind of thing myself. I hadn't realized Mel had been dealing with the murder scene all day. No wonder she looked so frazzled.

"I'll get through it," she said. "Probably going to take some time off when this is all over."

"How long will that be? They must have interviewed pretty much everyone by now."

"They're doing a complete search of Fred's cabin, and then they're apparently doing a sweep of the grounds."

"Looking for clues?"

"Murder weapon," she said flatly.

Wow. This was pretty serious. "Anything I should look out for?" I asked.

"We're not supposed to talk about it," she said, then shrugged. "It's something big, like a baseball bat or something. They don't know how anyone could have moved around the resort with it without being seen…"

"Because it's kind of hard to conceal a baseball bat when you're naked," I supplied.

"Exactly."

"That's completely crazy."

Mel nodded, and pushed her chair back, easing herself back onto her feet. "Just don't spread it around, okay? I probably wasn't supposed to tell you."

"I won't," I promised.

Mel looked like she was going to say something else, but then she shrugged and walked away, leaving me alone at the table. I decided I didn't need to hang around any longer; and knowing Fred had been murdered made me feel quite uncomfortable.

I got up and left. For as long as I'd known Mel, she had been unflappable in any crisis—drunk visitors, the craziness of the annual volleyball tournament, nothing seemed to faze her. Of course, a murder was a big problem, but somehow I expected her to handle it more easily. As I walked back to my trailer, I tried to think of everything I'd ever seen or heard about Fred. Nothing made sense.

***

I next saw Mel a couple of days later, and she looked even more haggard. She was wearing her usual uniform, the long Sunny Valley t-shirt that hung down to her thighs, but her pained expression was visible from yards away as we approached each other outside the club house.

"You look like you've been through the wringer," I said, as sympathetically as I could. "Have you even slept in the last two days?"

"You see this?" She waved a newspaper at me, undoubtedly the local paper, as she came within conversational range. "You can just imagine how the story was reported."

"Let me guess. 'Sexual deviant gruesomely murdered by other sexual deviant.' Something like that?"

She continued waving the paper around, but I couldn't see the article, even though it was right on the front page. "You just wouldn't believe it," she said. "All the usual stupid jokes. Butt out, walking abreast. They used a photo from our website, and my huge butt is right in the middle of it."

"That's awful," I agreed.

"Even the headline—*Murder at Nudist Colony*. Can you imagine? Is it still the sixties here, or what?"

I rolled my eyes. I agreed of course, but I had gotten used to the media misunderstanding nudists. I could easily imagine the sensationalism in the article about Fred's murder.

"I'm going to call the editor. I'd go into town and strangle him myself if I didn't have so much to do."

Mel was obviously nearing the end of her tether. "Any way I can help?" I offered.

"How about you go inside and quiet Gary down," she said, motioning with her head towards the clubhouse behind her. "He's on my to-be-strangled list as well."

"What's he up to?"

"He's holding court right now," she said. "Enjoy."

She hurried off down the path, and I headed towards the clubhouse door, wondering what I would find inside.

I was right to worry. Gary was in his sixties, and was a little wiry guy whose hair was salt and pepper all over. Many times I'd seen him try to make up for his size by being loud and aggressive, and today was no different. He was standing in front of Stan, a quiet, easygoing guy who wore shorts and a t-shirt. Gary's finger was in his face as he spoke.

"This is exactly the problem, though!" he was bellowing. "We shouldn't be changing what we do just because some reporters and cops come in. In fact, *they* should be getting nude."

"Just trying to make people comfortable," Stan muttered.

"This goes for everyone," Gary said, whirling around. He scanned the room, where about twenty people were sitting and standing. "I can count… three, four, five people who are actually nude in here right now. And that includes me and Marie."

His wife sat just to the side of him, blushing deeply and looking at the ground.

"If everyone was nude all the time, you know, this probably wouldn't have happened. Someone hid something—a, bat or something, the cops say—and killed Fred with it. Couldn't happen if people were nude the way they're supposed to be."

Much as I hated to engage Gary, I felt like if I didn't say something, this would get out of control. I had a towel on my shoulder, and flip-flops on my feet, but I quietly kicked them off and dropped my towel on a chair before I strode forward. "It's clothing-optional everywhere but the pool areas, Gary," I said as cheerfully as I could manage.

He turned towards me furiously, but when he clocked that I was fully nude as well, he lost a bit of momentum. "Huh, well," he said.

"I don't think—"

Before I could say more, Gary turned back to Stan. "So what about you? You going to take those things off, or what?"

Stan's gaze fell to the floor, and he frowned deeply. I didn't really know Stan, but he was such a quiet guy, he was probably incredibly uncomfortable with Gary singling him out.

"Gary," I said, putting a hand on his arm. "Lay off."

"Here's what I think," Gary said, spinning around and facing the room as well as he could, his hands on his hips, which he pushed forward, putting himself on display way more than necessary. "I think that if you're wearing clothes at a nudist resort, you're a suspect. You're not acting normally. And maybe you don't belong here at all."

His gaze swept the room again, slowly, and all eyes were locked on him.

"The cops won't know or care. No one will get it but actual nudists," Gary went on. "But I'll be watching, and other people—real nudists—will be watching, too."

He turned back to Stan, glaring at him expectantly. I held my breath, and felt like everyone in the room was doing the same.

Stan met Gary's eye, and then he sort of slumped down. He slowly pulled his t-shirt up and off his body.

Then Marie got up and took Gary's hand, saying something to him quietly. Gary finally turned and, without another word, strode out of the room, Marie right behind him.

After a few minutes, people started chattering again, first in hushed tones, then more loudly. But I wasn't happy at all about what I'd just seen. And I noticed that after Gary's tirade, a few more people had discreetly taken their clothes off; half the room was nude or at least topless now.

I needed out. I picked up my towel and flip-flops, and headed out the door towards the hot tub. As I passed him, Stan looked up at me, a small, embarrassed smile on his face. I smiled and nodded at him. Maybe if Fred's murder was solved, Gary—and everyone—would relax. But until then, Sunny Valley would not feel like home.

***

There were already too many people in the hot tub and the indoor pool, and I changed directions before I even went into the large pool enclosure. The outdoor hot tub was a possibility, but it was probably full as well. I didn't feel like I could handle a group of people, all fretting and chattering about Fred. I needed some peace. I headed out the back door of the club.

The late spring sun was flowing like liquid gold, and I realized that's what I needed more than anything: a bit of vitamin D. I would take a walk around the grounds of the resort, I decided. The long roadway that wound around the clusters of cabins and trailers would take me maybe twenty minutes to walk. I'd get a little fresh air, get the blood flowing again.

I started near the volleyball and tennis courts, all of which were empty except for one older guy, someone I didn't know, returning balls one after another from the automatic launcher. I wasn't close enough to see him well, but his pale skin suggested that he was a newly-arrived visitor.

The road forked, and I took the outside path, in among the trees. The first trailer belonged to Arlene Nowak. She stood to greet me, and we chatted for a few moments.

There was only one subject of conversation, of course. "Poor old Fred," she remarked. "Who would believe it?"

"It's crazy," I said.

"Granted... I won't miss him coming around and staring all the time."

"Staring?" I asked. I tried to make my tone of voice light, but this was a surprise. People here didn't stare at each other. We've seen it all.

"Maybe it was in my imagination," she said, suddenly very interested in picking bits of dirt from her hands and arms. "But when I was gardening—you know, kneeling down, bending over, and whatnot—it seemed like Fred was always just coming up the road. And he was always sort of…" She trailed off, made some motions with her hands I couldn't translate. "I felt very vulnerable, you know?"

"You're the second person to say they didn't feel comfortable around Fred," I told her. "Did everyone but me know that he was a creep?"

"Not really a creep—just…"

I didn't want to push her further. She had already revealed a lot. "In any case," I said, "I hope this whole thing hasn't upset you even more."

Arlene grinned. "I'm okay."

"Enjoy this fine day," I told her, and ambled off.

I couldn't get it out of my head as I walked through the shady glade. What had Fred been up to? If he was such a creep, how come no one had ever talked about him before?

And now that I had rounded the bend in the road, I was approaching his cottage. The yellow POLICE LINE tape fluttered in the slight breeze; it was the only sound and the only movement in the forest.

I walked closer. I had never seen a murder scene before; the rumours floating around Sunny Valley suggested that it was grisly, with blood everywhere and Fred's corpse all but dismembered. Exaggerations, probably.

I approached slowly and carefully. The front door of his cottage was slightly ajar, open enough to slip a finger through, maybe. I could go in and see for myself. The police had wrapped up their work for the time being, it seemed, so I doubted that this would affect their investigation.

Why bother? What right did I have? It was like seeing a crash on the side of a highway, maybe. It was absolutely possible not to look, but I often felt compelled, far more than I should.

But standing in front of the cottage, facing the door, I hesitated.

And heard something.

The noise had come not from inside Fred's place, but from somewhere else. Beside it—yes, leaves were rustling.

My first impulse was, of course, to run off, but it was only a moment before my thoughts congealed: they were hiding, I was just walking along.

"Is someone there?" I demanded, my voice carrying more authority than I felt.

The rustling became a full-on shaking, and I could hear footsteps—bare feet slapping against the hard-packed dirt path that ran behind Fred's cottage. Intrigued, I followed.

I pushed through the bushes and rounded the corner of the cottage, and almost skidded to a stop, one of my flipflops flying off to the side as I tried to keep my balance. I had almost smacked straight into Mel's backside.

She whirled around. "Oh! It's you again."

I paused before I answered, trying to figure her out. Did she look guilty? Or was she just surprised to see me? I thought I could see a tremble pass through her, but maybe it was just the slight chill in the shade behind the cottage. It was a truism that nudists had nothing to hide, but I knew it was just that, a truism. In fact, people were people, whether you could see their genitals or not.

"I was just passing by, and saw someone running behind Fred's house," I explained. "Thought I'd make sure everything was okay."

"I was just…" Mel looked around, and her shoulders slumped a bit. "I was trying to see if there was anything the police missed."

"It's very upsetting," I agreed. I was still unsure of what to think of all this. We stood there across from each other as though we were in some kind of standoff, even though I wasn't accusing her of anything, nor she me. She was nervously brushing some bits of dirt and grass off her breasts, which probably signalled how uncomfortable I was making her.

"I heard that Fred wasn't the harmless old guy everyone seemed to think," I offered at last. "Kind of like you were saying. Seems he upset a lot of people."

She put her hands on her hips and sort of puffed up her chest at me. "A lot of women, you mean. Men were just fine with him."

I mentally flipped through my memories of Fred. Had I seen him interacting with other people much? I had lived at Sunny Valley for a year and a half; Fred had lived there for that long, as well as maybe a hundred other permanent residents. I had seen him here and there, but I kept to myself a lot, and he seemed to as well.

"We had a handful of complaints over the years," Mel said. "Nothing major, just the sort of…we get these complaints mostly about visitors, not residents."

"Why did no one talk to him?"

"Jeff did, I think," she said. "But…"

Her voice trailed off. Jeff—in fact his name was Gottfried Fischler—was the original owner, having opened the park about forty years before. He and his wife had lived at the park since it opened, and raised their two kids there. Those kids were grown but were still residents too, and they had a bunch of kids of their own now, ranging from toddlers to teens.

I didn't have much to do with Jeff—I understood his role to be mostly in the background, letting Mel and the other managers be the ones dealing with people. He struck me as a very serious, unfriendly sort of guy, and I wouldn't want to be on the receiving end of a talk from him.

"But Fred didn't change? Why did Jeff put up with that?"

"It's…complicated, I guess." She looked around, and spotted a large log standing on its end. She plopped down on it with a sigh. I didn't know how her bare butt could be comfortable on a roughly-sawn log, but I didn't need to get into that at the moment.

"So there's a story here," I prodded.

She nodded slowly. "Fred invested in the club years ago, and Jeff was paying him back. But the last few years have been tight, and Jeff's been unable to pay. So he couldn't really do anything when people complained about Fred."

"It seems someone decided to do something themselves."

"Yeah." Mel looked away. "It's not a good situation."

"How many women have complained?" I asked. I didn't want to be too forceful—my midsection was around her eye level, and I was uncomfortable making that seem aggressive. But Mel was clearly holding something back.

"Several," she said, looking down at the ground.

"I'm sorry," I said. "I really had no idea."

"Jeff's granddaughter," she said, her voice just above the whisper of the breeze through the trees. "She was the last one."

I knew instantly who he meant. Emily was a tall, attractive young woman, and got plenty of stares from the day visitors to the club. After living there for a while, you tended to sort of forget to look at other people's bodies, but Emily was statuesque, and even I noticed her when I happened to see her.

"Should we maybe go talk to her?" I asked.

"I don't think so. Poor girl—I'm sure the police…" Her voice trailed off but I didn't disagree.

"Do you think Emily told Jeff?" I said. "That would seem suspicious, I'm sure."

"No," Mel said. "She didn't tell him."

The light switched on for me. "She told you."

"Yes. So I couldn't say anything to the police, and I couldn't—couldn't—"

She got up and tried to walk away, but burst into tears. I held out my arms, and she sank into my embrace, sobbing, her tears soaking my shoulder. I patted her back. "It's okay," I said soothingly. "You're under a lot of stress. It's fine."

She said something into my chest, so muffled by her sobs that I couldn't make it out. "You were what?"

"I was there," she said.

Suddenly, she drew back, wild-eyed. "You can't say anything."

"I'm not—hold on." I really wanted a towel to wipe off my shoulder, but that could wait. "What do you mean, you were there? Where?"

"I saw it happen," she said. She sank down onto the log again. "I was here that night."

"You didn't…"

She looked up at me, her eyes puffy, her mouth open. "I need you to be a friend right now, okay?"

I knelt down in front of her. "Okay. I'm here."

Mel closed her eyes and talked as if in a trance. "Emily came to me and said Fred cornered her, talked about—oh, you know the things these guys say. You're *developing*. Are you going to start shaving soon? Just...everything like that."

"Creep."

She nodded but barely broke her stride. “And he started touching her—grabbing at her. She got away and ran off, but she didn’t know who to tell, so that evening she came to me.”

“What’d you do?”

“I told her I’d take care of it, and I went straight over to see Fred. I told him I wanted him out of the park—and he came at me. I didn’t wear my staff shirt—I should have, but I wanted to keep it low-key. He put—put his hands…”

She hung her head and wept for a few moments. I patted her leg gently, knowing it was a lame gesture but needing to do something, anything.

Mel took a deep, shuddering breath. “Someone came in, and found him on me.”

On me. The words made me sick.

“They grabbed—something. Hit Fred, and he just went down. Boom.”

“What was it?” I guessed she didn’t want to tell me who saved her. To keep her talking I asked about weapon instead

She looked up, cold calculation in her eye. “It’s gone. We took care of it. And if I don’t tell you, you won’t know.”

The bits of dirt and grass on her. The sneaking around Fred’s cottage. She’d been covering for—

For whom? Emily’s father, her grandfather? Mel’s husband, Chuck, wouldn’t have stood for any nonsense either. If any of them had come upon Fred attacking her—well.

“I don’t think Fred deserved to die,” she said.

My mind suddenly stopped racing, and I turned my head to look at her. She was defiant, her hands on her hips. I suddenly knew who had killed Fred.

“You won’t tell anyone,” she said. “You won’t say anything. Right?”

How could I? A teenaged girl, killing a man who had assaulted her, and was in the middle of assaulting another woman. There was no reason ever to reveal it, to anyone.

I stood up, and patted Mel's shoulder. "I won't say a thing," I said. "There's no reason to."

"We need to keep the heat off her," she said, nodding slowly. "If people keep snooping around and speculating…"

We stood there, together. What would get everyone's attention, and stop everyone worrying about Fred?

It came to me like dawn coming through a window. "Gary," I said.

"What about him?"

"His crusade to force everyone to go nude all the time. That's the distraction."

I hadn't formulated the plan, but Mel already got it. She stood up, was practically hopping around. "Yes. Gary."

"We'll join his crusade. Distract everyone," I said.

"They'll hate it. They won't talk about anything else."

"Emily can be our spokesperson," I suggested.

She laughed, which made me feel much better. "Let's not go that far. We'll figure it out." She stopped suddenly, and looked up at me again. "You're sure."

"It may not be what we'd choose. But…it's justice, isn't it?"

She lunged at me—and hugged me, hard. "I won't forget this," she said.

I hugged her back. "There are some mysteries," I said, "that are better to remain mysteries."

Murder in the Nudist Colony

Ana Jurić

At first, Lisel thought it was just new guests arriving and not knowing what to do, how to shed their clothing or where to go to check in. But as she rose from her hammock, she realized it was something more serious.

There was big Giles, the 50-ish man who was a regular at the resort. He stood with his muscular arms folded across his broad chest, sun reflecting off his bald head. His position there blocked her view of whatever they were looking at. When he turned slightly, as if looking back over his shoulder in her direction, his expression was astonishing; she had never seen him so upset. Perhaps someone had broken a rule of the resort. Of course, there weren't many rules to follow at a resort for nudists: just be clothes-free and act nice. And don't stare. Even Lisel had stared the first time she visited five years ago. Now she was used to the sight of naked bodies all around her, her body among them -- just ordinary people doing ordinary things but without the constriction of clothing.

Enjoying the feel of her feet pressing down into the soft grass, she wiggled her toes as she stood straight and stretched from her nap, arms to the sky, breasts out, narrow hips leaning to the left then over to the right, breathing the cool mountain air deeply. The nap was perfect after a morning hike through the woods, down to the lake and going for a swim with a few other guests sunbathing there. It was a lovely afternoon!

Except for what was happening at the front gate. She stepped along the curving path of flat stones that wound its way across the yard and came up behind Giles. Several other guests had gathered beside him.

"Is he asleep?" asked someone as Lisel arrived. Another person dared push on his shoulder, no response.

"Not sleeping," grunted Giles. "Dead." He was a retired policeman, so of course everyone accepted what he said.

Lisel, on summer holiday from her job teaching primary school in Hamburg, rose on her toes to see over the shoulders of the others. There on the bench beside the tall wooden fence that surrounded the resort, next to the gate and its sign, stating "Happy Valley Naturist Resort" in German, French, and English, lay a middle-aged man with a thin moustache, eyes closed, apparently not breathing. What was odd, however, was the man was fully clothed. His khaki trousers were not so wrinkled that he had been wearing them long. His shirt was Hawaiian style with red palm fronds on white, buttoned up. There were no shoes or sandals anywhere around the bench, so it couldn't have been that he took them off to walk barefoot on the grounds of the resort. No, someone likely brought the man to the bench and laid him there.

Giles was stating the same idea as Lisel lowered herself from her stretched peek, feet flat on the ground again.

"What happened?" she asked.

Giles heard her and turned. The others also turned to see who had spoken. There was Frau Heinz and her daughter, Gretel. And the Americans, Joe and Susan, with their little boy, Jack. But Susan gathered up her son and left the gathering, a worried look on her face. Anton, a regular guest, turned to let his gaze follow her as she ushered the boy away. The elderly couple from England, Martin and Alice, stood beside Giles. Lisel heard Martin ask what the problem was; his German was getting better. She sidled up to Vic, the tall Italian, who had a tattoo of a boat on his butt. Nautical tattoos covered his thighs and arms, too. He wore rubber sandals. She wished she wore sandals, too; footgear and hats were allowed at the resort.

"Not sleeping," said Vic in good English as a group of teenagers, two girls and two boys carrying badminton equipment, paused to see what the commotion was about. "Looks like he's dead. And not for long, I suspect. He looks quite fresh."

"Ew," one teen girl sneered. One of the boys pulled her away and they continued up the path to the badminton area.

Lisel looked around Vic's elbow at the bench and the man on it—the same bench where some of the older guests liked to sit for their breakfast tea to enjoy the morning newspaper.

"Why is he wearing clothes?" Lisel asked in English. "He looks so uncomfortable. Maybe he only just arrived here. He was waiting to meet someone?"

Nobody knew him, had ever seen him before. Giles checked but found no identification on the man. "Either he died outside and found his way here or...." He looked around the group. "He died inside this resort." A gasp went up from the group. "All the way up that road? Through the forest? That's a steep climb."

"Anyone know who he is?" asked Giles, trying his German. The English couple asked what he said and Lisel translated.

"Good heavens!" cried Alice. She grabbed Martin's arm. "What happened to him?"

Giles bent down to have a closer look. "I think his name is Gerhardt. I saw him in town a few days ago." He blinked. "Yes, I think it is the same man. He sat at the same café as me, asked me where this nudist resort was located. As though I'd know! I was dressed, certainly."

"Was he planning to be a guest?" asked Vic. "Or come here to cause trouble? Like that TV reporter a few months ago."

"He looks like the sort of fellow bent on complaining about our lifestyle," Alice cursed.

"Some people are merely curious," Lisel spoke up. She tried to see the good in everyone. "I mean, they may wish to try going clothes-free in nature as we do, but they...maybe they are too shy?"

"That's it." Joe gave a huff. "Susan and I were curious, too, at first. But we are so glad you all welcomed us the way you have."

"Still doesn't explain how he got here," Giles growled.

"Then he just collapses inside the gate?" Joe glanced at the others. "Maybe heart attack? Too much stress hiking up here? There's no automobile parked outside."

"Anybody see him arrive?" asked Giles, looking around. His eyes settled on Lisel. "You were here. What did you see?"

Lisel crossed her arms over her breasts, pouting. “I was napping in the hammock over there. I didn’t see anything. All I heard was the gate swing open and, I guess, swing closed after. I heard no words spoken.”

“Well, he’s not going to stay here,” said Giles, standing. “Not dead. Better notify the constable.” He faced Lisel. “Could you make the call?”

“Sure.” Lisel, being from Hamburg, could explain the situation to the town constable in fluent German. Everyone knew of the nudist resort and no one minded its location behind a gate, hidden in the thick forest, with plenty of trails to hike, a small lake for swimming and wide shore for sunbathing. The cabins were convenient for temporary guests. Guests could cook their own food if they brought it from the town, or they could enjoy what the owners cooked. Friedrich and Beata were friendly owners and excellent chefs.

“What’s going on?” called Friedrich, approaching the group from the cabin that served as the office.

“Someone has arrived,” Giles explained with an edge to his voice, “but, at present, he appears to be dead.”

The owner stared down at the silent man. “That’s very odd. We usually get a call before anyone comes up here. Maybe he was trying to sneak a peek.”

“It’s possible,” snorted Joe. “We have some attractive people here enjoying the naturist lifestyle.” He chuckled but the others did not share his humor. There was a dead man before them.

“Someone get a sheet to cover the body,” Giles instructed. “Lisel is going to call the constable. Someone should go outside the gate and look for any clues.”

“Martin and I can do that,” said Alice, gesturing toward the gate.

***

Within an hour a constable car pulled up to the gate and an officer in a blue uniform stepped out, eyeing the gate, keeping a hand on his sidearm.

“Welcome, sir,” called Friedrich, coming out through the gate in his resort costume: a full birthday suit plus sandals.

“You called about a dead body?” asked the officer whose name badge identified him as Schmidt, a sergeant in the patrol squad.

Lisel jogged out to join Friedrich outside the gate and Schmidt’s eyes widened at the sight of the nude young woman, her blond hair flowing in the breeze and breasts jiggling. She stood with her hands on her hips beside Friedrich as he explained the situation. She added details he missed. Sergeant Schmidt kept his eyes on Lisel, which made her feel uncomfortable.

“You never saw a naked woman?” she finally had to say. “Everybody has a naked body. Some of us enjoy being free of clothing, that’s all.”

“Yes, I understand the idea,” said Schmidt. “I apologize.” He averted his eyes, like he had been caught sneaking a peek.

“You don’t need to act like looking at me is wrong, either,” Lisel admonished him. “Just don’t keep staring.” She waited for him to recover and start to act normal. “I suppose you will need to enter our resort to investigate. You better prepare yourself.”

“Prepare?” The officer was puzzled. “How?”

“You need to obey our rules when you come inside, sir.” Friedrich gestured that the officer should disrobe. “All guests must be clothes-free. It wouldn’t be fair if someone wore clothing. It would seem as though they thought they were better than those who are nude.”

“Or like they are just here to catch a glimpse of nude bodies,” Lisel added. “Like when a pervert sometimes tries to sneak in. There was a guy with a camera one time last summer.”

“But I’m on duty,” Schmidt responded curtly. “I must remain in uniform.”

“You can wear your utility belt, but all the clothing must be removed before you enter. That is the rule. The other rule is to be nice to everyone. For example, don’t stare. Also don’t comment negatively on someone’s body type. If you were to come inside wearing all that awful clothing, our guests would become alarmed. We don’t want to make any of our guests feel bad. It's disturbing enough to have to call you up here in the first place."

Schmidt frowned, scratched his forehead. "I understand your thinking, but...."

"I can escort him," Lisel offered. "Please, sir. First, you must remove your uniform. Don't you want to be comfortable like me? I come here every summer for my holiday. Teaching children keeps me so busy, I need some time alone in nature to relax."

"Yes, I see," He gave a smirk. "You must have a lot of fun up here in the woods, everyone being naked. Lots of games, yes?"

"We do. We hike in the woods, swim in the lake, play all sorts of games. There's a volleyball pitch and a badminton court. We sing and dance in the evenings. And we enjoy some of the finest food ever cooked by a pair of nude chefs."

"Nude chefs?"

"Yes, the owners do the cooking." She gestured to Friedrich, who blushed. "He was once head chef at a five-star Michelin restaurant in Strasbourg."

"But I didn't like the frantic pace of that career," Friedrich spoke, "and I always enjoyed hiking nude, so I decided to abandon that hectic life for this one. This used to be my grandfather's land. Now my wife and I love welcoming guests from around the world. They get time to relax and be one with nature. That is the reason we like to call ourselves 'naturists'."

"As natural as the day we are born," Lisel added. She flicked her hands up and down her body. The officer's eyes followed her hands. "Try it, won't you?"

The officer pursed his lips. "All right. As long as no report gets back to my supervisor."

He returned to his patrol car and began undressing as Lisel looked around the parking area, asking Friedrich if Alice and Martin found anything unusual outside the gate.

"No, nothing unusual," Friedrich responded with a shrug. "It looks like that man was delivered here. That's better than having him die inside our gate. We have enough problems with what people think of us."

"So...like this?" asked Schmidt. He stood unclothed except for his utility belt and black boots. His hand rested on his holster, his other hand hanging shyly in front of his crotch.

"The belt may give you away," Lisel laughed, "but otherwise you will fit in nicely and not cause any alarm to our guests."

"Let's go." Friedrich led the way.

***

Schmidt knelt before the bench, examining the prone man inch by inch, starting with his face. At first, he hesitated about getting into a position with all his 'bits' hanging down, but once he focused on ascertaining the circumstances of the man's death, he forgot his concerns about how he may have appeared to others. He checked the man's eyes, inside his mouth, looked under fingernails, spent time on the clothing, as though it was something odd. Then he stood up. Giles had shooed away everyone to give the policeman privacy.

"I don't think he died of natural causes," said Schmidt. "Pardon the pun."

"Maybe it isn't a pun," said Giles. "Anyone who dies in a naturist resort must die of natural causes, right?" The teens were returning from the badminton court and Giles rushed to steer them away from the dead body.

"It might be true," said Schmidt, staring down at the body. "You say you don't allow any clothing to be worn here? Yet this man is wearing clothing. That's strange, don't you think?"

"Not really. People arrive clothed, of course," Friedrich explained. Beata joined him, took his arm in hers. "When they check in is when they usually take off their clothing."

"Some even sit right on that bench to do it," said Beata in a sad voice. "We should get a new bench. Nobody will want to sit on a bench where somebody has died."

"Where someone has been murdered." Schmidt grimaced, hands on his hips. "There is something strange about the shirt and slacks he is wearing. It seems he was put into those garments."

"Put into?" asked Lisel, surprised.

"Like someone dressed him, maybe after he was dead." He scratched his forehead. "But there's something odd about the clothes, too." He gazed at Lisel. "Nobody knows him?"

She shook her head. "Giles said he saw him in town a few days ago but they didn't talk."

"Perhaps someone wanted him dead," the officer thought aloud to himself. "Enemies?"

"What's that?" asked Lisel, focused on the officer. He was already too concerned with the case to notice he was nude like the rest of the people. "Are you saying he didn't die of natural causes but...he was murdered?"

Schmidt looked up from his thoughts, met Lisel's eyes. "Yes, I think so. But I'll need to have some tests run. I need to call for assistance."

"Sure," Lisel responded. "Let me show you to the telephone."

As they walked across the compound, a quintet of naked children ran by, laughing and shouting. Schmidt turned to let his eyes follow them. "They look happy," he said.

"And you notice you don't feel any self-consciousness about being nude yourself, do you?" Lisel asked him. "It always happens. I was so shy my first visit. Now I can't wait to come here for my summer holiday."

"Yes, I can see why. I understand now. But let's solve this crime first."

"So, it is a crime?"

"Yes," said Schmidt as they came to the phone hanging on the wall of the office cabin. "I believe this man has been murdered."

"Murder?" Lisel was still in shock. "What makes you say that?"

"He doesn't look natural." He gave a dark chuckle. "I mean, not as though he simply laid on the bench and died. No, I believe he was already dead when he was put on the bench. Which means someone killed him elsewhere and then carried him to the bench. But why...?" He fell into thought.

"But why what?" asked Lisel, handing him the phone receiver.

"Why would anyone want to murder him?" He took the phone and punched in the numbers, requesting a coroner to come to Happy Valley.

***

"Deputy Constable Schmidt," called the woman with the short red hair, wearing the smart white dress of the coroner's office staff, coming from the van, "I'm surprised to see you so...so natural."

"Famke Neuburg. I should've known it would be you they sent." Schmidt stood with his hands on his wide utility belt, his genitals resting against his thighs as he stood in his boots before her. "Don't stare," he said with a frown. "It's the rule here."

"Yes, I know." She gave a sneer. "I know about these 'colonies'."

Lisel stepped forward. "Happy Valley is a resort, not a colony. We're not trying to colonize anything. We're here to enjoy being natural in nature."

"Yes, as she said," Schmidt nodded with a wave of his hand to Lisel. "But I came here to investigate a death. That's why I called you."

Famke laughed. "I certainly didn't expect to see you in all of your glory!"

"There's nothing strange about being clothes-free, ma'am," Lisel spoke in his defense. "We are all born without clothes and, as long as the weather is good, there is no reason not to continue being without clothing on our bodies. Our skin likes to be free to breathe."

"That's a nice advertisement. But it's really about the old men leering at the girls."

"No, it's not. We have many people here. All kinds. Families with children. And grandparents. All levels of society. But without clothing we are all the same."

"Ladies!" Schmidt exclaimed. "We are here to investigate a death. You can debate this nudism thing later."

"He's right," said Lisel. "But you'll need to remove your clothing before you enter or everyone will be alarmed. You won't fit in here. People will be upset and they will bother the camp director. You wouldn't want to upset anyone, would you?"

"Ah hah, Famke!" cried Schmidt. "Time to get naked. Strip down. Let's see what you've got, girl."

Lisel glared at Schmidt. "That's not very polite. She should follow our rules, yes, but not with you ogling her. What she does is not for your entertainment."

Schmidt lowered his head. "Sorry. You're right. I had to get out of uniform to do my job here, so I suppose you must also. We are both still working." He nodded at Famke. "I apologize. I'll look away while you strip down."

"We like to say 'remove our clothing'." Lisel grinned at him.

Lisel helped Famke return to nature by holding her clothing as she discarded it, then folded everything neatly. The coroner kept her low-heel shoes on but slid off her stockings. She turned to the van to get her bag, appearing to try to hide her wide posterior. Some people were still shy about how they looked to other people, thought Lisel. But enjoying the resort was not based on how fit or beautiful a person's body was.

Famke stepped forward, bag in hand, her face grim. "All right. I'm naked. Satisfied?"

"Please relax," said Lisel, joining her after setting the folded clothing on the driver's seat of the van. "You won't even think about being clothes-free after a while."

"She's right about that," said Schmidt. "I hardly notice I'm nude. Except for this damn belt cutting into my skin. At least the uniform buffeted the leather."

The three of them entered through the gate and Lisel showed Famke the dead body, which had been covered with a cloth. Famke pulled back the covering and scanned the face, then looked down the body. She took a voice recorder from her bag and began dictating data, describing the middle-aged male who wore clothes inside the nudist colony.

“Well, what do you think?” asked Schmidt, hands on his belt.

“The clothing has an odd smell. I’m not sure what it is. Chemicals.” She asked questions about when they found the body and how long it had been there before anyone noticed. The sun would have started to affect its condition. “Strange he is dressed in a nudist colony.”

“We already established he was not a guest here,” said Friedrich. “At least he hadn’t checked in. He had no reservation, either. We don’t even know who he is. No identification.”

“These clothes seem out of place for a wooded resort like this. Hawaiian shirt? Are they even his own clothes? Seems a size too large.” She put her hand up to her chin, squinting at the body. “Perhaps someone dressed him after he died. Perhaps anticipating someone like me having to carry him away. So perhaps his death was not so natural. Perhaps someone killed him, then put these clothes on him to make him seem more like an outsider, to shift any blame.”

“Wait! Are you saying he was murdered by one of us?” Lisel put her hands to her face.

“I think it is possible,” Famke replied. “Although there are no visible wounds, a clever person, like a spy, has many ways to slip something into a person that makes them appear to die by, say, a heart attack. He’s not too old, I guess. Or.....”

“We definitely have a murder then? A murder in the nudist colony?” Schmidt seemed amused.

“It’s not a colony,” Lisel corrected him. “We don’t live here year-round. This is not a nude village, it’s a resort.”

“But we can’t have this news get out or we’ll lose more business,” said Friedrich. “That fellow snapping pictures and putting them on the internet nearly ruined us.”

Schmidt frowned. “If it is a murder, then someone must be the culprit.”

Vic spoke up: “Someone who had the time and the means—”

"And the motivation!" Friedrich jumped in.

"--to do such a dastardly deed."

"Couldn't be one of us," said Martin, with Alice by his side. "We have no negativity toward anyone. And none of us knew this man. There is no record of him here. No reservation. No phone inquiry."

"Giles said he saw the man in town a few days ago," Lisel spoke up.

They turned to her.

"I told you he said so. He didn't have a good word to say about the victim."

Schmidt squinted. "Giles? That big fellow I met first by the body?"

"Yes, him," Lisel responded. "One of our longest standing guests. As soon as he retired from the military he wanted to relax in a forest--go completely natural, he said."

"Military?" asked Vic. "I heard him talking one night last year, when he was drunk, saying he did this and that for some spy agency. Missions, you might say."

"No, Giles is just an arms dealer," said Friedrich. "But retired now. He told me so."

"Where is he now?" asked Lisel and everyone gazed in a different direction around the camp entrance.

Famke clapped her hands. "I will need to take the body down to the lab and run some tests. I suspect something natural killed him. I mean, some natural agent. Like a microbiological something. Deliberately applied."

"A germ? Like the flu?" asked Lisel, her face tense.

"No, what I suspect—look at the rash all over his skin, following the line of the shirt, the V of the shirt making an exact V on his skin, like sunburn, but it's not. I suspect this rash is an allergic reaction."

"He was allergic to...to the fabric?" asked Lisel.

Vic laughed. "We are all allergic to wearing clothes."

"But this man was literally allergic to the fabric," Famke explained. "Or to whatever chemicals were in the fabric. I've seen that in spy movies. Spray-on allergen. The skin absorbs the chemicals and, voila, death."

"Wait!" Friedrich was shaking his head, fingers rubbing his forehead. "We have a man dead in our resort and you think it was a murder? And the murder was done by some sneaky means of triggering his allergies to...to chemicals in his shirt? That's preposterous!"

Famke lowered her arms to gesture as she argued, forgetting she was nude. "Not so preposterous. I've read a lot--"

"A lot of trashy novels, I'll bet!" Vic said with a grunt.

"No, I mean academic articles on secret bioweapon research," Famke continued. "We have to be ready for anything -- to recognize everything, and be ready to deal with it. You all could be exposed to whatever this agent is already."

"But we aren't dead," said Lisel.

"No," Friedrich agreed, "but we might have some of the stuff on us just by being close to the body and the breeze scattering the...what do you call it? Allergens? all over us."

"We should all wash off," said Beata and Friedrich gave a nod. "And stay away from the others until we're thoroughly clean."

"To the showers!" Vic announced, starting the march.

"Bring a strong soap," said Beata. "We must wash each other, make sure every bit of skin is cleansed, especially the tiny crevasses where dust and pollen can collect."

"I, for one, do not collect dust and pollen," said Lisel, crossing her arms over her breasts.

"Everyone does," said Famke. "It's part of nature. Hah! I'm surprised you folks haven't thought of that. Being nude all the time out here leaves your bodies subject to all kinds of contaminants. You need to wash yourselves constantly."

"Don't be so dramatic," Friedrich snapped.

"Let me prepare the body for transport and you go get your shower," Famke suggested.

The group headed over to the outdoor showers: a concrete square with four tall spigots set between the housing area and the edge of the forest. They took turns standing under the water spray, soaping themselves and scrubbing each other with rags, turning around and rinsing off. They shook the water off themselves as Alice returned with an armful of fresh towels to dry themselves. After twenty minutes the group returned to the gate and the bench where the body had lain. They stood back a ways.

"All clean now," said Lisel, sweeping her wet hair back.

"Be careful not to contaminate yourselves again by coming too close," Famke warned. She stood comfortably, forgetting she was in her natural uniform like the others, unconcerned with being unclothed. Schmidt wanted to point out that fact to her, he told Lisel, but she waved him off. No need to state the obvious.

"I've notified my office about the situation," Famke told them, hands folded behind herself. "I was able to conduct one test with the equipment in my bag and the results prove that something nefarious happened to this man. He died from an allergic reaction to these articles of clothing touching his skin."

The group gasped. Lisel threw her hand to her mouth. Shocking! To actually be allergic to clothing! Poor man! To die because someone put clothes on him, or persuaded him to put on these clothes. Maybe the fabric was treated with a deadly chemical, who knows? Lisel couldn't believe it. But worse was the idea that someone in this happy place had done the foul deed.

"But who?" she asked. "Who among us would do such a thing?"

Friedrich cleared his throat. "Giles knew him, he said."

"And Giles was ex-military something," said Vic. "He knew things. Maybe secret things."

"Like how to poison someone's clothes?" asked Schmidt.

"Exactly!"

"We should find him," said Schmidt, turning to Lisel. "Where's he staying?"

She led the way, with Vic and Friedrich following.

The lights were off as they approached the cabin where Giles was staying. The door was ajar. When they turned on the lights, they saw the room was empty. His bag was gone.

"He's escaped," said Friedrich.

Vic sneered. "But not through the front gate."

"He knows the trails like the back of his hand."

"Better call the whole constabulary."

Barefoot prints marred the dirt. Someone had gone that way. Friedrich and Vic took off down the trail that started behind the cabin.

"We'll catch up with him," Vic called back. "And don't worry, we'll be cool, not let him suspect anything. But you call the police to meet us on the other side, by the highway junction. At the north gate there."

"Got it," said Lisel.

She ran with Schmidt to the phone at the office and he called for backup. Then they went to help Famke move the body onto a gurney and roll it into the rear of the van. Closing the doors, Famke paused to look over Lisel and Schmidt, nodding with approval.

"Look at me," said Famke with a chuckle. "I'm like a newborn babe and not embarrassed at all. In fact, it feels kind of good out here. I may have to come again, for a real visit. Let me see what this resort has to offer."

"You're welcome anytime" said Lisel. She regarded Schmidt. "And so are you."

"It would be my pleasure to return here," said Schmidt, "for a normal visit."

Famke and Schmidt looked each other over, apparently satisfied there was nothing weird about other people seeing their bare bodies. It had to be better than worrying about deadly textile allergies. They shook hands, knowing they would work together again sometime. Or they might meet again here at the Happy Valley resort.

Lisel and Schmidt watched the van drive off. Famke had showered but not bothered to put on her white uniform again before climbing into the driver's seat.

"She's nice-looking," said Schmidt, watching the van pause at the highway intersection before turning.

"Does that matter?" asked Lisel, her voice tired.

"No, I suppose it doesn't." Schmidt gave a smirk. "It's what's under our skin that matters. Our hearts, at least." He pursed his lips, thinking. "My name's Hans, by the way. Could I see you again? Meet you, not just look at you."

"But I'll be going home at the end of the week," Lisel responded.

"Oh, that's a long distance."

"I'll return here in the autumn for a few days. Otherwise, if you're ever near Hamburg, text me," said Lisel.

"I'd like that," Schmidt said, grinning.

"We can get a beer and talk about the murder in the nudist colony."

A deadly afternoon

Stan Muir

She was lying on her belly, her arms above her head. She looked like someone enjoying getting suntanned on a beach. A naturist beach. She was completely naked with the exception of a hat that covered her neatly cut, tousled hair

On this beach, the scene would have been entirely normal if it had been daytime. It was though close to 10 PM and it was stark dark, and he almost bumped into the lying lady if the sudden glow of her ringing cellphone did not reveal her presence.

He kneeled, putting his hand on her shoulder to shake her. Her skin was soft … and cold. He immediately felt that something was not right. The lady was dead! He suppressed a gasp, stood up and dialed 15. Ten minutes later, a small squad of firefighters were there, one interrogating the man, another one confirming the death of the woman and calling a doctor to establish a death certificate. It was the first time somebody died on the beach of the naturist village of Leucate.

***

Earlier in the day

"It's too hot, I'm going swimming. Are you coming?"

Myriam stood up and not waiting for the answer from Sophie, she walked to the sea. It was a hot day, but because it was autumn and a weekday, there were few people on the beach. Just two couples in their fifties, and a dozen men and women, all lying or sitting naked on their towels. Everybody was minding their own business.

Myriam was a seasoned swimmer, a former member of her college swimming team. Despite not pursuing a career in professional sport, she continued to swim regularly long distance to stay fit and maintain a toned body. After a few meters, she turned at ninety degrees and started crawling regularly parallel to the shore. Thirty minutes later, she was back on her towel.

"How was it?" asked the other woman, sitting next to her towel.

"Refreshing," answered Myriam with her natural demeanor. "You should come."

"Yes, I should, I'm just lazy, I guess."

Sophie had been Myriam's best friend for more than thirty years. Myriam's ex-husband was Sophie's cousin. Although Myriam divorced ten years ago, they remained good friends, seeing each other occasionally. The divorce was unexpected for Myriam. Her ex-husband did his coming out on the day of their fifteenth anniversary and introduced Myriam to his boyfriend. Despite her open mind, this came as a blow and a treason for Myriam. In less than a week, she had packed her stuff, resigned from her job and headed south, where the couple had a small apartment in the naturist village of Leucate.

Sophie was a long-time naturist and she was the influence behind the purchase of Myriam's house, next to hers, when it was put on sale. Myriam was living in Leucate, enjoying her life as a freelance designer, as Sophie was living in Toulouse, two hours away.

"You are not lazy, So, you just need some motivation," replied Myriam while drying her hair she kept long.

"Yes, you are right. I'm more motivated by improving my tan," acknowledged Sophie with a big smile on her face.

"When are you driving back?" asked Myriam to change conversation.

"Later today! I have some meetings tomorrow. Boring but necessary," said Sophie with a grin.

Myriam nodded and lied on her back, grabbing her hat to cover her face. She let herself relax entirely, her naked body absorbing the rays of the sun. In a couple of weeks, the temperature would be too chilly to come to the beach. The wind in the region was blowing most of the time from the north, carrying fresh air from the high grounds. It could be freezing cold in winter despite a deep blue sky. Her small garden was her piece of paradise. Facing south, it was protected from the northern wind and even in the deepest of winter, she could enjoy warm naked moments. Living in a naturist setting, she was spending most of her time entirely naked. And the more she could stay naked, the better she felt.

Her divorce had been a kind of a blessing, allowing her to discover her true naturist side and embracing the lifestyle to the fullest. Although she had a couple of affairs in the past few years, none were completely satisfying, and she was still living alone in the town house. She just had found something bigger. It had another bedroom that would allow her to invite some friends for the holidays and provide extra space for her work.

“I’m going to get prepared, Mimi. I leave you my bottle of water, I won’t drink it. I’ll come to say goodbye when I leave.” Sophie stood up, put her towel back in her tote bag, laid the bottle of water in Myriam’s bag, waved at her friend, slipped into her high-heeled sandals and walked away. Myriam turned on her belly to watch her friend going away. She was a beautiful woman for her fifties, thought Myriam. She grabbed the untouched bottle of sparkling water Sophie left, looked at the label, then put it back for later.

***

The next morning

On site, the doctor had issued a death certificate and voiced her concern about the cause of death. There was no sign of a stroke, the body did not present any sign of a sudden natural death, but the dried tears left her in wonder. She ordered an autopsy to be carried out.

The results had just arrived, and she was studying them carefully. The cause of death was asphyxiation. “You don’t die of asphyxiation by lying on a towel on a beach in the open air,” she said to herself. She looked at the blood sample analysis, but all seemed normal. She grabbed the phone on her desk and called the hospital laboratory.

“Doctor Lambert?”

“Yes?” said a deep male voice.

“This is Doctor Jarnac, who delivered the death certificate of the lady who was autopsied this morning,” said she as she was in a kind of a hurry.

"What can I do for you, dear colleague?" asked the doctor his slow delivery suggesting a cautious approach.

"Well, you see, the cause of death has been established as asphyxiation. But you don't die of asphyxiation by lying on a towel on a beach, particularly when you don't have preconditions, which seemed to be the case of that lady. However, the blood sample is normal. Do you have any idea about the cause of the asphyxiation?"

"Wait!" Now the attention of Doctor Lambert was caught. "I'm just the lab doctor, and I did not have access to the pathologist's report. Did he or she not mention the cause of the asphyxiation?" he asked Dr Jarnac with an edge of excitement creeping into his voice.

"Can I send you the report, so we have a look together?"

"Please do so, and I'll call you back in five."

Less than five minutes after she hit the Send button, her phone rang. She picked up. It was Lambert.

"Jarnac, there's only one explanation to this," Lambert replied, it sounded like he was choosing his words with great care.

"And what is it?" she asked anxiously.

"Poison. Nerve agent, I would guess. Mme Boyer has been murdered," said Lambert as if it was a completely normal thing.

"This is what I thought. We need to inform the police. Can we identify what agent was used?"

"We will need to do more analysis if the coroner asks for it," replied Lambert, slowly and confidently.

"Thank you, Doctor," replied Jarnac while hanging up.

***

"Simon, we have a potential murder. Get your ass out of this chair and dash to the morgue. The number of the medical examiner is on the report." The police commissioner of the city threw the yellow folder on the desk of Simon Persan, the police officer on duty. "Call me as soon as you have more information," he said while turning and going back to his office.

Simon picked up the folder casually, opened it, and while keeping his feet on his desk, read through it. With eyes still on the sheet of paper, he grabbed his phone and dialed the number of the morgue. Five minutes later, he was on his motorbike, driving to the Narbonne hospital to get the bag belonging to the victim. Well, she may not be a victim, but the suspicion was a certainty in Simon's mind after having read the file.

On arrival, he presented his police card and was introduced to the doctor in charge, who handed him the bag.

"You never wear gloves when you hold deceased's objects?" asked Simon with a pinch of anger.

"Sometimes, but generally no," answered the man nonchalantly.

"Can you get me a pair of surgical gloves, please?" replied Simon while taking his backpack off his shoulder.

"Stay here, I will get you one," answered the doctor. He turned on his heels and went to the next room, grabbing two latex sterile gloves that he handed to Simon. While putting them on, Simon was glancing at the content of the bag. Only the towel was visible, covering the content. With the gloves on, he took the towel out and uncovered the rest of the bag. There was a copy of *Naturisme Magazine*, a half-drunk bottle of sparkling water, a pair of sunglasses, a bottle of sun lotion, a hat, an envelope where the magazine must have arrived in, and a set of keys.

The envelope had the name and the address of the victim. Simon took his notepad and jotted down the address. He then took out a set of plastic bags, wrote the name of the victim on each and put each object in its own bag, with the exception of the keys that he put in his leather jacket's pocket.

"Thank you for your help, doc. I'll keep the gloves, thank you!" said Simon while putting all the packed objects in the bag. He took the latex gloves off, threw them in the bag and put on his leather gloves. He closed his backpack, grabbed the bag and walked back to his motorbike at a fast pace. With a scorching noise, he left the hospital heading to the laboratory, where he would have all the objects searched for fingerprints and traces of poisonous substances.

He stayed a couple of minutes in the laboratory, left all the objects that he had gathered at the morgue and headed to Leucate. He entered the naturist village and parked his motorbike in front of the address he had noted down. It was a small townhouse, opening on a tiny garden that was tended with taste and a profusion of flowers. A round wooden table with two chairs and a lounge chair were standing in the middle of the terrace.

Simon pulled the set of keys out of his pocket and opened the front door. It opened onto a relatively large room that seemed to serve as a dining room, living room and an open kitchen. It was an open space, painted in white, with very little furniture and a flat-screen TV. Simon looked around, not touching anything. A at the back door opened into a bathroom.

He climbed the stairs to go to the bedroom on the first floor. A queen-size bed was occupying most of the space and the opposite wall to the staircase was a wardrobe. All was clean, neatly set with taste. The house was small and cozy. Simon walked down and noticed an address book set next to the telephone. He smiled. Many people did not keep a paper address book these years with smartphones. It was, though, easier than breaking into a phone, he thought. With his leather gloves on, he grabbed the address book and put it in his pocket.

He stepped out of the house, and carefully locked the door. He went to the house on the immediate right of Myriam's and knocked on the door. Nobody was in. He looked on the letter box and noted down the name in his notepad. Doing the same on the house on the immediate left, he did not have any further chance. He glanced around and decided to drive back to his office and see if he could arrange to interview the neighbors, he wanted to ask them a couple of questions.

***

Sophie's phone was in silent mode in her bag. It was only during her lunch break that she noticed the three missed calls. All from the same number, which was unknown to her. Who could be calling her? She pressed the screen and the phone dialed the number.

"Allo?" said a man's voice.

“Good morning, you tried to call me three times this morning,” answered Sophie.

“Yes. Thanks for calling me back. My name is Simon Persan, I’m a police officer, investigating the death of…” Simon opened the file on his desk to look for the name of the dead, “… Myriam Boyer.”

The other side of the line remained silent.

“Madam, are you there?”

“Yes,” said a very low voice, contrasting with the previous confident-sounding Sophie.

“You’re Mme. Boyer’s neighbor in Leucate, aren’t you?”

“Yes, but you said that Myriam was dead?”

“Yes madam. Did you know Ms. Boyer well?”

The line remained silent. Simon was used to it. Not that there were many murders or suspicious deaths in the region. It was frequent that people did not grab the situation immediately and needed time to think and reflect. He was used to it and remained silent. After a few seconds, Sophie started to speak again.

“Myriam is my friend,” said Sophie, with a trembling voice, tears in her eyes.

“I’m sorry madam,” said Simon complacently.

“When did that happen?”

“She was found dead on the beach yesterday evening. Hence my call, as it seems you have a neighboring house.”

“Yes,” answered Sophie almost like an automaton.

“Where are you now, madam?”

“I’m in Toulouse. This is where I live.”

“Do you have an opportunity to come to Narbonne in the coming days?” asked Simon, retaining his professional demeanor.

“Hmm, yes, over the weekend probably.”

"Can you come to my office on Saturday morning, let's say around 10 AM?" asked Simon, with a tone that sounded more like an order than a question.

"I guess so," answered Sophie, "but, what for?"

"It's the standard procedure in a murder investigation," Simon answered directly.

"Has Myriam been murdered?"

"This is what I'm trying to determine, madam. I will be waiting for you on Saturday at 10 AM at the police office, 1 Pierre Benet Street. You can ask for officer Simon Persan on arrival. Have a good day." Simon hung up and noted the meeting in his notebook. He then dialed for the sixth time the number of the other neighbor, with, once again, no success. Nobody was answering the phone.

***

Simon went back to the report and reread the medical examiner's comments. When Myriam was found, she had been dead for a couple of hours. Her body was stiff. What puzzled the examiner was the remains of tears on her cheeks. Now that the autopsy had attributed the death to asphyxiation, they needed to look for traces of poison, thought Simon as he was dialing the number of the laboratory, his eyes on the medical report.

After talking to the head doctor of the laboratory about additional tests on Myriam's blood sample for poisonous traces, he decided to look for clues back in Leucate. He switched his computer on and looked at the shops in the village. There were five restaurants and five shops in the vicinity of Myriam's house. This would not take him more than an hour to visit some, if not all, of them. He grabbed his helmet and walked briskly to his motorbike. Twenty minutes later, he stopped the engine in front of Myriam's house, as he had done a couple of hours earlier.

As he was walking down the streets, heading to the first shop to visit, he felt a little bit uneasy. He was the only one who was dressed. All the people he passed were stark naked or only had a flimsy sarong on. He was not a naturist and the idea of getting naked did not fit his brain. But now, he felt as if something was wrong with him. Despite his growing feeling of discomfort, he entered the bakery, Les délices d'Aphrodite.

"Good afternoon, Simon Persan, police officer," introduced Simon while showing his police id. "Can I ask you a couple of questions?"

"Yes", said the lady behind the counter. "Did we do anything wrong?" she asked with a trembling voice.

"No, it's not you. I was wondering whether you knew this lady," answered Simon while showing a full-page picture of Myriam's face he had extracted from the report file.

"It's Mme. Boyer. Yes, she comes every other day to get breads and cakes. A very nice and quiet lady. Anything happened?" the saleswoman asked eagerly.

"She was found dead on the beach yesterday," Simon answered abruptly.

The lady gasped and choked, putting her hand in front of her opened mouth. "No! it's horrible!"

"Yes, it is. Anything you can tell me about Mme. Boyer? Was she behaving strangely lately? Did she have enemies in the village?"

"Well, no!" said the saleswoman loudly and vehemently. "She is a very nice woman, nice with everybody. Do you think she was murdered?".

"There are suspicions, hence my questions. If you hear anything, please let me know. I thank you for your time." Simon handed her his business card.

"By the way, sir, you should not walk around fully dressed like that. It's a naturist village here. Try to respect nudity," she said, regaining her composure.

Simon did not answer, just nodded and stepped out of the shop, feeling even more uncomfortable than before entering. Getting undressed was not even a possibility in his mind. A police officer, naked! How credible can you be while entirely naked? He shrugged and walked in the next shop, the hairdresser salon, Le Salon de la Plage. People talk a lot generally while getting their hair done. It was maybe there that he thought he could learn more about Myriam.

"Good morning, sir. What can I do for you?" asked the shop owner cheerfully with a strong southern accent.

"Simon Persan, criminal investigation, I would like to ask you a couple of questions," answered Simon in his professional unemotional tone while showing his police id.

"Of course, officer," answered the lady with the same demeanor.

"Do you know this lady?" Simon showed her Myriam's picture.

"Of course! It's Mme. Boyer. A very nice customer. She comes every week to have her hair and nails done. Anything happened to her?" she asked.

"She was found dead on the beach yesterday."

The hairdresser wheezed and tears quickly showed at the corners of her eyes.

"I'm sorry," said Simon, trying to look more human. "Do you know if she had any problems with other people?"

It took the hairdresser a good two minutes to calm down and be able to answer the police officer. She grabbed a paper handkerchief, wiped her eyes and nose and answered half-sobbing. "No, she was nice to everybody. She had a difficult life, you know. Her husband divorced her and left her stranded. She had to rebuild her life from scratch."

"Do you have her ex-husband contact details?"

"Maybe. Let me check," said the lady, while flipping through the pages of the notebook that was sitting on the desk. "Yes, here: Franck Mistour, you can see his cell phone number."

Simon noted down Franck's number. He noticed that Myriam's last name, Boyer, was her maiden name.

"He still comes with his new friend sometimes. I heard he rents an apartment in summer. The real estate agent will probably be able to tell you more."

"Thank you, madam. It's been very useful. If you hear anything else, do not hesitate to contact me at this number," said Simon while handing her his card.

"I will, officer, I will. It's horrible!" she said again, sobbing.

"And by the way, you should undress. It's a naturist village here - people come here to be naked among naked people. Just saying!"

Once again, Simon did not answer, and his unease moved up one peg as he was stepping out. He looked around, saw once again only naked people walking around and headed to the restaurant next door, le Bar de la Plage, where he was greeted with the same cheerful demeanor by a fully dressed waiter. The same conversation he already had with the two previous people happened again: Myriam was a nice lady, she had been coming there frequently, and no, she did not have enemies.

The only added information he got was that she came in frequently with her friend Sophie, the one he was seeing on Saturday. That confirmed they were close.

Despite the fact he was sure he would get the same answers from the other restaurant, La Palmeraie, and the grocer's shop, he visited them. He came out with a growing feeling that if there were an answer to be found it would be with Sophie. Nothing was telling Simon that Myriam had been threatened in any form, and her ex-husband seemed to live his life. While standing just outside the grocer's shop, his cell phone rang. It was the laboratory.

"Simon Persan?" asked the voice as he picked up the call.

"Yes," he answered in a flat voice.

"Doctor Germon, from the forensic laboratory," replied the man.

"Good afternoon, Doc."

"I'm calling you, officer, because we have the cause of death and it's not common," said the doctor with a slight hesitation that Simon caught.

"What do you mean, not common?" asked the police officer while tilting his head as if he wanted to get closer to the phone that was already on his ear.

"Well, we found traces of VX in the blood sample. It's a nerve agent that is generally used by secret service."

Simon kept quiet, thinking.

"Officer, are you still there?" inquired doctor Germon.

"Yes, I'm here. Sorry, I was thinking. How do you think it came into her bloodstream?"

"Well, this is the other interesting fact actually. We found traces of VX in the bottle of water that was in the bag. It seems to have been poisoned and that's what killed Mme… Boyer," answered the doctor as he was looking for the name of the deceased.

"Any fingerprints on the bottle?" asked Simon in a nervous voice.

"Yes. Two sets. One belongs to the victim, the other is unknown."

The other belongs to the murderer, Simon thought immediately. If we can identify who it belongs too, we have him, or her, he thought.

"Thank you, doc, can you send the results by email?"

"It's already in your inbox, officer. But I wanted to give you the results by phone before you read it,".

"Thank you, doc. Have a good day," said Simon while hanging up. Now, he had results, he thought, pinching his lips. It's a murder and we are going to nail the one who perpetrated it. He then started briskly to the last visit he wanted to make: the real estate agency. The air was warm, and he continued to feel uncomfortable in his jeans, shirt and leather jacket, among all the people who were much more at ease than him, entirely naked. The idea of undressing was slowly but surely soaking under his skin.

He pushed open the door of the real estate agent and introduced himself with his police id. The real estate agent was a handsome man in his forties, with a strong accent of the region and a huge mustache.

"Yes, we have just found a new house for Mme. Boyer," confessed the agent. "She has been looking for a while, as she wanted to sell her small house to purchase a bigger one, with at least two rooms. We have found her a nice one, facing the ocean, with three rooms in perfect condition."

"Did the transaction happen?" asked Simon.

"Not yet. She has made a down payment to secure the transaction, but we are due to sign two weeks from now. Do you see any problem with this?" asked the man, keeping a big smile on his face.

"Well, Mme. Boyer has been found dead on the beach yesterday evening, so yes, I see a problem with this," answered Simon repeating the same words. "Do you know if anybody had any issue with the transaction happening?"

The man, surprised, started to stutter. "Well, nnnno. The p, p, previous owner is a very, very, very, nice … gentleman."

"Slow down. I understand you're shocked. Have a glass of water and we can continue this conversation," advised Simon.

The man stood up and went to the water cooler to drink not one, but three glasses of water. He swiped his mustache with a handkerchief taken out of his trousers pocket and went back to his desk.

"I'm sorry, it happens to me sometimes," he apologized.

"There's no problem, sir. My sister stutters too when she gets nervous. You were saying that the current owner of the house is very nice. Do you see any other people who would disagree with the transaction?"

"Let me think… Maybe her friend. A very beautiful woman as well. Both came yesterday morning and visited the apartment. She seemed unhappy with the purchase. I remember she blamed Mme. Boyer that they would not be neighbors anymore."

"Was that Sophie Daumier?" asked Simon?

"Yes, I think that was her name."

"I thank you sir, this has been a very helpful conversation," said Simon while standing up and handing out his business card. "Call me if you remember anything else."

"I will, officer. Take my card as well and a list of apartments and houses to rent. You should come to the village, you'll discover naturism, a great way to unwind, you know."

Simon grabbed the card and the leaflet, stuffed them in his backpack, and headed back to his motorbike.

***

A stunning woman knocked on Simon's door. In her fifties, her blond hair, clear blue eyes, perfect makeup and haute couture blouse, skirt and high-heel pumps, offered a sharp contrast to the grim police offices.

"Officer Persan?" asked the lady, almost whispering.

"Yes!" Simon answered severely, standing up and greeting her. "Madam Daumier, I presume. Please have a seat," he said, while pointing to a wooden chair in front of his office. "Thank you for coming."

"I would not say it's a pleasure, since my best friend died, but if I can be of any help," answered Sophie, while sitting, with the same low voice.

"This should not take long, madam. I just have a few questions that I would like you to answer."

"Sure, officer."

"Some water?" asked Simon while grasping a bottle sitting on the edge of his desk.

"Please," confirmed Sophie, picking up an empty glass with her perfectly manicured right hand.

"How long have you known Mme. Boyer?"

"Oh, ages! Myriam's ex-husband is a close cousin of mine. We met before their wedding but remained close friends when they divorced. Myriam is, was, a very good friend. We loved each other."

"When you say, we loved each other, do you mean you were engaged in a romantic relationship?"

Sophie blushed slightly and put her head slightly forward. Simon was under the impression she was acting.

"Well, it's difficult to say. We can probably say I wanted our relationship to become romantic, but Myriam did not have a lesbian inclination. I am a lesbian; in case you were going to ask."

"I thank you for your openness, madam," acknowledged Simon. "What do you do for a living?" he asked, changing topics abruptly.

"I own a pharmacy in Toulouse. I'm a graduate pharmacist." She straightened her back and chest, as she answered.

"Any field specialty?"

She was taken aback by the question and hesitated a fraction of a second. Imperceptible for a normal human being, but not for Simon, who was trained to detect those tiny hesitations and changes in facial expressions.

"No, not really."

Simon was not convinced, but he would come back to this later.

"I was told by the real agent who had signed Mme. Boyer's new apartment in Leucate that you did not seem happy by the transaction. Why was that?"

Sophie froze. She crossed her arms and legs and pinched her lips.

"I don't know why this stupid real estate agent has told you that," Sophie said defensively.

"Maybe because you did not like that Myriam was distancing herself from you?" Simon cut in.

"No!" Sophie almost shouted. "I was happy for her that she could find a larger place,"

"And start a new life without you around?" asked Simon while leaning forward toward Sophie.

"What are you implying, officer?" asked Sophie, on the defensive.

"I'm not implying anything, madam, we are holding you in custody to question you about the murder of Myriam Boyer. An investigating magistrate will take this over. You may want to call your lawyer."

"They will never be able to prove I killed that slut," said Sophie as Simon was handcuffing her.

"Maybe not, but another one may. You'll have time to ponder this, madam."

He grabbed her by the arm and led her to an interrogation room. Sophie knew deep in her heart that it was not the end she envisioned, but at least she was free of the suffering that Myriam had started by refusing her love.

***

Back at his office, Simon opened an evidence bag and with a gloved hand, picked up the glass that Sophie used. He was sure the fingerprints on the glass would match those on the bottle.

Then he opened the leaflet that the real estate agent had given him. “Why not give naturism a try?” he asked himself. He needed some rest. He picked up the phone and dialed the number of the agency.

Pest Control

Will Forest

The dirty white van sped by, forcing Nate to swerve dangerously close to the Noonay Noo Naturist Park welcome sign.

"Someone's trying to get out of there in a hurry," observed Beverly from the passenger seat.

"Did you get a look at the sign on the van?" asked Nate.

"It said 'Regal Pest Control," Beverly replied, and laughed a little. "There's a royal termite emergency somewhere."

"Curious," said Nate, furrowing his brow.

Beverly kissed his cheek. "Don't worry about it."

The rest of the drive down the Noonay Noo access road was uneventful. Nate always enjoyed coming to this corner of the island - it was a 45-minute journey from his apartment in Port Trésor, but the payoff was being able to hang out *au naturel* at a beautiful spot he considered his home away from home. As usual, he parked his Jeep in front of his friend Dr. A's house and bolted out, throwing his clothes off in such haste that he almost ripped his shirt.

"Dr. A, I'm here!... Dr. A?"

Nate stopped yelling long enough to get his shirt over his head and completely off. He threw it on a pile with the rest of his clothing, just inside the front door, and called out for his eccentric friend a few more times as he moved through her home.

"Better check the kitchen," he said to himself out loud, "and the stove that's probably on…"

In the kitchen he found a sticky note: "Nate, I know you'll be here soon. I'm at Ernestine's. Please grab Ladybug and come join us."

"Typical," said Nate, referring to Dr. A's request about Ladybug, and also referring to the stove that had indeed been left on. "What's odd is that Ernestine is *not* one of Dr. A's favorite souls, as she likes to put it…"

Nate pushed through the hanging plastic flaps into Dr. A's greenhouse and butterfly garden, and found Ladybug, her pet praying mantis, in its little carry-cage. He brought it back through the house and closed the front door behind him, then returned to his Jeep, where Beverly had already removed her clothes. "Dr. A's at the neighbor's," Nate told her, and so they set off on foot with Ladybug, walking along Noonay Noo's only road to Ernestine's house five doors down.

Noonay Noo had been established as a naturist park on the southwest coast of St. Ethel, an independent island in between Cuba, Haiti and Jamaica. There were many cabins and tenting areas for park visitors, and also a dozen homes for permanent residents. These houses occupied the seaview side of the long gravel road, each with its own backyard opening directly onto the coast.

"Who's Ernestine?" Beverly asked as they walked along under palms and flame trees. The Caribbean sun was still low in the east but already toasty warm.

"Remember how I told you Dr. A and her late husband founded Noonay Noo? Well, there were a few other founders too - people who fronted funds to get the place set up. Ernestine is one of the founders," Nate explained. "But Dr. A doesn't like her at all."

"Interesting," mused Beverly. "You'd think everybody out here gets along just fine. Like-minded naked people, and all that."

"Yep, you'd think," Nate agreed. "Here, this is her place."

"The front door's wide open," noted Beverly.

As they passed Ernestine's front-yard sculpture--a tree made of upended glass bottles of varying hues--they heard Dr. A calling from inside: "Oh, Ernestine! How could you do this to me?"

"Hello," called Nate as they moved inside. "Dr. A?"

"Nate! Beverly! Just look at what this woman has done!"

Dr. A was pointing at the floor behind the couch. Nate and Beverly exchanged a curious glance as they approached.

There, sprawled out along the rug, lay Ernestine, and she was as dead as she was nude, which was to say, completely.

“Oh holy mother of god…” muttered Beverly.

“Well, yes, she was many things, including a mother,” began Dr. A, “but…”

“What happened to her?” interrupted Nate.

Dr. A stared at him. “Well, I don’t know, do I? What took you so long? When are you two getting engaged, anyway? And have you eaten?”

The couple exchanged grins even in spite of the circumstances. They both knew Dr. A’s habit of tripling or quadrupling her interrogations.

“First things first,” answered Nate. “Here’s Ladybug.”

“Thank you,” said Dr. A. “I am always lamenting forgetting remembering her.”

“Uh huh,” said Nate. “Now, tell me how it was you found Ernestine like this.”

“Alright, young man. You’re so insistent, and it’s a good thing I like that about you. But you tell me first, how did you know I was here?”

“You left me a note, remember? It said, ‘I’m at…’”

“I know perfectly well what it said - I wrote it, didn’t I? And you better damn well have brought Ladyb… oh, of course, yes, you did bring her...I bet I left the stove on, didn’t I?”

“We need to call the police!” interrupted Beverly, who had squatted down to check for a pulse. “There is a dead body here! We’re all going to be questioned, but we’ve got to do it!”

Nate cocked an eyebrow at Dr. A. “And you think I’m the insistent one.”

“You’re quite right, Beverly,” said Dr. A, “and in fact I already have called the police. It was the first thing I did.”

“Thank goodness,” she replied.

“Yes, but it’ll probably take them another half hour still to get here from Port Trésor. In the meantime, just have a look at her,” said Dr. A. “I haven’t touched anything. This is how I found her. Her door was open, and of course there was no answer when I called out, so I was coming through here to look for her out back, when I almost stepped on her!"

Beverly knelt to look more closely. Ernestine lay face-up, and did not appear to have been dead all that long. There were no wounds on the front of her body. She was elderly - as old as Dr. A or even older.

"And so I think it was obviously a burglary," said Dr. A.

Nate looked around the room. He saw a TV set on its shelf and a laptop on the side table. None of the bureau drawers were open. "Why would you think it was a burglary?"

"Well, just look at her nipples!' Dr. A exclaimed.

"I see them," said Nate calmly. "They are… entirely the number and shape I would expect."

"No, no," protested Dr. A. "Her perchings are missing!"

"You mean someone ripped out her piercings?" asked Nate.

"Ouch!" said Beverly, instinctively covering her chest.

"Not piercings. Perchings. She was a fan of that, what's it called... body jewelry?" Dr. A sighed and shook her head. "Just one of her many quirks. In any case she always had something perched there, and she certainly doesn't now… But she did have a piercing, in her navel, and that's gone too. And she's missing the charm belt she wore around her hips, and also the amulet she almost always had on."

"Lots of bling," said Nate.

Dr. A gave a blank look. "He means jewelry," Beverly clarified.

"Yes, well, she had a ton. Always wearing something different, at least on her nipples, or adding new charms to her belt. I asked her once where she got all that stuff and she said something about an inheritance."

"Is it possible she just wasn't wearing any jewelry at the moment she was killed?" asked Beverly.

"I suppose it's possible," mused Dr. A, "but so is having transparent governance and quality healthcare here on St. Ethel."

"In other words, not likely," Nate surmised.

"But, who knows?" said Dr. A. "And why are her feet so sandy, here in the middle of her house? Anything's possible… including an invasion of ants! Oh my goodness, quickly, help me lift her onto the table to get her away from these ants!"

"News of death travels quickly in the tropics," Nate muttered.

"But we're not supposed to move her!" said Beverly. "The police will need everything as it was, won't they?"

"We can't just leave her to the ants!" insisted Dr. A, while nonchalantly scooping some of them into her hand and dropping them down into the carry cage for Ladybug to hunt. "Oh she was not one of my favorite souls, not even close, but I can't just let the ants…"

"We need a spray, or a barrier of some sort around her body," continued Nate. "What would work?"

"A spray would also really mess up the crime scene for the police, though," said Beverly.

"Olive oil!" said Dr. A. "Look and see if she has any in the kitchen, and if she doesn't, we can ask Jimmy next door."

Beverly quickly found some olive oil in the kitchen.

"That should be enough, but barely!" said Dr. A when Beverly showed her the almost full bottle. "Just pour it gingerly around her perimeter… I'm afraid at this point the rug she's on is ruined anyway."

"Hey," said Beverly, squatting on the carpet. "These are tunneling ants. I've never seen them on St. Ethel."

"Thank the stars for an entomologist when you need one!" exclaimed Dr. A.

"Dr. A," interrupted Nate. "You're an entomologist yourself..."

"A retired entomologist!" Dr. A huffed. "Although, can one ever really retire from entomology?"

"I'm sure I wouldn't know." Nate sighed and looked around Ernestine's home while Beverly spread the olive oil around the body. "Dr. A, why did you come over here, anyway?"

"Ernestine is not… oh my, she *was* not… one of my favorite souls, but I needed her to sign the Noonay Noo board report, so I came over. Now where did I put that report? Oh, there it is, on the coffee table, over there by the statue on the floor... That was one of her favorite things, that statue, a Taino piece she got in Santo Domingo. Why would it be on the floor?"

"Hmmm..." Nate said, eyeing the rather hefty effigy that looked to be made of dark wood, about a half meter in length. "Good question. And while we're thinking of it, when you came in, did you see anything else that was odd or different about the place?"

"Well," said Dr. A, "Jimmy."

"What? You mean the guy who lives next door?"

"Well, of course, Nate! You think I'm talking about Jimmy Cricket?"

"That was Jiminy… oh, never mind. What about him?"

"Well, on the way over here, I saw him on his front porch and I called out to him, 'Hello!' because why wouldn't I? And you'd think I was the devil, the speed with which he jumped up and ran inside his house."

"Odd," mused Nate.

"Oh," continued Dr. A, "and then here in the house, I noticed the cabinet under the kitchen sink is open and there are some tools lying around over there. Is that where the ants are coming from?"

"On the way into the park, we saw a pest control van speeding away," said Nate. "Maybe Ernestine had contracted them?"

"Maybe," said Beverly, still down on the carpet, "but I see where the ants are coming from, and it's not the sink. They're coming from under this couch. And like I said, they're tunneling ants - they need a deep underground structure to build their colonies. Does this house have a basement, or a cellar, or anything like that?"

“None of the homes here at Noonay Noo has a basement,” said Dr. A, “and I should know, since I saw them all get built. The soil here just isn’t good for it, especially on the edge of the sea like this.”

“It’s very odd, then,” said Beverly, “to see these tunneling ants... Nate, can you please help me move the couch?”

“What about not disturbing the crime scene, and all that?” said Nate.

“We can put it back…” said Beverly.

“Go ahead,” said Dr. A. “It’s just one mystery on top of another around here.”

Beverly and Nate grunted as they lifted the heavy sofa and set it down a few feet away.

“There’s something loose there,” said Nate, looking at the spot where the couch had been, and as he spoke, they all saw more ants coming up from below the floorboards.

Beverly kneeled back down and pulled the edge of a plank. It lifted easily, and so did the one next to it. Nate helped her remove another four boards, and there it was: a staircase leading down. The primordial smell of the ocean wafted up clear and strong from below, and they heard the sloshing of the waves.

“Well for goodness sake,” said Dr. A. “All the times I came and sat my bare bottom down on this couch, and I never knew what lay underneath.”

“I hope that what lay underneath your bare bottom,” observed Nate, “was a towel.”

Dr. A ignored this. “But did Ernestine know? Did she herself even know there was a staircase… Wait a second, I’m remembering something…” Dr. A looked up, and then out toward the ocean. “All those years ago when we were laying out Noonay Noo, Ermestine was very particular about her home being on this exact spot… What a sneaky soul! And I never suspected… What did she keep down there…?”

“Alright!” said Beverly. “Well, it looks like we've got to go down there, and we need a light.”

"And we need to hurry if we're going to do it before the police get here," added Nate.

Some five minutes later, after a quick run back to Nate's jeep and Dr. A's house for a couple flashlights, they were ready to descend.

"I don't think we need to bring Ladybug," said Nate.

"I'm glad you can express your opinion, Nate, but I didn't ask you for it," said Dr. A. "Ladybug is coming with us."

"Dr. A, no offense, but at your age, how are you going to carry the case while you climb down…"

"Oh, I'm not carrying her case." Dr. A opened the little cage door, pulled out the mantis, and placed it on her bare shoulder. "There - all set."

"Careful," said Beverly, who had already gone down a few steps. "It's slippery."

She took Dr. A's hand, and the three of them descended slowly. There was a curve in the staircase, and then another, and as they wound around it grew lighter, until they stepped onto the very narrow and irregular shore of a cove where they could see out to the open sea. Right in the middle of the cove was a shipwrecked skiff tilted away from them.

"My stars, Ladybug," said Dr. A. "I thought it was all a hoax."

"What was a hoax?" asked Beverly.

"The Sea Witch," came the reply. Dr. A shuddered. "But this is it. This must be her cove."

"Never heard of a sea witch," said Nate.

"Well, Ernestine talked about her all the time," said Dr. A. "I imagined it was because she was a little concerned about living all alone out here, and so she'd talk about the Sea Witch haunting her home to scare people away."

"Understandable," said Beverly. "So who was the Sea Witch?"

"According to Ernestine," said Dr. A, "the Sea Witch lived on this island centuries ago, during the colonial period. She was from West

Africa, had been enslaved and brought here to the Caribbean, and escaped. Supposedly she was the captain of her own ship..."

"And what about this cove?" asked Nate.

"I was just getting to that part! Really, Nate, you should work on your patience. Now, as I was saying… Don't you roll your eyes at me, young man!"

Dr. A laughed in spite of herself.

"The cove?" prompted Beverly.

"Oh yes, thank you, Beverly," said Dr. A. "This cove was allegedly where she hid her treasure… But, it all makes so much sense! Ernestine's body jewelry - it was always exquisite, and she had so many different perchings and piercings… she must have been borrowing from the Sea Witch's stash down here!"

"Her 'inheritance," added Beverly.

"I'm wondering where the stash would be," said Nate.

"And I'm wondering how long that little motorboat has been here in the cove," said Beverly. "Looks like it hit something under the water that sliced the hull."

They watched the boat's bulk for a moment, but there was no movement, and no sound other than the gentle waves… until a new sound, faint at first, grew steadily and unmistakably.

"Why do they have to turn their sirens on? Oh, this is such a scandal for Noonay Noo, to have the police barging in here," complained Dr. A.

"We'd better get back up there quickly, and put the couch back where it was," said Nate, already climbing the stairs.

"I don't know how we can avoid telling the police about all this," said Beverly as she helped Dr. A begin the ascent. "The stairs, the cove…"

Nate and Beverly had just managed to move the couch back over the floorboards when there was a knock at Ernestine's front door.

"I'll get it," said Dr. A, but the door opened before she had even moved, and in walked two men dressed in their police uniforms.

They stopped immediately upon seeing the trio of naked people before them.

“Lieutenant Tipton, Port Trésor Police,” said the shorter of the two, holding up his badge. He then nodded toward the other man. “My associate, Officer Cointreau.”

Nate, Beverly and Dr. A introduced themselves and explained their presence at Ernestine’s house. Dr. A showed them the Noonay Nay board document, with the line where she had needed the deceased woman to sign, right below her own signature, *Dr. Miranda T. Alcántara*. Both officers seemed to make a show of being very business-like as they quickly and professionally took photos and fingerprints, and asked questions, without commenting on anyone’s lack of clothing.

“Olive oil,” said Officer Cointreau as he knelt down by the body. “That’s a big help, thank you.”

“Uhmm… are you being sarcastic?” asked Beverly.

“Not in the slightest, ma’am,” he replied. “We use it all the time to keep bugs away from the cadaver. But I’ve never seen ants like these before… Well, Lieutenant, there are no wounds on her front, so let’s turn her over, shall we?”

The two policemen rolled the body to one side as the others looked on.

“Oh my…” Dr. A covered her mouth.

There was a large gash on the back of Ernestine’s head, and her hair was matted with all the blood it had soaked up.

“Blunt trauma,” said the lieutenant. “We need to get samples from that statue lying on the floor.”

“Yes sir. And from the edge of this table behind her,” said the officer, who, still on his knees, had the tabletop at eye level.

While Cointreau took the samples, Tipton continued to interrogate. “So, regarding a motive, do any of you have any idea?”

Beverly shifted her arms. “I don’t know that we’re being entirely forthcoming here.”

At the lieutenant's raised eyebrow, Dr. A blurted out, "Jimmy! I mean, the neighbor. He was acting very suspicious."

"I see," replied Tipton, jotting down a note.

"And there was the pest control van we saw speeding away from the property this morning," added Nate.

"Do tell…" muttered Tipton, scribbling away.

"But mostly, lieutenant," began Beverly, "it turns out that there's a stairway hidden under the couch here, to a cove that may have a treasure, and that's where we were just before you came... investigating."

"Well now, did you hear that, Cointreau? There were quite a few things these naked folks were covering up…"

"We have a match from forensics, sir," said the officer, peering into his phone. "There were two sets of fingerprints on the statue, belonging to the deceased herself, and also to one James Ferreira."

"That's Jimmy!" said Dr. A, pointing toward his house. "Oh my…"

Cointreau looked through the kitchen window and saw Jimmy's car. "Looks like he's at home."

"You go question him, officer Cointreau," said Tipton.

"Roger that," he replied, already on his way to the door.

"I'm going with these three down into the cove," continued the lieutenant, "to see what we can find."

"Well I hope very much that we find Ladybug," said Dr. A, "because Nate, you didn't remember to bring her when we came back up."

"What?!" said Nate. "I… You… She was on your shoulder… It's not my…"

"Yes," interrupted Beverly. "Let's go find Ladybug."

She and Nate moved the couch and floorboards again, and then Beverly explained to Tipton about the mantis, and the ants, as they made their way back down the curving stairs. "Oh," she added, just as it came into view, "there's a beached boat in the cove."

"This is all very odd," mused Tipton. "I'm rather glad I took this assignment today. A bit… out of the ordinary, all these goings-on and clothings-off!"

"Well, yes," said Dr. A, "please do feel welcome to remove your uniform. Being able to enjoy freedom from clothes is the reason we founded this park in the first place."

"I appreciate the invitation," replied Tipton, "but I may still need my badge and belt and etc. I'll keep my clothes on for now at least."

"Suit yourself," Dr. A replied drily. "Ladybug! Ladybug!," she began to call as she moved around the narrow beach. There were sandy areas that led under archways of rock, some quite large, others more like very short tunnels, and still others that were quite small. "She can't have gotten very far."

"I don't see any treasure," stated the lieutenant as he looked around, "nor much of anywhere to hide one. These interesting arches would be good for hiding behind, though, in an emergency."

"I found Ladybug!" yelled Nate. "And Ladybug found…"

"Don't move!" yelled a new voice. All eyes focused across the water, where a man now appeared, his torso visible from the waist up over the tilt of the wrecked boat. His gun was trained on Nate.

Tipton's hand flew to his holster in an instant, but the shipwrecked man simply changed targets. "Put your hands up!" he yelled to the policeman.

Beverly spoke in a voice that she hoped was low enough for the others to hear but not the gunman. "It should be obvious that we naked people are unarmed. Why did he aim at Nate?"

"What do you want?" called Tipton.

"Everybody back up the stairs and don't come back!" the gunman called out.

"How long have you been out there? Do you need help? What happened to the boat? Do you need something to eat? Are you a nudist?"

"No questions, lady," the gunman replied to Dr. A. "Start moving back up the stairs. All o' ya. But one at a time. You first, officer."

Tipton walked back over to the stairs and began to climb. Just beyond the first curve, he saw Cointreau crouched on the steps with his left index finger over his lips and his gun in his right hand. The gunman could not see him.

"Your turn, old lady," the gunman was saying.

"Who are you calling old, you impertinent…"

"I said no questions! Get moving!"

Tipton and Cointreau motioned for Dr. A to pass by them on up the stairs, and Beverly and Nate as well. Then the two policemen rushed down the stairs and fired into the boat, dodging and weaving their way to safer positions behind a couple of stone archways. The gunman fired at both of them but missed.

"You're outnumbered," yelled Tipton, "and you're under arrest for opening fire on officers of the law!"

There was silence from the boat, until a splash was heard, followed by the distinct sound of the man swimming away.

"Add resisting arrest to the report, Cointreau," the lieutenant said to his associate, who was already on his phone communicating with the precinct office.

***

"Well then what were Jimmy's fingerprints doing on that statue?" Dr. A wanted to know. She set down the tray that she had brought out from her kitchen--holding a carafe of fresh-squeezed orangeade and several glasses--and sat on the chair where her towel was already spread, joining the others on her front lawn.

"I'm happy to explain," replied Lieutenant Tipton as he helped himself to a glass. "But let me say first, thanks for your cooperation on this case. It's been rather an exciting morning! And thanks as well for your hospitality."

"Of course!" said Dr. A. "I know it's a long way out here to Noonay Noo. Better to make it a memorable visit for you."

"Yes. It certainly has been memorable, to say the least," he echoed. "Alright, about the fingerprints: Jimmy told Officer Cointreau that he went to check in on Ernestine to ask if she'd been satisfied with the quality of the pest control service. He knocked, got no answer, and went inside. When he saw the statue on the floor, he picked it up without thinking and then set it back down. He never saw Ernestine and assumed she had gone for a walk. He also said he had wanted to borrow her tape measure, and he knew she kept her toolbox under the sink, so he got it out and left. He seemed terribly upset to learn she's died."

"And you believe him?" asked Nate.

"Yes, for the moment we do, because his fingerprints weren't all we found on the statue. There was a bit of blood we've matched to a man with a criminal record for breaking and entering, and for robbery. Our working hypothesis is that this man went to Ernestine's home under the guise of the pest control service. Then he tried to rob her, they struggled and she hit him with the statue, at which point he must have knocked her backward, and she gashed her head and knocked herself out. She bled to death."

"Poor Ernestine," said Dr. A. "For crying out loud."

"But then who was the guy in the wrecked boat?" Beverly wanted to know.

"I bet it was the same guy, or else his associate," said Nate.

"I mean, aren't we making a big assumption here?" Beverly followed up. "Why would Ernestine have told the pest control guy about the cove, or the rumored treasure? Apparently, it was a big secret. And also, if it was the same guy we saw speeding out of Noonay Noo in the service van, how could he have made it back around so quickly, in a boat?"

"Excellent questions," said Tipton. "Back at the precinct, there's a full investigation going on into this Regal Pest Control business, to see who owns it and who the employees are. But in the meantime, here comes a man who may have some more answers for us."

Walking up the road from Ernestine's house came Officer Cointreau, completely naked except for a mantis on his shoulder and his phone in his hand.

"Ladybug!" cried Dr. A. "Oh, I am so happy to see you!"

Cointreau used his finger to pass the mantis to Dr. A. "Thank you, ma'am, for trusting me to get her back for you. That mantis gave us a key piece of evidence!"

Tipton cleared his throat. "Officer… uh… where is your uniform?"

Cointreau laughed. "I have to say, lieutenant - you should definitely try this walking-around-naked business. Don't waste your opportunity out here today!"

Amid nods and smiles of agreement from everyone else, Tipton asked, "Well, how did you get up the courage to do it?"

"The answering of that question will, I think, answer several other questions you probably have," Cointreau replied. "It happened like this: When you, lieutenant, went back up the stairs to the patrol car, I was left waiting for the police boat, which I knew would take a while. I couldn't hear the gunman swimming anymore. So, I looked around for the mantis, just as this young man had asked me to do when he passed me on the stairs."

"Thanks," said Nate.

"Yes, well…" continued the officer, "when I found her, she was eating what I thought to be some sort of plant, like a grass or something, growing out of the rock wall. But I looked more carefully, and for all the world, it looked like hair. Human hair."

"That sounds about right," said Dr. A. "Don't you agree, Beverly?"

"I don't know why there would be hair coming out of the wall, but I can attest that mantises have a quite varied diet," Beverly confirmed.

"So, I got out my knife," officer Cointreau continued, "and started to pry. It took a while, but I had some time on my hands, right? I loosened some rocks, pulled them out, and I almost fell over from the shock of what I found. An entire cache opened up, of coins and jewels and goblets and all the kinds of things you would imagine in a pirate treasure."

"My stars," said Dr. A. "Ernestine really did have an 'inheritance,' as she called it, down there."

"But what was the hair?" asked Nate.

"The hair was… hair," said the officer. "At least, I think it was real hair. It was attached to a kind of a large doll, like an effigy, of the kind they call around here a zemi or cemi. The Taino people used to make them as objects of reverence. We'll definitely need to get the archaeologists involved. Here, look at these photos!"

Cointreau pulled up the pictures he had taken on his phone and passed it to the lieutenant, who swiped through while the others looked over his shoulder, astonished. The officer took a moment to help himself to some orangeade.

"Wait… is that a note?" asked Tipton. "Here, in this photo. I can't quite make out what it says."

"Ah!" said Cointreau. "Yes. The note says, 'Ere you dare to touch my lair, your mind, your soul, your body bare.'"

"Ehr… what?" asked Nate.

"It's a rhyme, like… instructions, no?" said Beverly. "Like, get naked if you're gonna open this cache."

"That's the way I understood it, too," said Cointreau.

"Impressive," said Tipton. "So that's all it took, then, for you to doff your kit? Some old ditty that somebody left underground?"

"Actually, no, not quite. I was considering it. I was definitely tempted to throw my clothes off right then and there. But as it happened, just at that moment I heard vigorous splashing. It was the gunman, returning… and behind him I heard the motor of the approaching police boat. Then I heard the gunman call out in pain. So, I yelled to him. "What happened?" And I got no answer. There was no more splashing sound either. So that was it."

"What do you mean?" said Nate.

"I made up my mind. I pulled off all my gear and clothes and jumped in the water. I quickly realized I had to swim slowly because there are large rocks in that cove, and they seem to be randomly located, like pillars that go up almost to the surface. I swam toward where I had heard him, just beyond the boat, and found him. He must have slammed his head in his hurry to get back to the boat, because he was unconscious. Big gash on his head."

"Oooooh, karma," said Beverly.

"I managed to pull him onto one of the rocks and monitor him while at the same time waving to the police boat as it came into view and gesturing to cut the engine. Once they could hear me, I shouted to them about the dangerous rocks, and showed them that I had the assailant unconscious right next to me. The driver of the boat was able to maneuver close enough for me to float our gunman over to them, and they lifted him on board."

"Strong work, Cointreau!" said Tipton.

"So, then I swam back to the tiny ledge of shoreline where I had left my things. I grabbed my clothes and was going to put them on, but I was still wet, and I knew once I found you, lieutenant, we'd still need to go back to the crime scene where the car is parked so I just left my clothes there. I decided to see what it feels like to walk around naked and just air dry."

"And…?" asked Dr. A.

"It feels absolutely wonderful," said Cointreau with a big grin. "I'm hooked. And it makes me very curious to know more about that treasure and who would have left that note."

While Dr. A filled him in on what she knew about the legend of the Sea Witch, Tipton's phone rang. He answered, and then he listened more than talked. After he ended the call, he turned to the group.

"Here's the next chapter... hopefully the final one," said Tipton. "Cointreau, that man you dragged onto the rock is indeed the match to the blood sample from the statue. He was running Regal Pest Control as a way to get into people's homes. Under interrogation at the precinct, he confessed that he pretended to seduce the victim until she told him where she got her body jewelry, then he attacked her."

"I see…" said Beverly. "She must have said there was a cove below her house, but without mentioning the secret stairs under her couch."

"Except that her feet were sandy - had you noticed?" said the lieutenant. "We know he had a gun. He must have forced her to show him how to get to the treasure, and then made her come back up to the house, where they struggled and he pushed her. And after he realized that he had killed her, in his desperation to act quickly, he drove back out the access road and then stopped at the first boat he could steal for his own use."

"And without knowing about those rocks, he wrecked it as soon as he entered the cove," added Cointreau. "Case closed, lieutenant!"

"All but the paperwork," said Tipton, who then drank the rest of his orangeade. "Let's go back to the crime scene to take care of the last details, and to get your clothes, shall we?"

"Boss, listen to me. You've got to try walking naked under the sun. It's fantastic! Don't leave here without giving it a try."

The lieutenant stared expressionless at his officer for a few seconds, then broke into a big smile. "I'll do it!"

A few minutes later, as Dr. A and Beverly watched the two officers and Nate walk off leisurely and *naturally* down the road, the two women began a long conversation about entomology, the fate of Ernestine, and the newly manifest legacy of the Sea Witch.

Don't miss Nate and Dr. A's first mystery, "Bugs and Bares," free online!

If you'd like to know more about the Sea Witch, stay tuned for my next naturist novel, *Skinners*!

Revenge for Stan

Hannah Steenbock

It was a lovely morning, Lydia thought, as she stepped out of her house and slung her purple backpack over one shoulder. It served as her purse and as her pockets, she wasn't wearing anything else.

It contained a towel, her cell phone and a little snack. Breakfast would have to wait until after her first round of the grounds. That was a habit that served her well, ever since she had started out as the manager of this resort.

Now, it was all her own, and she had worked hard to make it the place of her dreams. In fact, just this year, she had renamed it "Circle of Life".

She strolled down the well-maintained path, reveling in the early sunlight on her body and the light breeze caressing her skin. It would get hot later today, but for now, the weather was perfect.

The path wound around the cottages she rented out and then curved down into the small valley that contained the jewel of her resort, the pond that had replaced the old swimming pool.

Lydia was especially proud of it, since it was the most obvious sign of her efforts to turn her resort not just into a nudist paradise but also into a haven for wildlife and nature.

Crows were squawking in the willow tree leaning over one corner of the pond, and she frowned. They didn't normally like sitting in that tree.

And it wasn't just one, it was a whole murder of them.

Lydia walked faster, a sense of foreboding destroying the joy she had felt at this perfect morning.

Something was lying in that pond.

She hurried closer, and then her breath caught.

That something was someone, a man dressed in clothes that were familiar. And he was lying face-down in the shallow water.

"No!", she gasped. "No."

She had folded that shirt last night. Her hand went to her mouth, and then tears started falling.

A moment later she remembered she was the owner and manager of this place. And so, she pulled her backpack around, dug out the cell phone and called the police.

Once she had been reassured that someone would come, she called Jill and James, her capable workers. She ordered James to take up vigil at the pool, and Jill to inform the guests that the pool was off limits for the day, claiming the appearance of a rare bird.

James arrived quickly, also wearing just a backpack. He stared for a moment, then lifted knowing eyes to Lydia.

"What do you want me to do?"

"Just stay here, make sure nobody touches Stan or his things. And shoo away those damned crows."

"Got it. Lydia, I'm so…"

"Not now!" She interrupted him harshly. "I don't have time to fall apart just yet."

He simply nodded, gave a little sigh and stared out at the pond.

Lydia put a tight rein on her feelings and marched towards the entrance of the resort. The police should be arriving soon.

She was relieved when they didn't use those darn lights. Instead, a black car pulled into the parking lot, marked only as police by the light attached to its roof by a magnet.

Two people got out of the car, walked up to Lydia, and very obviously did their best not to stare. One of them was in uniform, and the other was a woman in plain clothes, who wore a frown that had left deep grooves on her forehead.

"Thank you for coming so quickly," Lydia said. "I'll take you there."

"Just like that?" the woman asked, looking her up and down.

"Just like that." Lydia lifted her chin. "And no, you're not expected to undress."

The man accompanying her gave a little chuckle. “That’s good, I suppose. I’m Sargeant Brown and this is Sheriff Lanning.”

Lydia nodded and introduced herself as well. “If you’d follow me.”

She started walking and had to give the Sheriff kudos for staying right at her side.

“So, you’re the manager?”

“The owner and manager,” Lydia corrected her.”

“I see. And what were you doing out so early in the morning?”

Lydia glanced at her. “I walk my property every morning, preferably before people are out and about. That way I can fix anything troublesome.” She bit her lip. Finding Stan in the pool did not exactly fit the category of troublesome.

“That makes sense,” the Sergeant said, who was trailing close behind them.”

“I am proud of this place,” Lydia said, not caring how fierce she sounded. “I created it, I made it into something special, and I’ll do my best to keep it that way.”

The Sheriff nodded. “It does look nice and well kept.”

“Thank you.” Lydia felt something inside her relax a little. “We’re restoring native grasses and trees,” she explained, waving at the landscaping. And we just recently finished our natural pool. Which is where we’re going.”

“I see.”

A moment later, the path curved and allowed the first view of the pool. Lydia was relieved to see that Jeremy was simply standing next to the edge of the pool, and that the crows were gone.

“Oh,” the Sheriff said a moment later. “Did you call an ambulance?”

Lydia shook her head and gritted her teeth. “I could see he was dead. Face under water and no movement. And the crows were already interested in him.”

“I… see.” The woman glanced at her. “Did you know him.”

Lydia swallowed hard. “Yes, I did. But I think that maybe I should have a lawyer at my side before we talk about that in detail.”

The man nodded. “I understand.”

“Ah. You think you’d be seen as a suspect?” The Sheriff threw her a hard look.

Lydia said nothing, and the woman sighed.

Moments later, they had reached the pool. The man looked away from James immediately, while the Sheriff focused on his face, with a bit of an effort.

“And who are you?”

Lydia quickly introduced James, and the Sheriff made him describe the events of the morning. At the same time, the policeman started taking pictures, which made it quite clear to Lydia that he wasn’t just an ordinary policeman.

When James had finished, the Sheriff took out her cell phone and arranged for both a coroner and a forensics team.

“So, what made you think this was not just an accident?” the Sheriff asked after she was done with her phone calls.

“Why would you ask that?”

The Sheriff smiled a tight, hard smile. “You called us. Not an ambulance.”

Lydia sighed. The Sheriff was right. “I do not think it was an accident because Stan knew this place. He wasn’t ill or anything. And we talked last night. He was excited about building a new future.”

The woman nodded. “So, you’ve known him for some time.”

Lydia just nodded. “I did. As I said before.” She certainly wasn’t willing to explain they had been lovers years ago, and that they had only resurrected that relationship the previous night.

“So, you did.” The woman nodded. Lydia tried hard not to compare her with a TV inspector who always had one more question.

"I would like to be alone for a while now, if you no longer need me." Lydia knew she would cry for hours but had no intention of starting while that woman was looking at her.

"I understand. We might have to come back for more questions."

Lydia's cell phone rang. "Yes?"

It was Jill, telling her that the coroner wanted to drive onto the grounds.

"Absolutely not!" Lydia said. A moment later, she was speaking to the coroner himself, and repeated those words.

"You realize that we do need to pick up the body, don't you," the man said quite condescendingly.

Lydia took a deep breath and pushed down the rage that consumed her instantly. This was Stan he was referring to.

"Mr. Coroner," she said, making her voice as friendly as she could with the rage filling her veins with fire. "I do realize that. But you don't seem to realize we have no roads on the grounds. And in fact, what you might take for grass is native prairie we have painstakingly restored. Your car would cause immense damage to it. I do not allow any kind of car on my grounds. And that is the final word."

"But… but…"

"Your car carries a gurney, does it not?" she asked sweetly.

"Yes, it does, but…"

"Oh, it's not terribly far. Jill will show you the way. And I am sure she'll help you move it, if you cannot do it alone." She deliberately added that insult at the end.

The man sputtered on the phone, and Lydia smiled, just as hard as the Sheriff had a moment ago.

"Can you handle that, or should I send more help?"

The coroner obviously got a grip on himself, but Lydia could imagine the effort it took. "Yes, ma'am," he said, weakly. "We can handle it."

"Good." Lydia hung up on him.

"James, do you think you can help the coroner and see him out?"

"Sure, Lydia. Go get some rest." He gave her a sincere smile.

The policeman was done taking pictures.

"What about the forensics team?", the Sheriff asked.

"No cars," Lydia repeated and stared her down. "They can borrow wheelbarrows, if necessary. We have ones with special wheels."

Obviously, the Sheriff could read body language well enough to know when she encountered an immovable obstacle. "That should work," she said simply.

Lydia gave her a nod, turned on her heel and hurried back to her house. She was relieved that she had given Stan a cottage, even though they had dinner together at her place, and had eventually found their way to her bedroom. He had left her around midnight, so she could truthfully say he had stayed in his cottage for the night.

And now he was dead.

Tears wanted to fall, but she didn't have time for them. Because she knew very well that whoever had caused his death would do her best to blame it on her.

Which meant she had to figure out who it was and how they had done it as fast as possible.

She sank into the armchair she used for reading and thinking and pulled up her feet, remembering their rambling conversation of the evening before.

Stan had talked about his wife, and how he had filed for divorce, fed up with their constant fighting. And he had dropped hints of having applied to a patent that could be worth millions.

That was motive enough, she thought. Annie would want in on the money, and Lydia didn't doubt her desire to see Stan dead. But how?

She hadn't seen any blood, not in the pond, not on Stan's clothes. And in fact, nobody should have been able to enter these grounds at night. They locked the entrance securely every evening, there had been too many attempts by people trying to sneak in and take pictures of her guests.

Lydia shook her head. "Think harder," she told herself.

If police found out about the patent and the divorce, she, Lydia, should be in the clear. There was no chance whatsoever that she could profit from that situation. But she had no idea what traps Annie had laid. She assumed that somehow, Annie would suggest that Lydia was the murderer.

But how had she killed Stan?

Poison. That was the only way, she realized.

And something the forensics lab wouldn't find easily. Something they wouldn't check automatically. It might even look like a heart attack.

Lydia gnawed her lower lip. She would have to do a lot of research fast. With a sigh, she got up, grabbed her laptop and sat down again.

Moments later, she was delving deep into the internet, looking on author sites for ways of killing someone in the most subtle way. She didn't bother to hide her trail. It would be easy to prove that she had started to look after Stan's death, not before.

There were several poisons that authors like to use, she discovered. Thallium, aconite, lead, arsenic, death cap… But few of them worked fast. She kept returning to aconite, because Stan had died quickly during the night, without showing symptoms when he left her. And yet… how had Annie managed to poison him when he had been at the resort for the entire day?

Lydia frowned.

It could not have been the food. They had shared dinner, and she had not felt anything. They also had shared a bottle of wine, so it wasn't that, either.

And why in the world had Stan walked to the pool?

Nothing made sense right now. At all.

And yet, she was certain that Stan had been murdered. Even if she didn't know how. Or why she knew this so clearly.

She closed her laptop and got up. A walk would help, she hoped, to sort out her jumbled thoughts. She left her house, slinging her backpack over one shoulder as usual, and stepped out on the path that led once around the entire resort.

Annie had killed Stan. She was sure of that.

But she couldn't prove it.

And in fact, she wasn't even sure if police were treating it as a murder investigation. That Sheriff hadn't returned.

Lydia walked faster, letting the exercise loosen her back and tense shoulders. The sun felt good on her skin, and the breeze had picked up enough to keep her from sweating. It blew her long hair back, which reminded Lydia of long-gone days on the beach with Stan.

No, she couldn't yet accept that he was gone.

She gritted her teeth and broke into a run. She needed to get to the forest at the far end of the resort, she decided. There, nobody would hear her cry.

Soon, the tall beech trees welcomed her in their green, warm shade. She slowed to a walk, found an old log to sit on and gave herself permission to feel her grief.

Moments later, she was bent over, hands covering her face, crying harder than she had in years.

Oh, Stan.

How cruel to have held him in her arms again, only to lose him forever a few hours later. How could the Universe do this to her? She cried out her grief and anger and loss.

She had no idea how long she had been crying, and she didn't care, either. This was her way of saying goodbye to Stan.

Now she just had to avenge his death.

Which meant finding out how Annie had done it.

Grim determination filled her, and she got to her feet. Stepping out of the small grove of beech trees, she discovered that the day had turned hot. The sun was blazing and she hadn't brought any sunscreen.

Quickly, she decided to jog back to her house to reduce the time beneath the scorching sun. It worked, she got home quite fast. She quickly went to her shower to wash off the sweat and cool down the skin. Under the warm water, she discovered that her backpack had chafed her shoulder.

She dried herself carefully and dug through the drawers of her bathroom cupboard to find a soothing lotion. Among a bunch of tubes she discovered an old one that had belonged to Stan, and remembered that he had always put lotion on his elbows and knees where his psoriasis had been worst.

That was one reason why he liked nudism. All that sun really helped keep those sores in check.

Lydia sighed and put that tube back. She chose another one and sighed with relief when the lotion took the sting of those spots away.

Her head hurt from all that crying, and so she made herself some tea and a sandwich and sat down in her armchair again.

If she wanted to kill Stan, how would she go about it?

Tears flowed again, but she just let them roll. What would be a way to get rid of him without being found out? Or a way that would pin his death on someone else? Preferably someone Annie hated.

Lydia knew Annie hated her. She had always tried to undermine the connection they had, even if they were no longer lovers. Annie hated the ease of their friendship, the way they could reconnect even after years of little contact.

Thus, it made sense that Annie would try to send Stan to his death here at the resort. Even if Lydia didn't get accused of the murder, the negative publicity would hurt the resort, and ultimately her.

But how?

Lydia racked her brain.

Annie had used aconite, at least that's what she thought. But how had she got it into Stan's body?

She jumped up with determination. She had to look at everything Stan had brought here. Maybe she had given him cookies.

She grimaced.

No, Annie wasn't the homely, caring type.

Just as she had reached the cottage she had given Stan for the night, her cell phone rang.

"Yes?"

"There's someone here who says she's Stan's wife. She wants to pick up his things."

Lydia frowned. "I'm not sure the police have cleared us to hand them out," she answered. "Let me check that real quick. And do not let her in until I tell you to."

"Got it. I'll stall her."

She gritted her teeth. Of course, Annie wanted to remove any evidence. She had to be fast.

Instead of calling the police, she dashed into the cottage and stopped the moment the scent of Stan's shower gel hit her.

Tears flowed again, and she dashed them off angrily. This was the only chance she had to nail Annie for murder, and she had to use it.

She ran into the bathroom, checking what he had brought.

Shower gel. Toothpaste. Shampoo, for what little hair he had left. Body lotion. Psoriasis lotion.

She shook her head and checked the bedroom. He had turned back the cover, but there were no wrinkles in the sheet.

He had never even laid down in bed.

She bit her lip and hurried back to the bathroom.

Yes, he had taken a shower. Why had he put his clothes back on?

Samples. Her mind went into overdrive. She needed samples!

Quickly, she grabbed a few glasses from the kitchen cupboards and squeezed a sample from everything into them taking care to remember every color. She checked the fridge just as quickly, and found it practically empty, except for a bottle of water and a can of soda.

She nabbed the water, as well, and took it and the glasses back to her house and put them into her fridge. Then she called James again.

“Let her in. Make her undress.”

That was at least a small dose of revenge she would get. Watching Annie look flustered in the nude would give her much satisfaction.

It didn’t take long for Annie to march through the resort to the cottage. Lydia had positioned herself at the entrance.

“You,” Annie said with as much disgust in her voice as Lydia had expected.

“Yes, of course.” Lydia gave her a sweet, false smile. “I am the owner of this resort. Please let me express my deepest condolences on the death of your husband.”

Annie glared at her. “Thank you,” she managed to say. “Now let me pick up his stuff.”

“Certainly.” Lydia pushed open the door to the cottage and allowed Annie to walk into it. She followed her.

“What do you want?” Annie turned and glared at her.

“I want to make sure that the cottage will be left in good order,” Lydia explained, lying through her teeth.

Annie glared at her, then picked up Stan’s bag and stuffed his few belongings into it. “Did you have fun together?” she growled.

Lydia smiled again. “We had a lovely evening.”

Rage filled Annie’s eyes. “You fucked him.”

Lydia shrugged and kept smiling. “If you want to believe that, feel free.”

Annie marched to the bathroom and threw all the tubes into Stan’s bag.

Lydia watched her in the mirror above the sink and noticed a fleeting look of relief and satisfaction cross Annie’s face.

That was enough.

Lydia quickly moved to the kitchen and started looking through the cupboards, checking their content as she always did.

Annie came out of the bathroom, put the bag on the bed and added the small alarm clock to it that Stan had put on the bedside table.

"Got everything?" Lydia asked, straightening up.

"You can keep anything I missed," Annie growled.

"Thank you."

Annie hefted the bag, slung it over her shoulder and gave Lydia another glare. "Good riddance," she grated, turned away and stalked out of the cottage.

Lydia checked the wardrobe and found a shirt that Annie had indeed missed. She lifted it to her face, sniffed it and allowed her tears to flow again.

She waited only long enough to make sure that Annie was no longer in sight before leaving the cottage and hurrying over to her house.

Once there, she put Stan's shirt into a plastic bag and put a clip on it, to preserve his scent. Next, she spooned all those samples she had taken into small plastic containers.

What if she was wrong?

No, she told herself, she wasn't. Annie was not the grieving widow, she was the angry divorcee, and she had killed Stan.

Two days passed, and Lydia became more and more impatient. She went through her work mechanically, stuffing down the grief over Stan, and quietly nursing her anger.

Finally, the Sheriff herself called.

"Am I talking to Lydia Heidenger, the owner of the "Circle of Life" resort?"

"Yes, that's me."

"I have news."

Lydia gritted her teeth. Why else would she call? "Yes?"

"We got the coroner's report today. He says it was a heart attack and an accident."

Lydia couldn't help it. She burst into tears.

"I'm sorry," the Sheriff said. "But that means the case is closed, because it never was a case."

Lydia fought for her voice. "Tell him to check for aconite. I'm serious. Stan wasn't sick. He never had heart issues. He also was a good swimmer. This doesn't compute."

The Sheriff sighed. "I'm sorry, Lydia. There's nothing I can do. And it's her."

"Please. I know why he got killed."

"He didn't." The Sheriff's voice was gentle but firm. "He just died. I know that's difficult to accept, but these things happen. It's a tragedy but not a murder."

"I… is there anything I can do?"

"No. I am sorry. The case is now closed."

Lydia bit her lip so hard she tasted blood. Now she was truly on her own. She suddenly remembered about being civil.

"Thank you for letting me know," she managed to say.

"It's the least I could do." The Sheriff hung up, and Lydia was both relieved and devastated.

She stared at the phone, mind whirling. Thoughts raced and crashed into each other.

How could she get her samples tested?

And how could she trap Annie into confessing?

Slowly, she put the phone down, feeling trapped in an evil nightmare. Just as slowly, she walked to her armchair and sat, pulling up her feet and sitting cross legged.

Police had let her down.

The coroner had let her down.

And they had let Stan down.

She would not let Annie get away with murder.

Furious determination rose in her. Stan would get justice, she vowed to herself.

She had to prod Annie into a reaction. And the easiest way would be to tell her that she had taken samples of Stan's lotions and gels and sent them off for testing. Even if that wasn't technically true yet.

With her lips pressed firmly together, she opened her laptop and composed an email to Annie. She read it several times, edited small things, and finally hit 'send', while her heart beat faster.

Next, she found a forensics lab willing to analyze her samples, and finally went out to tell James and Jill to watch out for Annie.

After a quick trip to the post office to send off the samples, and a detour to a hardware store to buy a surveillance camera, the waiting began.

Oh, she had things to do, after all, running her own resort took time and effort. But she did all that almost on autopilot, while her mind waited for Annie to arrive.

What else could she do to protect herself?

Late in the afternoon, Annie called the office. Lydia was doing her bookkeeping and listened to James taking the phone call. She shook her head when he offered her the handset.

"Ah, she's busy right now," he improvised quickly. "But do tell me what's up."

"I need to come up and look at the cottage again," Annie explained, sounding both flustered and sad. "I think I forgot something that belonged to Stan."

Which was true, Lydia thought. Except that Annie wouldn't give a rat's arse for that shirt. She nodded at James.

"Oh, I understand," James said. "Of course, you can come up and look for it."

"Thank you so much. I'll be on my way, then."

After Annie hung up, Lydia exchanged a look with James.

"What was all that about?" he asked, and she took a deep breath and told him about her suspicions and how she had baited Annie.

"She'll kill you," James said, wide-eyed. "If you're right, she killed once, so she'll kill again."

"Not if I can help it," Lydia said grimly.

"We should call the police."

Lydia shook her head. "They closed the case. They will only reopen it if I bring evidence."

James sighed. "I'm not at all happy with this."

"I know. But this is the only way I can get justice for Stan."

He nodded. "I'll come with you."

"No, she won't talk in front of witnesses. But do put that spy-cam into the cottage. It's a good thing we didn't rent it out again just yet."

James practically ran to do that task.

Lydia gave up on the bookkeeping. She was much too excited and worried to focus on numbers and receipts. Instead, she got up and walked the shortest circular path in the resort, staying fairly close to the main office, doing her best to shed the adrenaline rushing through her body. It would take Annie about an hour to drive up from where she had moved with Stan.

Finally, she saw a car pull into the parking lot, and she just knew it was Annie. She hurried to the office, pulled her cell phone out of her backpack, set it to recording and put it back in. With luck, it would get some words.

"Hello Annie." James greeted her just as cheerfully as he would have greeted any resident, and Lydia gave him full kudos for acting.

"Hi," she said, and her face darkened when she saw Lydia.

"I'll take you to the cottage," Lydia said quickly, implying that James knew nothing about the trap she had set.

"Ah, thank you." Annie managed to reply, and they left the office together. Jill waved to them from where she was emptying garbage cans and weeding a flower bed, and Lydia was grateful for that. Annie wouldn't hurt her in plain sight of anyone else.

They reached the cottage quickly, and the moment Lydia closed the door behind them, Annie whirled.

"You bitch!" she growled. "How dare you imply I killed Stan?"

Lydia's heart was pounding, but she crossed her arms and did her best to sound calm. "I simply won't believe he died like that. And I didn't imply that at all. I just said I sent samples of his lotions for testing. Is there something wrong with his lotions?"

Annie blushed furiously. "I know you were lovers. You're just trying to get back at me."

Lydia managed a shrug. "If you're innocent, why are you even here? Your arrival is a clear sign that you did something with his stuff. Dare I say aconite?"

Annie sputtered. A moment later, she dug into her purse and pulled out a gun.

"Ah." Lydia took a deep breath. "A gun. That is a very bad idea, Annie."

"Really?" The word was a mere snarl, and Annie lifted the gun higher, aiming at Lydia's heart.

"Because there's a letter with my attorney in which I explain everything. To be opened in case of my death. There's also a camera recording us."

Annie stared at her. "You're bluffing."

Lydia smiled, even though she was. But she had learned that poker face from Stan. "Not at all, my dear. I knew you had killed once. A second time would be so much easier."

Something changed in Annie's face, and Lydia suddenly knew she was in immediate danger. In one fluid movement, she slung her backpack around and into Annie's face, pushing her hand with the gun aside. Then she dropped to the floor.

Annie fired her gun, but the bullet only shattered the glass of a kitchen cabinet.

The door flew open, and Jeremy and the Sheriff burst in.

Annie whirled, pointing her gun at the Sheriff, and dropped it the very next moment.

The Sheriff nodded. "Smart move." She arrested Annie, reciting her rights, while James rushed to Lydia's side.

"Are you okay?"

Lydia got to her feet. "Never better. Did you call her?"

He nodded, blushing. "I had to. Did it while you were walking. She said she'd come right away."

"Well done." Lydia smiled. "Stan has been avenged."

And that was all that mattered.

The Anniversary

Robert Payne

Morning

Poor Dan. Seeing him being his happy go lucky self on the outside, but so lonely on the inside is heartbreaking. I love him so much. I keep telling him his life is not over since I died. But, my death and the legal circus that followed took a lot out of him. I am so glad Ron was able to step in and help him. Now, finding out that cancer will diminish his independence and eventually take his life is a serious blow. Being married to him was paradise in itself. We had a beautiful partnership starting with the first time we met on Lake Travis in Austin, Texas.

Now here having our daily mid-morning talk, as usual in our Florida home. Not as nice and spacious as our beautiful house in Texas perched on the edge of a cliff, it is a nicely appointed mobile home. Park Model they call it, with a porch across the front and floor-to-ceiling windows. Inside is a spacious living area with a loft and open concept kitchen and dining. Past the kitchen is the large master suite. It sits snuggled into a lush green spot of manicured lawns and year-round flowers, this home could be in a scene right out of a retirement community brochure. But this is not like most retirement communities. Bordering a stretch of sand bar, bay and ocean on the Florida west coast, this community is home to just as many young families and seasonal vacationers as there are retirees. Gulf Breeze Nudist Resort is one of Florida's premier nudist gathering spots and that is why we bought our vacation home here. We have been nudists ever since we met at Hippy Hollow those years ago.

Dan spends most of his time in the Loft. It is a small cozy space with an easy chair, small desk and chair, books and items of the past scattered about. My Urn and our fur babies' Urn are prominent on an altar at the far end of the room.

Dan is always talking, but, as usual is not listening to me, but maybe he will.

"Well, babe, our anniversary is tomorrow. I got some great plans for today and this evening."

"Oh, Dan, you always surprise me on our Anniversary. Never a dull moment! I so hope you don't get carried away celebrating this year.."

"Yes. Yes. I know. I won't overdo it. I will have a good cigar and your favorite vodka."

My favorite vodka! That rascal knows I hate vodka!

"Just one cigar, they stink and are so expensive. Not to mention causing you breathing problems."

"No. Cigars can't hurt me anymore. They say I'm in stage four. It's not bothersome. I am OK! I may surprise you and come knocking on your door sooner than they predicted."

Laughing is interrupted by a hacking cough that takes his breath away

For almost 40 years I have been trying to convince Dan to exercise more, drink less and stop smoking so many cigars. If he would just listen to me when we were younger he would not be facing his death at the young age of 60.

"Dan! You here?"

Ron opened the front door, hearing Dan coughing.

"You OK?"

Ron is a tall lean tanned man with a down home Texas drawl. His wife Cathy, also an ex native of Texas, became best friends with us that day over 10 years ago when Dan and I happened to "inadvertently" trespass onto the resort property from the public beach. OK, not completely true. Dan and I loved walking on beaches. One day we saw this beautiful resort off the beach with a tidal basin separating the resort property from the beach. Dan had heard that this was a nudist resort. Against my better judgement, Dan was looking for a way to sneak in to see what the resort looked like and we got caught by Ron, Cathy and their friend Stephie. As it was, everything turned out nicely. A beautiful friendship flourished from that encounter. The three made the long trip from Florida to Texas when I died. They helped in getting things in order at the house. Ron, an expert in civil and Texas state constitutional law, helped Dan with the wrongful death lawsuit.

"Come on in, buddy." Yelled Dan after a kiss and pat on both urns, "Coffee?"

"Please. I never asked, why do you use a French press? Why don't you use drip?"

"I fell in love with the process after Gayle and I visited Ireland. All the B&B's served coffee this way. It adds another level of richness."

"It's so nice today, Ron, let's sit outside. Where else can you sit outside totally nude and drink coffee, waving to a passerby who is just as naked."

"That's why Cathy and I moved here. We can be ourselves. We can be around people who believe in this lifestyle. We are safe here."

"Well, except for recently. Have they figured out what happened the other day at the beach? I know the resort has spent a lot of money to build up the wall there since Gayle and I made the wrong turn ten years ago."

"Yep, wrong turn my ass." Laughed Ron. "It really wasn't much of a problem to separate our mangrove from the beach when the beach was foot traffic only, but when they opened the beach to cars it really has presented a problem. They are going to put rock and barbed wire up to stop them from driving around, and fencing to stop them from wading across."

"Hell, Ron, those gators should be enough to stop them. But I heard some idiots are actually shooting them."

"Yep. They think those same punks are the ones who attacked and robbed that couple who were staying here last week. Stole their golf cart in broad daylight even!"

I watched as the two men fell into silence. I have begged Dan to tell Ron about the cancer.

"Dan, tell me what the doctor said. It's been two weeks. You asking me to update your will and wanting me to be your power of attorney and all these instructions on what to do with your personal things, send up red flags."

"OK. OK. I was going to tell you and Cathy, but just couldn't find the right time.

Pausing to compose himself, Dan takes a deep breath

"There is no good way to say this, Ron. Lung cancer. They say I don't have much time left."

"Oh, Dan."

"No. No. Don't. It's fine. I am still in my 60s and I am in great health. I think they got it wrong. Gayle may be disappointed in me, but I think with these new medicines and treatments I can live longer than they think. I am also doing some holistic stuff from Stephie."

"I have seen her stop by here. Was wondering what you two were up to."

Dan just leaned back, smiled and changed the subject.

“Look at this place! Perfect manicured park, three pools, tennis, Bocce Ball, Lawn Bowling, miles of trails to walk, a fantastic restaurant and our own police force. Say, are they going to beef up patrol at the lagoon?”

“Yep. Starting this weekend. On Friday, Saturday and Sunday. It seems that is when we get trespassers on the property. The county is also beefing up patrols. They are having problems with cars being broken into on the beach and down at the county park. They think it’s some gypsy types who wandered into the area.”

“They will catch those bastards. So. Where’s Cathy and Steph? Let’s go to the restaurant and grab breakfast.”

“You mean lunch?”

“Lunch? Already? I need a watch.”

“You won’t look at it. I will give Cathy a call. Let’s start walking that way.”

Ron reaches in his shoulder bag and pulls out his phone and to call Cathy

“Hi. Do you want to eat lunch? Yep, Dan and I are walking that way. OK. I will tell him.”

“Cathy and Stephie are already there and waiting for us.”

Ron notices a faint smile across Dan’s lips

“Come on Dan. Are you and Stephie having a go at it?”

“Just friends.”

“She is beautiful, Dan, and she seems to really like you. I know I would in a heartbeat.”

"Well, well, Ron! What would Cathy say?" Dan laughed as he teased his best friend.

Lunch

Dan and Ron entered the restaurant. It's a beautiful appointed open-air establishment, typical of the Florida Keys style. Sitting at a table for four on the veranda are two women in their 50s. Both thin and athletic. Cathy has a deep dark tan and light brown sun-streaked hair. Stephie is tall, dark skin, hair and eyes, revealing her Seminole Indian and African heritage.

Taking their seats, the men noticed an already empty wine bottle on the table.

"So what are we having besides wine?" Asked Ron.

"We are sharing the Chicken Fettuccine." Replied Cathy.

"As well as another bottle." Piped in Stephie.

Dan closed the menu and asked "Second bottle? Soup and Salad and tea for me. I got to save room for tonight. How about you, Ron?"

"The same for me. I guess the girls aren't going to eat much."

All four laughed

Pouring wine for Stephie and herself, Cathy remarked, "Ron, we have to go into town to buy groceries for tonight."

"As long as I am driving." Teased Ron, "Nothing but the best for our friends."

"Dan, are you going to watch the sunrise tomorrow?"

"Yes. Just like every year since I moved here. Tomorrow will be 40 years to the day that Gayle and I got married."

Dan leans back in his chair with a grin

"You guys already know how Gayle and I first met. But there is something we never told. After we met and started talking, I asked Gayle if she wanted to get a burger."

"Now, wait." Interrupted Ron, "You guys were at Hippy Hollow skinny dipping and you both put clothes back on to go get a burger?"

All four laughed

"Well, no. Not really. We went naked and used the drive-through."

The others stopped and stared at Dan. Then burst out laughing.

"Really. We did. Gayle was pretty adventurous back then."

"Oh, my. Sweet Gayle, a wild child." Remarked Cathy.

"She was very sweet, Cathy, but that girl could not keep her clothes on back in our younger days."

Laughter from the four filled the restaurant

Afternoon

With lunch done, Ron and Cathy went to their place to put clothes on and left to go shopping.

Dan and Stephie went for a walk on the resort grounds.

Oh, look how my Dan and Stephie look as they stroll about! I remember how we three would spend the late evenings here hands in hands walking and talking. Stephie is not only beautiful, but she is a strong independent woman. She had owned a place at the resort even longer than Ron and Cathy. She knows it to be the safest community in all of Florida. She took over her mother's herb and rock shop in Tampa at the young age of 19. Her family, prominent members of the Seminole Tribe, have been active in the community for over three generations. She was married to the love of her life, Jeff, a real estate developer and the architect of the resort, almost as long as Dan and I. Stephie moved here permanently to the resort after he died in a commercial accident.

I so wished they had married after I died.

"Thanks, Stephie, for being here for me. Hey! You know Ron thinks we are having a thing."

"Well we will just let him keep thinking." Stephie replied laughing her contagious laugh, which prompted Dan to join in, until his cough once again took over.

"Dear, dear, Dan. If I was going to have another man in my life, it would be you, but after Jeff died, I found that I really do not want another man sexually."

"I am glad you and Gayle found each other. She really loved you."

"Me too. Me too."

Both hugged and stayed quiet for a bit.

"This is such a lovely place. I can't imagine living anywhere else, with or without clothes. They really do care about the residents here."

Stephie simply nods in agreement

Their meandering walk ended at Dan's house.

"Steph, do you have what I need?"

"Are you sure you want to do this?"

"Nature has made up my mind. I won't let cancer kill me."

"Ok, then, my sweet man."

Pulling out a sack from her bag with three small plastic bottles of colored liquid, "The bottles are marked. Take the first when you wake up, that's at 5, right?

Dan nods in agreement

"Don't eat anything. Have coffee. Take the second bottle after you get to the beach. That will be between 5:15 and 5:30. Be sure to throw the bottles in separate trash cans. After about 15 minutes you will feel very relaxed. Sit and make your fire. Set up your spot. Open the vodka. Drink a couple cups. Take the last bottle. Be sure to pitch the bottle in the fire. Enjoy watching the sky change colors. Sip on your vodka. Relax, watch the sunrise and let the potions and the vodka take effect."

"Do you have any questions?"

"What is in each bottle?"

"They are tinctures using vodka and certain herbs. The first bottle will relax you. The second has sort of a hallucinogenic effect. The third will slow down your heart. It will take about 15 minutes before your heart stops. You won't even notice what is happening. The more vodka you drink the faster it will work. By 6-6:30 it should be over. When they find you, no one will think suicide."

Tears run freely down both of their faces as they hug and kiss each other.

"OK. Stop." Dan struggled to stop the tears, "It's best this way. But Ron and Cathy cannot know! Agree?

"Yes."

"You said you have helped others, but are you OK with doing this for me?"

"I know you need this. You want this. So, yes, I am definitely OK." Stephie nodded through sobs.

Dan and Stephie spent the rest of the afternoon talking, totally comfortable in each other's company. Soon the sun was getting low in the sky and it was time to go to Ron and Cathy's.

Dinner

Ron and Cathy were busy cooking and setting up for their two guests when Ron finally decided to tell Cathy about their friend dying from cancer.

"I can't believe this." Wept Cathy, "It's so wrong. Poor Dan."

"We can't let this ruin the evening, Cathy. Dan thinks with his health and the new treatments out there that he can live a long life. So we must act normal. OK?"

Cathy nods in agreement

The evening was pleasant with good weather, great food, conversation and lots of drinking among four friends. Ron and Cathy did not let on their sadness of knowing Dan was dying and Dan and Stephie did not betray their trust of knowing his plans to end his life.

Sunrise

It's 5 AM. At this time, on this date every year for the last seven years Dan would get up and go to the beach in his golf cart. There he will drink himself into a stupor watching the sun rise out of the horizon. This year will be different. He will not return.

Dan followed Stephie's instructions. Up before sunrise, coffee in hand. He is drinking the first bottle. Everything he needs is already in the golf cart.

Kissing goodbye to his fur babies and Gayle, "I will see you soon babe."

"Wait, don't go just yet! Wait a bit, please."

Dan stops. He felt himself shudder. Did he just hear Gayle's voice? Should he not go? He waits a minute. The sensation subsided. He sets off for the beach.

"Good morning Dan!" Officer Johns spoke in quiet tones so as to not wake the neighbors, "Going to the beach?"

"Good morning, Frank. Yes my yearly ritual you won't find me up this early for any other reason."

Both men laughed

"I will swing by to check on you after breakfast."

"Thanks, Frank. See you then."

Frank has been on the police force and been a resident of the resort for a long time. He understood Dan's yearly ritual and would not think about bothering him until later in the morning.

Dan hated that Frank would be the one to find him, but it will be better than some passerby.

After taking the contents of the second bottle, Dan set up his spot looking east, made his small fire, and set up his phone to record the transformation from night to day. No he will not be in all of the video. As in the past he will record himself talking about Gayle and their life, then he will let the camera see and hear what he sees and hears.

He realized that he had not taken the last bottle. He hurriedly drank the liquid and took a few sips of vodka.

Dan settled down, feeling very light and nostalgic. He watched the horizon and talked out loud about his wonderful life with Gayle.

"Oh, Gayle you should see this splash of color. It's beautiful."

These were his last recorded words.

The potions were taking hold of his senses and body. He could no longer speak, nor feel, but saw beautiful amazing colors on the horizon.

Soon his pulse began slowing even as his mind was racing with the beauty he was seeing.

It was 6:15AM. It will soon be all over.

The Two Disturbing Men

"Damn! What's that over there?"

"Shut up! Be quiet. Let's go and fuck someone up."

Two young men eager not to live to an old age, slowly approached Dan's little camp. One had a pistol, the other had an ax handle.

"Hey you! Don't move, fucker!"

Dan, still alive, but now deep in a trance responded with only a blank stare and smile.

The axe handle connected with his head.

"What did you that for, you dumb shit?"

"He pissed me off. He just stared at me."

Both men bent over to look at Dan just as his body exhaled.

"Shit he is alive. Give me that towel."

The man with the gun wrapped the barrel with Dan's towel and pressed it to his chest and pulled the trigger. A muffled pop sounded.

Satisfied that Dan was dead, they looked for any valuables. Finding nothing but the almost empty bottle of vodka, they jumped into the golf cart and sped off.

"We should get some good money from Steve for this cart!"

Celebrating their good fortune, drinking the vodka, the two, now murderers, drove down the beach in the morning twilight to the county park where their truck was parked. They had ramps in the truck bed and, from past practice, they know the cart will load easily.

Frank Johns was making a last round before breakfast when he stopped at a port-a-potty near the beach and heard a noise, like a muffled gunshot, and then the sound of an electric golf cart speeding off. Fearful Dan, he quickly exited the port-a-potty and drove over to the beach.

He started scanning the beach, water and trees. As the sun cleared the horizon he found Dan.

To their surprise, the young men found that the cars and trucks at the park had been broken into, including theirs. Deputies have already been by. Following normal practice in this type of situation, they left a card on the windshield with a case number and contact number.

"Damn it! What the fuck! They broke out both windows to steal nothing!"

"What are you going to do?"

"Load this fucking cart and take it over to Steve's. Then go file at the sheriff's office."

"What for?"

"Insurance, stupid."

As their luck had it, Steve's shop was not open. Steve was never very prompt.

After Sunrise

Ron was making coffee when Cathy came out of the bedroom.

"Good morning, babe. Coffee?"

"Yes, please. I drank too much"

"We all did. I wonder if Dan made it to the beach."

"Did you hear the sirens this morning? I thought they were right outside."

"Yes, but I think they were down aways."

"Ron, is that Frank walking up to the house?"

Both Ron and Cathy met him on the porch.

"Ron. Cathy." Tracks of tears running down his face. "It's Dan. Someone killed him this morning"

Total silence and shock went through Ron and Cathy. Then sobs and tears.

"How, why?"

"We are not sure of anything yet. The sheriff's office is taking over."

"Who found him?" Asked Cathy through her sobs.

"I. I did." Frank broke down crying, "He was beaten and shot."

Neighbors were soon out asking questions and staring in disbelief.

Stephie, nursing a mild hangover herself, was watching The Morning Show on TV while making coffee, thinking of her friend, Dan.

"I hope, sweet Dan, that you had a beautiful morning."

The Morning Show was interrupted with local breaking news. A body had been found on the beach, near the resort.

"On TV? Surely it was Dan's body, but this soon and on TV?"

Listening closer, Stephie found out what happened. She immediately ran over to Ron and Cathy's.

Frank met Stephie in the street, "I was on my way to see you. I am so sorry, Stephie."

"Frank, when did this happen?"

"Right at 6:30."

Stephie stared into space. She was prepared to hear that Dan died, but not this!

If Dan had gone by his timeline, which he always did. He was a stickler for schedules. If he did. He would have been dead by then. He would not have lived to feel the horror of being murdered.

Tears of sadness and joy ran down her face.

Ron walked out of his home to meet Stephie.

"Come in. Sit. We can't help Dan, but we can hold on to each other."

The Police Reports

The two killers decided to stop by the sheriff's office to complete the paperwork for the truck insurance as they waited for Steve to get to the shop. Filling out the report, the deputy saw the cart in the pickup.

"Was that golf cart in the truck when they busted out the windows?"

Continuing the lack of intelligence they have been demonstrating all morning, they had completely forgotten that the stolen cart was in the pickup. They gave, what they hoped was, a plausible explanation: that they had stopped to get the cart for a friend.

As part of the report, another deputy went outside to take pictures of the damage.

Frank had completed writing up his report. He was pulling up to the sheriff's office to drop it off. He was surprised when he saw a deputy standing next to a pickup with a golf cart that looked just like the one stolen from Dan! Talking to the sheriff deputy, he quickly examined the cart. It was the stolen cart! Dan had his name stenciled on the side.The two young men walking out of the sheriff's office came face to face with two guns pointing at them. The authorities found the ax handle, gun, Dan's bottle of vodka and his towel. Earlier, Dan's phone was recovered at the murder scene. It was still recording.

Afterwards

Dan's body was cremated and a memorial was held at the resort chapel with both his and Gayle's urns in the sanctuary. With the help of the lead investigator, Frank was able to acquire the video of Dan's last hour before he was killed to be played at the memorial. Ron, Cathy and Stephie were carrying the urns back to Dan's house after the service. Their ashes are to be combined later with the ashes of their beloved fur babies and will be sprinkled about on the beach.

"The sheriff's office has allowed me to take possession of Dan's things." Ron told the two women.

"What are we going to do with his things, Ron?"

"Do you think Dan left anything to chance?" Ron laughed. "I have everything written down."

Cathy came to a stop in front of Dan's house. "I just feel so sorry for Dan to have his life ended this way."

"I don't think he knew what happened," said Stephie.

"What do you mean?"

"I have to tell you guys something. Here. Come in the house. Let's have a cup of coffee, Dan's way.

Stephie prepared the coffee and, as they sat in Dan's living room, she told Ron and Cathy Dan's grand plan of exiting this life.

They were stunned into complete silence.

Cathy was the first to speak "Stephie! Really! Dan was gone before those guys showed up? Should we tell anyone?"

"No. No. Definitely not, Cathy. Stephie, does anyone else know this?" Ron asked with a quivering voice.

"No one but us three." Stephie replied, trying to reassure her friends.

"Then his secret is ours. Those punks get what they deserve. Dan is with Gayle. And. And." Ron was unable to finish his thought.

"And we had the immense privilege of knowing them both."

The Beauty of it All

"Oh my, Gayle! How beautiful!"

Dan then realized what he had said. It felt as if he was dreaming.

"Gayle? Gayle! It's really you!?"

"Yes it is, sweetie."

They fell in a long embrace.

"Oh, Dan. I so miss you. It's about time you came home."

Looking around the beautiful beach that he and Gayle were sitting on, he realized this was not a dream. His fading memory of his life before seemed to be a dream. In the distance were some small animals running towards him.

"Are these our babies!?"

"Yes, Dan. We are all here." Replied Gayle, "But I so wish you had listened to me. You did not have to get Stephie involved."

"I know now!" Dan was being attacked by paws and licks from the animals. "Who would think..... OK. I should have listened."

"Yes, you should have. But it's done."

Looking around, "You did good, Gayle, my love. Thank you."

With their little fur babies scurrying about, Dan and Gayle began walking hand in hand down the beach in perpetual bliss, never looking back into the past, nor looking into the future.

The Chase

Wallace M Greensage

July, Southern France

'Bonjour, monsieur. Vous enregistrez?' the young lady behind the counter asked politely.

'I'm sorry, I don't speak much French,' the tall, well-built man replied. In his early thirties, his pretty young wife and two young daughters had followed him into the reception office, pleasantly open air in the wonderful Mediterranean climate. 'Do you speak English?'

'Of course. Are you checking in?'

'Yes, please' he replied, placing the family's passports on the counter. 'And glad to be here at last, I can tell you.'

'You are welcome. And I see that you have a reservation here for ten days in one of our premium camper locations. Let me show you on this map.'

The young lady came from behind the counter and took them to a wall map of the site. She was bronzed all over, nothing on her feet. The two little girls took one look and immediately peeled off their shorts and tops and everything else, including footwear. Their parents, Charlotte and Todd, glanced at each other and smiled, a family completely at ease with their naturist lifestyle.

'May I ask about the campers who left shortly before we arrived?' Todd asked, after the formalities had been completed.

The young lady frowned. 'Yes, they were in a big hurry and would not wait to check out.'

'And in so much of a hurry that at that narrow bend near the entrance,' Todd added. 'The driver did not slow down and hit our motorhome a glancing blow.'

'I am sorry to hear that. They were very rude people. Unusually rude, because most of our residents are always so polite and friendly.

They did not belong here, I think. They did not stay long. Only for one night.'

'Do you know their nationality?' Todd asked.

'I'm sorry, but I'm not permitted to give any information about guests. But if you have a problem and wish to make official claims, please let the camp manager know.'

'That's OK. Thanks anyway. I will report the damage to the vehicle rental company and if they need information, I may come back.'

By the time that they had driven out of the reception car park, Todd was also nude and that's how he intended to stay for the full ten days. Charlotte was as eager but waited until they set up camp. As they searched for their spot, Charlotte pointed out a similar motorhome. 'Looks just like ours,' she commented. 'Same colour and everything.'

'Same model too. And the plates are also Dutch, like ours. Maybe the same rental company.'

After a quick lunch prepared by Charlotte, she and their two young daughters headed for the adjacent naturist beach to explore and swim and play in the waves. Todd would join them later but wanted to check out the van and to report the damage. Todd had stopped after the incident, but the other driver had not. He had checked that the damage was not bad enough to stop them from continuing even though it had been a sharp jolt; a dent and scratches would not stop their progress. He suspected that the front wing of the other vehicle would be damaged too. Now he checked more thoroughly and photographed the damage with his phone. He called the rental company in Amsterdam and spoke with the manager.

'Thanks very much for calling in your report, Mr. Mathersley,' the manager said. 'I agree that there is no need to report this to the police unless you want to for any reason. By the look of the photos, we will not make an insurance claim.'

'OK, that's fine then. Thanks very much.'

'One more thing, Sir. Did your colleague find you?'

'Colleague?'

'Yes, the one who called this office to find out where you are staying. He said that they knew you are travelling around and wondered where you are exactly.'

'Oh? And what did you tell him?'

'I told him the area that you were heading for, but I told him I did not know where exactly or when you would arrive.'

'Sorry, but isn't that sort of information confidential?'

'Well yes, but he called you a Chief Inspector of police and said that he is an Inspector in your team. I thought that as it was the police calling, it would be OK to at least tell him the general location.'

'Did you get his name?'

'No, sorry. He didn't give it.'

'Well, thanks for letting me know, but if anyone else calls, please give out no information about our whereabouts. OK?'

'OK and I apologise if I should not have said anything.'

After the call, Todd sat at the table under the van's awning, and gave thought to the information about the call that the rental company manager had received. All his colleagues had his roaming number, email address and media connections. The necessity for such a call simply did not exist. Someone else wanted to know where he was, and this unsettled him. A court case against a senior mob boss was looming. Could it be connected? The date of the case was imminent, and the case files were closed. The case had taken months of hard work over long days and many long nights to prepare. Todd had taken the opportunity for ten days holiday with his increasingly impatient family, to spend quality time with them and to make up for his long hours of absence. He was now concerned that this break was in jeopardy and that he would have to be on his guard.

As Todd was preparing to lock up and head out to join his family at the beach, he noticed a guy of about his age and build, with the same dark hair, walking towards the similar caravan he had noticed on the way in, his arms laden with beach toys, inflated boats and umbrellas. Coming through the reed bed and over the stream by the low dunes behind the beach, a lady and two young girls appeared, the girls chasing around and in no hurry, their mother stopping to wait for them. I'll go over later and chat to them, thought Todd, mildly curious about whether they had the same rental company.

The man disappeared behind the caravan and as Todd left his motorhome to join Charlotte and the girls at the beach, he was watching the domestic scene in front of him, the two little girls still holding up their mother. Moments later, the blast of a huge explosion hit him. The woman started screaming; the shattered remains of the similar motorhome were completely engulfed in flames.

***

In the aftermath of the explosion, people ran to help the hysterical woman and girls and two men from the camp office ran with fire extinguishers in a futile attempt to control the fire. The intense heat prevented them from getting near to the already destroyed vehicle. Todd had no doubts about the man's chances of survival. If he was in the vehicle, his chances were zero.

The rescue services were quick to respond, and the paramedics immediately turned their attention to the despairing woman and children, realising that they were not needed at the fire. The man was not found immediately by the fire team and it would be many hours before his charred remains could be retrieved. It would be a long, distressing clean-up.

Onlookers congregated in groups. Todd gathered his family together and they all retreated to their camp, away from the scene of devastation and the small groups. On arrival of the police, he had informed them that he had witnessed the event and was available to make a statement.

Charlotte prepared snacks but no one ate very much. Todd packed them off to the beach again, away from the disruption and turmoil in the camp as rescue services, police and media milled around.

It was late afternoon when the vehicle had cooled enough to be loaded and removed. The camp manager laid the charred ground with tarpaulins and at least a look of normality returned to the camp, even if the guests were far from settled. Many departed that afternoon and evening, leaving mainly residents and a handful of holidaymakers.

It was after the motorhome had been taken that a policeman eventually called Todd to the camp office, where the police had set up their base. Todd, experienced as he was, gave a full and concise statement, omitting nothing. He also reported the motorhome that had struck his on his way into the camp, but that fact did not make its way into the police report. He was told to exclude it from the witness statement as irrelevant. He debated with himself whether he should voice thoughts that were growing in his mind. He was turning more to the notion that in fact this was no accident and that he had been the target. The wrong person had been killed if his suspicions were right. Before he could say anything, it was taken out of his hands.

'Why did you mention the vehicle incident outside the camp?' a man he had not heard approach, asked. He was leaning casually against the doorframe.

'In case it becomes evident that this was not an accident. Maybe the person or persons leaving in such a hurry have material evidence.'

The man, wearing plain clothes, walked over to the desk and picked up Todd's statement; the room was silent as he read it. 'Very professional, Chief Inspector Mathersley.' His title was spoken with acidity. 'Do you suspect that it is not merely an unfortunate accident?'

Todd paused before answering. The man's attitude was clearly cool towards Todd. 'It's not my place to suspect anything. I am not party to your findings, nor should I be.'

'That's the point isn't it?' the man replied loudly, almost before Todd had stopped speaking.

'This is my job, my country and my case, so don't forget that!'

Todd stood and faced the man. He was a head taller. 'If you have finished with my statement, I would like to get back to my family.'

The man walked past Todd and handed the statement to the policeman still sitting at the desk. 'Merci, Inspecteur,' the policeman said. Without glancing at Todd or speaking further, the Inspecteur left the room. 'Merci à vous aussi, Monsieur. You may go back to your family now.'

Todd paused, hesitant about voicing his suspicions. He let it go. They were simply unfounded suspicions at this stage. The attitude of the Inspecteur was not conducive to throwing around such possibilities. 'Here is my card with my phone number if there is anything else,' he told the policeman. He put his card on the desk and left the office.

***

That evening, after a sombre meal and with the girls in bed asleep, Charlotte and Todd sat outside in the evening warmth, sipping dry red Collioure wine. Nude as always, they sat without lights, the darkness matching their moods. They had spoken little, lost in their own thoughts. To Charlotte, Todd had recounted the conversation following his witness statement and his disappointment with the Inspecteur's attitude. He had not voiced his fears to Charlotte, but she was an intelligent woman and she looked over at Todd and reached out, touching his hand resting next to his wineglass.

'Are we having the same thoughts about what happened, Darling?' she asked quietly.

Todd sighed. 'If you mean, as I'm sure you do, that the accident was no such thing and that he was an innocent victim, then yes, we're having the same thoughts.'

'I feel so terrible for that poor family,' Charlotte whispered, clearly distraught. A sob escaped from her and Todd stood and went to her quickly, wrapping his arms around her.

She recovered slowly and as she reached for her wine, Todd resumed his seat opposite her, took a long draught from his own glass and topped up both glasses.

'We are not safe, are we?' she asked quietly.

'We are for now,' he replied reassuringly. 'If it really was what we are both thinking, and I hope to God that it wasn't, the perpetrators will think that they were successful and got away with it. The police will no doubt report this evening that it was an unfortunate accident and the media will get hold of that and report it. His name will not be released until the autopsy, which will be no earlier than tomorrow. His name will probably be released after that so by no earlier than noon tomorrow, the perps will know that they failed. Although it's unlikely, we can't be sure that the name won't be leaked earlier though, so we should be wary.'

'Oh! You have it all worked out! So, what will we do?'

'First thing tomorrow we will join all the other escapees and move out.'

'And then what?'

'I'll go online this evening and see if I can find another campsite far from here and book us in. I'll use a false name until we get there and have to divulge our true identities but by then we will be hard to trace. We can move every two or three days until we go home. I know that we don't know for sure but best to be cautious.'

'There's little doubt in my mind, Todd. The call to the rental company, the explosion. It adds up to enough for me to be as sure as I need to be. Yes, let's move out tomorrow as early as possible.'

Todd spent an hour using the free wi-fi at the resort social area and was not surprised that, at the height of the vacation period and at short notice, no naturist campsites on the Mediterranean Coast were available. Without much expectation, he decided to try inland sites before checking out textile grounds. Even those were unlikely along the tourist coast and he was ready to look in Spain and Portugal too. At least they could find plenty of naturist beaches in those countries. He was surprised, then, to discover that the first inland naturist campsite in France that he tried actually had three recent cancellations, a party of touring Germans, and he booked one of the berths immediately for the two available nights.

***

They left early next morning and headed inland, stopping after an hour in a layby by a wooded river for breakfast. An experienced cop, Todd was on the alert for anything suspicious, but he was not expecting the killers to know they had missed their target yet and was not overly concerned, even when he spotted the same car twice while they ate, travelling in opposite directions.

An hour later, they stopped at a filling station for fuel and Todd bought a local paper. His French was not great but good enough to find the report he sought. The victim had been named. While he was reading, and while Charlotte and the girls were using the washroom and buying snacks for the road, he received a call from a French number.

'Hello.'

'Is zat Monsieur Mazzerley?'

'Todd Mathersley, yes. Who is this?'

'Inspecteur Gignac wants to speak you. 'Old please.'

Todd waited and in moments, Gignac was on the line. 'Monsieur Mathersley, we talked yesterday when you gave your statement, I am Inspecteur Gignac.'

'Yes, good morning.'

'Monsieur, I would like for you to come to see me at my office.'

'I'm sorry, Inspecteur, but that's not possible. I am no longer in the vicinity. We have left the campsite. What's this about?'

'A camper van was discovered overnight abandoned twenty kilometres away. It 'ad been burnt completely but damage to the front wing was still clear to see. I want to 'ear more about the incident you mentioned yesterday.'

As Todd stopped to think about this revelation and its implications, he again saw the car he had spotted twice earlier, travelling in the opposite direction. He knew now for sure that he was being tailed. This changed everything. He was now also as sure as he could be that he was the intended target and that they were onto him. He and his family were in mortal danger.

'Allo, allo!'

'Yes, I'm still here, Inspecteur.'

'Can you come and meet me. Monsieur? I 'ave some questions.'

Todd hesitated. What was the safest thing to do? 'I cannot come today, Inspecteur, but in a day or two perhaps. Or I can call in at a police station near where we plan to stay.' He was playing for time.

‘Tell me where you are or where you will be, and I will inform you of nearest police post.’

‘Very well, Inspecteur. I will text the address to you. I’m sorry but I must go now. Au revoir.’

Todd decided to say nothing to Charlotte until he had done some more checking. They found a mall with a family restaurant and he used the wi-fi, to Charlotte’s puzzlement.

‘Let me check something, Angel,’ he parried. ‘I’ll tell you everything when I’ve checked out a couple of things.’

Charlotte sat quietly, watching their daughters in a children’s play area of the family restaurant, eaten up with curiosity. ‘Come on Todd, tell me what’s going on.’

‘OK, but don’t freak out. I have a suggestion to make when I’ve explained.’

He told her about the Inspecteur’s call and the revelation about the burnt-out campervan. He also told her that he was sure that they were being followed. Charlotte was shocked at first then increasingly afraid. ‘Todd, what will we do? These people were prepared to allow the whole family to be killed yesterday. It could have been us. They will stop at nothing!’

While Todd watched the girls playing, at his request Charlotte went back to the motorhome and packed her own and the girls’ belongings. As soon as she was finished, Todd and the girls joined her, and they headed out. Three hours later, by which time Todd had worked out that they were being tailed by three different vehicles, they reached the city of Toulouse. They stopped at a busy roadside restaurant in a shopping precinct on the outskirts of the city and managed a late lunch, Charlotte looking at her watch constantly, anxious about the next crucial stage of the plan.

***

Todd kissed his two daughters tenderly, cheerfully promising to see them again in a few days and entreating them to be good for their mother. He took Charlotte in his arms briefly and kissed her too.

‘I love you, Todd,’ she whispered. ‘Please stay safe, don’t take any risks and call me constantly!’

Todd kissed her once more, patted each daughter on the head then left the restaurant. At the motorhome, as planned, he took his time to check the van over, including the engine oil and water, and then drove the van to park as close to the restaurant door as possible. He hoped that the probable watchers were far enough away and that they could not see what was actually going on. He opened both van doors on the passenger's side and then went into the restaurant with the suitcases, leaving moments later. He closed the van doors after allowing enough time for his imaginary passengers to embark and, before climbing into his driver's seat, he pretended to call something to those inside the vehicle. Hopefully, the subterfuge worked, he thought to himself as he left the carpark and headed away from Toulouse towards the Pyrenees.

Ten minutes later, the pre-arranged taxi arrived and whisked Charlotte and the girls to the Gare de Toulouse-Matabiau railway station. With careful timing, Charlotte quickly collected her pre-booked tickets from a machine, validated them at the barrier and they settled into their seats on the Paris-bound train. Minutes later, the high-speed TGV train pulled out of the station. They were to be met by good friends at Paris Montparnasse, to spend a few days at their small city-centre apartment. It would be a squeeze but manageable and the girls would enjoy the beautiful sights of Paris. They were out of trouble and safe.

***

Todd realised that, although his family was safe now, he was far from out of trouble and that he had to be very cautious. He was the real target. After fifty kilometres, he relaxed a little as he realised that all three cars were still on his tail, exchanging their positions from time-to-time. He had conflicting emotions, firstly relief that the watchers had apparently been taken in by the subterfuge at Toulouse but countered by growing anxiety about what was to happen.

He refuelled en route and was on his way within minutes. Before dark, he arrived at his chosen campsite, high in the hills. His GPS had helped with following the twists and turns and he was surprised that the following cars seemed to have disappeared. He realised that he had not seen them since he refuelled and then it dawned on him; they had probably sneaked a tracking device under his vehicle, probably when he refuelled before heading into the foothills. That was OK by him; if he was to put a stop to this, he needed them to know his location, even though he was ostensibly trying to hide away. He would check for the device later at the campsite.

The campsite was beautiful, in wooded foothills of the huge Pyrenees mountain range on the French-Spanish border. He checked in and asked if the other two cancellations had been filled. They hadn't. He parked and set up camp, less concerned that the watchers, if indeed they were watching that evening, noticed that he was alone. He left the GPS tracker, discovered as expected under his vehicle, in place.

***

Early next morning, a motorhome with local plates arrived. The man and woman parked within sight of his van, he noticed. He also noticed that they didn't set up camp very quickly and that when they did, they were clearly not familiar with erecting the awning. They also did everything dressed in shorts and tops, unlike most naturists, who usually couldn't wait to be nude as soon as possible and certainly when tackling jobs around their camping location. The man eventually removed his shirt in the heat, but the woman didn't.

Todd was reasonably sure that the couple were there for reasons other than nude relaxation. At the office, he mentioned the new arrivals and learned that they had made a late booking the previous evening. He doubted that they would try anything during the daytime and so, after lunch, he risked a brief siesta, knowing that he would probably sleep little that night. He spent the rest of the afternoon exploring the surroundings, becoming totally familiar with them. At the back of his motorhome, the ground sloped gently down to a shallow mountain stream and he could see that it was a well-used area for picnicking and playing in the small pools.

He also kept a surreptitious watch on his new neighbours and the more he saw, the more that he realised that they were not naturists. Not even close. The man was naked briefly but soon threw a wrap, probably hers, around his midriff. She removed her top to lie in the sun for a while, but as soon as she rose, her shirt was on again. Very few people at the resort, including Todd, wore anything at all, except in the heat of the day when one or two put on tops and hats to protect themselves from the sun's midday glare.

***

Todd waited in his motorhome until the lights went out in the couple's vehicle around eleven p.m. By that time, he had set things up in his own campervan and soon afterwards he slipped quietly away. He had selected a spot between the two vehicles, behind a stout tree, so that he had a good view of both. He had no doubts that very soon, events would become interesting, He hoped that he would not be spotted by the couple, but he was ready for anything.

Todd slid to the ground behind the tree, surrounded by everything that he would need, including a comfortable blanket to sit on. He had decided to stay nude; it was a warm evening with a slight breeze; perfect weather for a long wait. He had drinks and food, a torch, insect repellent and after-sting lotion, although he did not need the latter. He had also found a sturdy wooden club earlier in the trees near to the stream and this rested against the trunk, ready for anything unforeseen. Most importantly, his mobile phone was set up to record. He had practiced with it to make sure that he was ready and able to start his video in the dark at short notice. His phone's battery was fully charged.

The occupants of the other vehicle waited until the camp had finally settled and then for a further hour. At around one a.m., the couple made their move. Without switching on interior lights, they left their vehicle. The campsite's lights were enough to enhance the phone's video capabilities, even in the dead of night. Todd had switched on the video recorder feature as soon as he heard the couple moving around in the van and was already recording when they opened their camper's door. They moved stealthily towards Todd's motorhome and Todd recorded everything. He wanted a continuous recording. Still recording, he silently crept through the trees to their vehicle and took video of the registration plate. Without pausing the recording, he returned to his hiding spot, by which time the couple had reached his van and were looking around it.

It was too easy for them. They found a conveniently open bottom-opening window and lifted it. The curtains were slightly apart and, with the woman holding the window open, the man looked inside. A convenient dim interior light allowed him to see a prostrate body under a light blanket. Moments later, clearly satisfied that he had his target in sight, he raised a silenced gun and quietly lifted it through the window. Todd heard three quick pops as shots were fired into the apparently sleeping Todd, followed by one more, just to be sure. The man tried the door but on finding it locked, he turned away.

The couple hurried back to their vehicle, less concerned about silence and disappeared inside. Todd waited, his phone still recording video. Within a minute, the man left the motorhome and, torch in hand, made his way carefully down to the stream. Todd followed and from behind a bush, saw and recorded the man throw the gun into the stream lower down. The man returned as quickly as he could to the motorhome and ten minutes later, Todd watched as the engine started and the vehicle moved away in the direction of the exit. He heard voices and a sharp instruction, and shortly afterward the sound of the vehicle receded.

Still recording, Todd returned to his vehicle and ended the continuous video after recording the damage to the motorhome's interior and especially to the 'body' under the blanket. He downloaded the recording, saved it to his computer and a flashcard backup and sent the video by email, using the reception area wi-fi, to a colleague at his home police station with instructions on what to do with it.

***

Thirty-six hours later, Todd strolled into Wellingbury police station in his home city. He was there to watch the progress of the interview of mafia boss, Paulo Marcerelli. He sat watching the interview on screen from the adjoining room, waiting for the perfect time to make his appearance. The interview was routine, going over old material. Marcerelli, with his expensively dressed lawyer, was fielding the questions with a bored expression.

One of Todd's team, Inspector Davies, was interviewing Marcerelli. Davies suddenly changed tack. 'What do you know about the recent murder of a man in a motorhome in Southern France?' he asked, maintaining the same calm questioning tone.

Marcerelli was taken aback for a moment, then turned to his lawyer with a smug expression.

'I have no idea what you are talking about,' he replied cockily, turning back to the interviewer.

'What is this about?' his lawyer intervened.

Inspector Davies spoke directly to Marcerelli. 'This morning, in France, suspects have been arrested and are being questioned about a campsite murder. Under questioning, and probably to save their own skins, they told police that they were working for your consigliere. They have agreed to give him up in exchange for a lesser charge. Your consigliere is known to us and we know that he works directly for you.'

'Bullshit!' Marcerelli exploded. 'Don't give me this crap!'

'That's a bit of a longshot isn't it, Inspector? Even for you guys.'

'No longshot. A true story. Would you like to take a break so that your fancy lawyer here can call your consigliere? He's in custody too, being questioned, but I'm sure you'll get confirmation.'

'What is all this?' Marcerelli sneered. 'It's all bullshit! I don't know nothing about no murder.'

'From the smirk on your face when I asked you about the recent murder of a man in a motorhome in Southern France, it is clear to see that you think you know exactly who was murdered! Come on, Marcerelli. It's all over for you. Murder is being added to your charge sheet as we speak. You're going down for good!'

'Fuck you, sbirro!' Marcerelli retorted, jabbing his finger at Davies. 'And all you cops should think about this very hard. Being a cop can be hazardous for your health!'

'That's enough, Paulo,' his lawyer whispered, his hand patting Marcerelli's arm, trying to calm him. 'Don't say another word.'

Jimmy Davies hadn't finished. 'Should I take that as a threat, Marcerelli?'

'No, no!' the lawyer jumped in before Marcerelli could say anything more. 'It meant nothing.'

‘Oh, I think that it did mean something. Marcerelli, do you think that this murder is going to intimidate us? If so, think again. It is going to do you far more harm than us.’

Marcerelli couldn’t resist the taunt. ‘Someone was hurt very bad, yes? And that’s just the start …’

The lawyer lost his cool. ‘Shut up, Paulo!’ he shouted angrily, then moved his head close to his client’s to whisper into his ear but Marcerelli was not listening. He leaned forward in his seat and jabbed his finger at Davies, but his lawyer pulled him back before he could say anything more.

And that’s when Todd walked in.

***

Marcerelli was half out of his seat in shock for a moment, before strong hands jerked him back down into his chair and pinned him there.

‘Ah! I see that you are shocked to see me, Mr. Marcerelli,’ Todd said calmly. ‘Now why is that? Perhaps it’s because you’re trying to work out what has happened and how I’m here and not lying on a morgue slab somewhere in France, right?’

Marcerelli looked totally confused. He was too shocked to say anything. And he could be in serious trouble, he now realised. His lawyer was not so intimidated, and had regained his composure, however. ‘My client is merely surprised at this turn of events. You should not read anything more into it. What is all this about murder? I’m sure that he wants to know.’

‘I’m sure he does. So it’s clearly time for disclosure. Are you ready for this, Marcerelli, or do you want to talk to your lawyer first?’

Marcerelli hesitated. He wanted to hear what Todd had but he also realised that he was being backed into a corner and that he would need to discuss this privately with his lawyer as soon as he could. He made his choice; it turned out to be the wrong one. ‘What the fuck is all this nonsense, Mathersley?’ he demanded. His voice was now unsure, and his former belligerence had disappeared.

‘We have pieced this together with the help of the team sent by your consigliere, who are singing like songbirds now in the hope of minimising their charges. Here's what happened. I arrived at a campsite in France and on the way in, my motorhome was involved in a minor accident with another vehicle rushing away from the campsite. Soon after my arrival, an explosion in an identical motorhome to mine at the campsite killed a man and could well have killed his whole family if his kids had not been dawdling with their mother on their way back from the beach. The police initially put it down to an accidental gas bottle explosion but, after my report of the vehicle accident and the discovery of a burnt-out motorhome with accident damage, they began to suspect that it may not actually have been an accidental explosion. I, on the other hand, had suspected that I was being targeted, so I moved out next morning, only to discover clumsy attempts by three separate cars to follow me. I made my family safe and headed alone for an inland campsite in the mountains. Soon afterwards, your killers arrived and that night they made an attempt on my life, shooting four times into my caravan. They were not aware that I videoed everything. They left immediately. They were tracked and were arrested a few hours ago.'

'That has nothing to do with me.' Marcerelli retorted defiantly.

'Your consigliere is implicated and has been arrested. Are you sure that you too will not be implicated?'

'My client has absolutely nothing to be concerned about. There is nothing at all to link him with this rambling tale.'

Todd ignored this and continued to address Marcerelli directly. 'So you had the wrong man killed and his family were lucky to avoid the same fate. You had me followed across France and the people you sent, who were obviously not experienced campers, turned up right after me and pumped bullets into my motorhome.'

'Not me! I was here.' Marcerelli had regained some of his composure and his brain was starting to work again. 'Who were these campers who you say weren't campers? I have no idea!'

'They were killers hired by your consigliere, on your instructions, to remove your principal accuser and witness in the case against you, me, and to intimidate others. If I can be killed, so can others.'

'What rubbish!'

‘They failed first time and bungled the second attempt. It was easy to see that they were not proper campers. They stuck out like sore thumbs! They made it easy for me.’ Todd was dangling the hook. Would Marcerelli slip up and take the bait?

He did! ‘Perhaps they are a decent couple and not as deranged as you?’

‘Deranged? What do you mean?’

‘That’s all you should say,’ the lawyer instructed Marcerelli. ‘Let’s take a sidebar …’ but Marcerelli wasn’t listening.

‘Everyone knows you are a weirdo nudist. I bet that’s where you were. In a nudist colony! Right? And that would make anyone who isn’t the same stick out! Especially a woman…’ He stopped abruptly, realising that he had said too much. ‘What I mean is, I’m guessing it was a couple, I don’t know though.’

‘I said killers. I didn’t mention a couple or that one was a woman. I didn’t mention where I was staying. How do you know all this if you weren’t involved?’

‘My client refuses to comment further,’ the lawyer interjected. ‘We would like some private time now.’

Todd continued to address Marcerelli. ‘Paulo Antonio Marcerelli, you are being charged with murder and attempted murder. Anything you say will…’

‘You bastard,’ Marcerelli hissed at Todd.

***

Todd returned to Paris and, unable to continue their camping holiday because their rented motorhome had been impounded by the police as evidence, for the remainder of their break, he and his family booked a rental car and spent a relaxing time at a wonderful seaside naturist site on the Atlantic coast north of Bordeaux, enjoying the sunshine, beaches and excellent facilities.

Marcerelli went to prison for a very long time.

N-00-D-1 Station

P.Z. Walker

Calamity report.

Location: N-00-D-1 Station.

Responsibility: Clony World.

Galactic calendar: 298002.173.

Incident: Suspected murder.

It all started like a simple assignment. I needed to follow up on a disturbance at one of the space-stations. Nothing difficult, I thought. Until I discovered it was one of the deep-space places. N-00-D-1 Station. Scarily close to a sun and hard to get to. Also, hard to get away from - at least alive. Shuttles only went there a few times per week but this case couldn't wait that long, so I was brought there as a special delivery.

Three days of FTL travel later, we arrived near the sun, a decent K-class one. As soon as we dropped back to a more comprehensible speed, the shuttle warmed up quickly and it would get hotter soon if the shuttle were to get any closer to the sun. The pilot laid in a course to keep us at a safe distance. The internal cooling system of the craft wouldn't be able to cope with the star's extreme heat.

"Sir," the co-pilot said, "Nudy station is hailing us. They want to speak with you."

"*Nudy*?" I said. "What kind of name is that?" The co-pilot explained that N-00-D-1 looked like NOODI and so all pilots had adopted that name for the place. Nudy. I laughed. It was definitely funny. "Okay, put them on my comm."

The LED lit up and I accepted the incoming transmission. I was prepared for a lot. Not for a naked man.

"Detective Rodriguez?" the man asked.

"Ehm. Yeah. That would be me." No denying it; I had been a Rodriguez since birth. "Excuse me, but didn't you forget something?"

"Forget?" The man shook his head. "I'm not sure I understand."

"Clothes. It looks as if you're not wearing anything," I pointed out,feeling stupid for having to do that.

"Oh. That." The man grinned. "Detail. We'll get to that soon enough. My name is Johansen. Brent Johansen. Manager of N-00-D-1. We'll send over a pod to pick you up. Shuttles don't do well near the sun."

"Very kind. I'll await its arrival." The people on Clony had told me about that mode of transport.

"Wonderful. Now to my appearance. That is official dress code here. Which is why I contact you, detective. You will be required to leave your clothing on board the shuttle."

"What?" There was nothing wrong with my ears, I knew that, but had he just told me I had to get naked?

"You cannot enter the station wearing any clothes, sir." The man continued to tell me when the pod would arrive and where someone would be waiting for me upon my arrival. Before I could object to any of this or at least ask why this was, the connection was terminated.

"What the hell…"

"Changing room is in the back, sir," the co-pilot said. "That's also where the pod will dock."

"Okay, thanks, but hell if I will get into that thing naked," I muttered.

"Oh, I strongly suggest you do, sir," the co-pilot said. "Otherwise the pod won't leave."

Crap. They had actually rigged the thing like that? What kind of circus had I gotten into? And did the police force back home know about that? I decided to take my chances.

Once in the 'changing room' I waited for the pod to arrive. A round hatch opened and I slid into the thing, which was not much more than a tube. After pressing the 'go' button, a beep sounded and a display flashed at me. 'Clothing detected'. Repeatedly punching the button repeatedly treated me to the same message. Crap again.

I crawled out of the thing and cursed as I took my clothes off. What the hell was I going to get into? This was supposed to be a serious enterprise. A space exploration and surveillance station, not some kind of orgy-palace! As I stood there, hesitant to get into the pod, I wondered if the blasted thing would also object to carrying my ID-card and my weapon. There was only one way to find out…

Getting into the pod naked was… weird. I was acutely aware of the material I was lying on, and even though there was no one here, I felt utterly exposed. I even feared going out into space this way, which was an idiotic thing. A few layers of clothing wouldn't make a big difference in case anything were to go wrong, and those pods were insanely reliable and robust.

"Okay. Here goes," I told myself as I pressed the 'go' button. The hatch closed over my head, the pod pressurised, and a rapid countdown later I was on my way.

***

This wasn't the first trip in a pod for me but it felt like the longest, and so I had a tonne of time to think. How the hell had I gone through with this? I was going to arrive there butt naked! And maybe even worse (if possible), everyone on that station would be naked. Or would they have pulled a fast one on me to have a good laugh? But what if they didn't? What if everyone was naked, *including the women*? And why had no one told me?

As I said, a tonne of time for a load of questions - and no answers. A display in front of my face told me the distance to the station was rapidly decreasing and suddenly the thing was docked. As the pressure equalised to the station's, my heart pounded. This was it. I was going to have to get out of this pod and face the naked truth.

The hatch opened and I got out of the pod. There was no way to do that in a dignified way, not even in a lower-gravity environment like this station. To my dread I was greeted by four people. Two men, among whom was Johansen, the station manager, and two women. All of them undressed. I didn't know where to look.

"Welcome to Nudy, Detective," Johansen said. He laughed. "Yes, we're quite aware of the name we've been given, and actually we're sort of proud of it. It does fit us, don't you think?"

Look at his face, look at all their faces, I told myself. I didn't want to stare at penises or breasts and I certainly didn't want to make an embarrassing scene of myself. "Yes, it does fit," I replied, forcing a smile. "Is there a reason for this?" *Please tell me there is.*

"Of course," the man said to my relief. "As you may have noticed, the station is quite close to the sun. That heats things up. Instead of spending a fortune on cooling systems, we decided to test going naked. And I must say, so far it works well."

Okay, duh, that sounded like a very simple and rational reason, but still… naked…

"Right," I said. "Now to the reason of my, ehm, visit. There's been a murder here."

"Indeed." Johansen turned to one of the women in the group. "This is Carly Moonis. She discovered the body, so I think it's best she tells you all about it."

The woman smiled and nodded. "If you could come with me… I'll tell you about it on the way. We've left everything as I found it, to make sure no traces or bits of evidence are removed or disturbed."

I asked her to lead the way. She walked off. None of the others were following so it would be her and me. How embarrassing and weird, walking along naked behind a naked woman, passing lots of other naked people and species. Now, I knew for several of those species being naked was normal, but not all of them had their *physical traits* hanging out for everyone to see. Closest to the Earth humans were the Razolians, but nearly everyone who had seen them was used to them being naked. The Razolians had never developed the concept of clothing, and with their kaleidoscopic skins, their *bits* didn't attract so much attention.

As we walked along, Miss Moonis told me she had been assigned to doing preventive maintenance in one of the standby reaction chambers. "We check them four times per sun-revolution, to be certain they are operational in case we need them."

My understanding of these chambers was very limited. I knew stations like this one were powered by a number of small fusion reactors, and this reaction chamber was clearly part of one. I shivered for a moment, realising we'd go into a room that might have been used for nuclear operation. A senseless fear of course, because this technology was as safe as a baby's crib.

We stopped at a transport tube and waited for the door to open. We stepped inside and she told the system where we were going. "I was doing the usual visual check of the coolant pipes when I found the body," Miss Moonis continued. "It was rather shocking. Not what you expect to find in such a chamber."

Her words gave me pause. The way she put it almost made it sound as if she expected dead bodies in other places. Just not there.

"Did you know this person?" I asked. "Have you seen him before?" That was one of the few facts I had about this case. The dead person was an Earth-human man.

Miss Moonis looked over her shoulder for a moment. "No. I can't say I have."

I was painfully aware that I was standing inside this transport tube with her. Alone, with a naked woman who didn't seem to give that a second thought. For me it felt even weirder than walking along with her when many others had been around.

The tube door opened and we got out. Again, I followed her. It was a bit easier to focus on her head and shoulders now, instead of on her curves. “And here we are." We were in front of a huge door. She typed in a clearance code and had a system scan her hand. No half safety precautions, clearly. That was something to note. If this place was so secure, how had the dead guy gotten in there? It had to be with the help of someone who had clearance to these chambers as well. I needed a list of people who had such a clearance.

The big door moved to the side and gave me the first glance into the interior of such a space. Miss Moonis walked in as if there was nothing to it. I had to take a deep breath before going forward. This was a space where nuclear fusion could happen. If someone pulled a wrong lever, we'd be taken apart. I knew that no one would be able to pull that lever as long as the door was open, or if there were lifeforms inside, but my instincts weren't connected to my logic at that level.

"There he is," Miss Moonis said, pointing up. I looked where her finger indicated after noticing she did not look up herself.

Twelve feet over the floor there was a dead body. Hanging upside down. It was an Earth-human male. Blood had run down his chest and face from the three metal rods that protruded from his stomach. I looked down and saw a dried-up pool of blood on the floor. Good grief, that looked sick. How the hell had he gotten up there?

"What is he hanging from?" An odd question, I realised.

"Stabiliser rods," she answered. "They are all around the room to…" she went off into a technical ramble that I didn't understand. Okay, baseline: those rods had to be there. Just without bodies hanging from them.

"Do you know who was in here before you found him?" I asked.

"A number of people, probably," she responded. "There was a maintenance crew in here to upgrade things. They didn't report anything out of the ordinary."

I nodded and thought. This was a technical complication that wasn't in my pay-grade but this case was in my hands and I was here, so I had to work with what I had. "Hmm. Did the maintenance people run any tests after doing their work? And would it be possible to see if the deceased up there was in here when those tests were performed?"

"Ehm. Of course they tested the systems. And trust me, Detective Rodriguez, if that man had been in here during those tests, we wouldn't have found him anymore."

"Not even that?" I pointed at the now solid pool of blood. She didn't look at it, she just shook her head. Wonderful. "I think I've seen enough for now, Miss Moonis. I would need a space to work from, do you think…"

"I am sure Mr Johansen has already arranged that for you," she said as she walked out of the chamber.

I followed her a bit faster than I had wanted. This place spooked me. My strange hurry made me run into her. "Oh no, I'm so sorry!" I didn't know how to apologise for being so stupid and rude.

She just smiled. "That's okay, detective. You're not used to touching other people's skin, are you? It's quite difficult to avoid that here at times."

I admitted that it was strange to me. Miss Moonis smiled as she closed the door via the touch-pad and assured me she'd had some issues with it at first.

"But you will get used to it," she said. "It's quite freeing to walk around like this."

I wanted to say I believed her but I couldn't. Simply because I didn't believe it.

***

We walked off to find the manager, Johansen. He was glad to hear I was going to take the case (what choice did I have?). They had already prepared a cabin for me and from the shuttle my stuff had been sent over. Everything except my clothes, of course.

"Another reason why we don't allow clothes here," Johansen said, "is that this cuts down on filter maintenance. Clothes, certainly fabric-based ones, release particles that can clog certain systems. And before you mention plastic-based clothes: those are not an option here at all. They will make you sweat too much, which would require even more installations to keep Earth-humans comfortable."

I asked him if there was a way they could get the victim down from the rods and put him somewhere safe. I wanted a station doctor to investigate the body as much as possible and get some information to decide if the victim should be sent on for further autopsy or if I could go on without that. Interplanetary body-shipments were expensive and should be avoided if possible.

Johansen said he'd make sure that would be arranged. He then turned to a seemingly genderless humanoid near him. "Larima, would you be so kind as to show the detective to his cabin?"

Larima was an amazing person to look at. He was from a distant planet, from a clan called something Earth-humans couldn't even pronounce. Bright red skin with a million tiny scales, light blue pupils surrounded by an unnerving dark blue instead of white and no hair anywhere. "Mr Rodriguez. Or do you prefer your title, Detective?" The humanoid nodded, showing a row of black, triangular teeth.

I shrugged, trying not to stare at the alien who looked so human. "Either is fine, as long as you include Rodriguez," I said. I didn't smile at the alien. I knew they didn't like that as their clan interpreted that as hostile. Larima probably had gotten used to it, but if this simple social interaction helped in making things easy between Larima and myself… I nodded. That was safe.

"Very good, Mr Rodriguez. Would you kindly follow me." Larima started walking. I nodded at the manager and Miss Moonis, then followed the red alien.

"There is a cabin prepared for you in the cold wing, Mr Rodriguez." Larima didn't look back as he/she/it spoke. "You will be more comfortable there. The sun-side of the station is warmer."

"Sun-side? You mean the station doesn't rotate?" That was odd.

"No. It doesn't. The fusion reactor needs the thermal energy from the sun to be started, as far as I know. That is what I know, at least." Larima made an odd move with an arm. "It seems to be very tricky technology. Maybe it's something I can't even understand."

Two more of Larima's kind stood to the side and looked at me as we passed them. Their faces were hard to read under all those colours. I wondered how many of them were on this station, and how many different species there were. I should have read up on this place a bit on the way over.

Larima stopped at a door. "Here is your cabin, Mr Rodriguez. Deck 6, cabin 149." He pointed at the large 6-149 on the wall. As he did so, the door opened. "Are you familiar with registering yourself into the room?"

I assured him I knew my way around places like this, thanked him for the help and went inside. Uninvited, he came after me and started pointing out all the facilities and utilities. At first I was annoyed by that but as it turned out, he knew a few things I had never heard of. On an impulse I turned to Larima. "Who do you think killed that man?"

The Razolian's colourful skin turned very dark. "You ask this of me? I don't know this, Mr Rodriguez."

"Sorry to upset you," I said. "It never hurts to ask, does it?"

Larima made a strange movement with his arm again; it was probably a habit of his species. "Our species is not aggressive even though we try to stand up against injustice." He offered to guide me to a restaurant. His words made me notice I could indeed do with some food. "Very well, make sure to remember to collect a 'tow-well from the shelf."

"A what? Why?"

"A piece of fabric, to sit on. For hygienic reasons." Larima pointed. I had been too busy looking around to notice the pile of towels.

"Oh. Of course."

***

By the time I was done eating, I got word that the body had been transferred to a special room in sick bay. Larima guided me there and remained outside while I talked to the doctor.

"The victim is identified as one Kalerem Bodrigon, from the Nergron System. He's from the fifth planet. That is why he looks so very Earth-human." The doctor had already had the man's arrival checked. He'd been on the station for a few months already, working in a warehouse dock to handle incoming goods. Bodrigon didn't seem to be anyone special, just a local worker finding temporary employment here. It was interesting though. The species from the Nergron system were wealthy through all their conquests of neighbouring systems. Why would he come here for such meagre wages?

"The cause of death is apparent. Not many species survive being pierced like that," the doctor said as he pointed at the several openings in the man's chest. "One went straight through the heart."

I asked if he had an idea how the body could have gotten up so high.

"Either he was thrown, or there was a very tall attacker, or he had an accident while zero gravity was on in the chamber. I would rule out the tall attacker, myself. Someone like that would attract a lot of attention."

"Wait. Zero gravity? Miss Moonis never mentioned that."

"Oh, most people who live here know that those chambers function best in zero grav," the doctor enlightened me.

"So could it be he knew how to switch that on, bounced around for fun and got, ehm, unlucky?"

The doctor thought that possible but not probable. "These chambers are secured. People only get in with proper clearance."

I had seen that. On a hunch I asked him if he had noticed anything special around the time the victim had been found. It took him a while before he recalled that one of the technicians, a male Volarian called Brimu, had come to see him with a head wound. The Volarian apparently had bumped his head during his shift.

"That was one day after the find."

I decided to seek out this Brimu. Larima was helpful again. He seemed to know everyone on board.

Brimu was off duty. We found him in a zero gravity game-hall, playing a kind of space volleyball. It looked insanely difficult. Larima explained a few of the rules, but soon lost me.

When Brimu finally left the playing field, I stopped him, introduced myself and asked him about his head wound. The man looked at me, showed me a row of teeth that had to be his smile, and told me he was fine.

"Can you show me where you got it?" I wanted to know if he had been on duty during the murder and if he had seen anything.

Brimu nodded, cast a hostile glance at Larima and led the way to the reaction chambers. He showed me a door identical to the one I had seen before, with Miss Moonis. "I went in here and I bumped my head."

"Can you show me exactly how that happened?" It looked odd since the door was very high.

"No. The chamber is in use." Brimu pointed at a display that showed incomprehensible signs.

"Is there a problem?" Somehow Miss Moonis came from somewhere. "Brimu?"

"Mr Brimu just told me this chamber is in use, Miss Moonis," I said.

"It is, indeed, detective." She looked at the display. "It's been active since almost an hour."

I noticed how Brimu and she exchanged glances. Odd glances. Not the kind you'd expect between two different species. Could they be in love? Was I interrupting something here? There was definitely a tension that felt strange, even for me, and I wasn't familiar with space station dynamics.

"Is there something I can help with?" Miss Moonis looked at me. I forced myself to look at her face.

"Mr Brimu…" I started.

"Just Brimu. We do not entertain your Earth manners of gender designation," Brimu said.

"Okay. Brimu said he bumped his head in the chamber where the body was found. Seeing how high the doors are, I would like to know how that happened."

Miss Moonis laughed. "Surely you don't suggest Brimu has anything to do with the dead person?"

"I'm sorry, Miss Moonis, but anyone is under suspicion at the moment." It was the simple truth. "I heard these chambers have no gravity when they are operational?"

"You heard right. I can show you." Miss Moonis glanced at Brimu once more and walked me to the chamber where the body had been. It wasn't operational yet. "I will set it to a test sequence," she said as we went inside. Brimu closed the door and sealed it. That made sense but at the same time I felt a bit unnerved. What was going to happen now?

"Have you been in zero grav before?" Brimu pointed at a few handles and held on to one himself. I grabbed one too.

"Not often," I admitted.

"Sequence is on," Miss Moonis said, also holding on to a handle. She stood very close to me, making it difficult to focus for a moment. A counter ran down from ten to zero. A soft sound reached my ears and my feet left the floor. "You can let go now, Detective Rodriguez."

I did. Immediately I drifted away from the handle. "How do I get back?" I asked.

She let go too and pushed off towards me. "You don't, unless it's by accident," she explained as she reached me and grabbed by arm. "The trick is to stay calm and push off from a wall while aiming for the handles. It takes some skill, of course." Miss Moonis gently pushed me away. I felt like an idiot, slowly flying through the chamber, rotating around myself with no way to stop myself until I bumped into a wall.

"And that is how I bumped my head," Brimu said, who was still holding on to his handle. He looked at Miss Moonis. "I feel we have to tell the detective."

"Tell me what?" I asked.

"We should," she agreed with the alien.

"Detective... Kalerem Bodrigon came from a planet that was in search of this technology. He tried to bribe Miss Moonis to hand him the information. He also tried that with me. We both denied him the access. He then tried to bribe another technician. His planet in the Nergron System is very wealthy, so when they offer a bribe, it is substantial." Brimu nodded as if he confirmed something to himself.

Miss Moonis took over. "Our colleague was quickly annoyed with the man so he told us he wanted to teach him a lesson. Scare him off. Brimu and I agreed it was a good idea so we made sure this chamber was offline. Our colleague invited Kalerem Bodrigon here, and made him experience zero grav, like you experience now. Then he told the man we will never hand over this technology, because his kind will most certainly use it for warfare."

That made sense. As I said before, the Nergron System was 'famous' for that.

"The person Kalerem Bodrigon panicked and struggled to get away. He managed to reach our colleague and threatened to kill him. Our colleague somehow was able to fight him off and push him away. Which made Kalerem Bodrigon end up on the rods."

I frowned. "Why didn't you say so before? Why didn't you report this immediately?"

Brimu shook his head. "We couldn't. Our colleague left the station on one of the shuttles that pass by once in a while, together with a number of other people who worked here for some time. We wanted to make sure our colleague was far away. By the time you arrived, we were quite certain our colleague was no longer traceable."

I was confused. Why did these people do that? If this had gone down the way they told me, there wasn't much to fear for the man who'd caused Kalerem Bodrigon's death. Although, man? They had only referenced this person as *our colleague* so it could have been a woman too. Strength didn't mean much in zero gravity. Skill counted a lot more. "Is there anything you can tell me about this colleague of yours?"

"No, sir." Miss Moonis shook her head. "We can't." I knew she meant *we won't*.

I realised this was the end of the investigation. Some shuttles could pick up hundreds of people from here in one go. Suppose there had been three shuttles, that could mean three to five hundred people had left. Going in all directions. Finding the person who had done the actual pushing of Kalerem Bodrigon would be close to impossible. "All right. I see your point." I felt weird saying that, hanging upside down in the chamber, looking at Miss Moonis who also somehow hovered somewhere.

"So, what are you going to do, detective?" Brimu was still holding on to his handle.

"Officially I'm not supposed to tell you, but this is one of those situations," I said. "This case will go into the archives as closed without conviction." Like so many others, I added for myself.

Knowing the warring spirit of Bodrigon's people, I thought it good that this spy had been stopped.

Somehow Miss Moonis managed to move close to me. She took my arm, pushed off from the wall and got us close to the handles again. "Be careful, detective," she said. "We'll bring gravity back, so be ready to land on your feet."

Gravity returned slowly. I was slower. I landed on my back. Brimu helped me to my feet and warned me to hold on to the wall for a while. "If you're not used to zero grav, you will feel nauseous for some time," he warned me. He was right.

***

I contacted my superior and reported. "Kalerem Bodrigon came from the Nergron System, tried to bribe people for classified information and became so difficult that someone decided to warn him. Which ended badly. The person doing it left the station a while ago, no identity available."

"So that is all you can report to this?" My boss didn't look too happy but he understood how I couldn't solve this case. Space was huge, murders happened all over the place, and the time for us to get to the crime scene gave killers as much time to get away.

"Indeed."

"Too bad, but it is how it is. You'll have to stay there for a few more days, Rodriguez. Not a high-traffic area where you are. I'll be in touch when I know more about a pick-up time."

"I understand, sir. I'll wait. Maybe some more information will come up." After terminating the connection, I lay down on the bunk. More information… Highly unlikely.

But I'd be spending more time here. With the naked people. Oddly enough, I felt comfortable with that. I even felt comfortable with myself.

Afterword

More about the work of our chosen charity

Médecins Sans Frontières/Doctors Without Borders (MSF) is an independent international humanitarian organisation that delivers emergency medical aid to people affected by armed conflict, epidemics, natural and man-made disasters or exclusion from health care in more than 60 countries. Every year MSF sends around 3,500 doctors, nurses, logisticians, water-and-sanitation experts, administrators and other professionals to work alongside over 35,000 locally hired staff. Together they run medical projects in more than 65 countries around the world.

In emergencies and their aftermath, MSF provides essential healthcare, rehabilitates and runs hospitals and clinics, performs surgery, tackles epidemics, carries out vaccination campaigns, operates feeding centres for malnourished children and offers psychological support.

When needed, MSF also constructs wells and dispenses clean drinking water and distributes materials like blankets, plastic sheeting and other basic necessities.

Through longer-term programmes, MSF treats patients with infectious diseases such as tuberculosis, sleeping sickness and HIV/AIDS and provides medical and psychological care to marginalised groups such as street children.

MSF was founded in 1971 as the first non-governmental organisation to provide both emergency medical assistance and bear witness publicly to the plight of the people it assists. MSF is an international network with branches in 24 countries.

Biographies

Cover art

Fabien Barabé is an artist and cartoonist living in Tantallon, Nova Scotia. Fabien has been a freelance artist since 1993. After discovering he had Squamous Cell Carcinoma cancer in November of 2016, he decided to embrace his passion and create art full-time.

As a member of the Peggy's Cove Area Festival of the Arts for the last nine years, he has fostered some amazing relationships and projects. His art journey led him to the Rainbow Reflections project Body Image for Queer Men in December of 2018, an Anthology of Queer Creators, a collection of short comics by 40-plus creators, which was conceived and edited by Phillip Joy.

He created online cartoons in 2018, *The Secret Life of a Naturist* and *The Spice of Life*, on various social media accounts. His own struggles with cancer along with depression and self-esteem have helped him using narrative medicine as a healing tool. Not only is Fabien an artist, he also poses for various Life Model Art Groups.

Last year he published two queer comics, "With This Ring" and "How it All Began". He was also commissioned to do the cover for Naturist Fiction author René Beauchemin, *René Reinvented.*

When he is not making comics and fine art you can find him spending time with his amazingly supportive husband John.

Websites:

https://fabienbarabeart.wixsite.com/fbart

https://fabienbarabeart.wixsite.com/secretlifecartoon

#

Murder in the Nudist Colony and N-00-D-1 Station

P.Z. Walker. I live in the Netherlands, where my main occupation is in IT (mainly healthcare). After reading a rather terribly made naturist book, I decided I could do this better and so, on a vacation on the Canary Island of Fuerteventura, I started writing my first naturist book.

This has evolved into a few trilogies, a set of 8 (almost 9) in a series called "Naked Crow" and various other publications. Curious? Have a look at **https://zjuzdme.org/pzwalker**!

#

A question of sex

James Gault. After spending ten years in the Czech Republic, James Gault, prize-winning writer born in Scotland, has retired to SW France where he enjoys the sunshine and writes.

In his time James has been an IT specialist, a businessman and a teacher as well as a writer. He has taught English to students of many nationalities. His international outlook on life is reflected in his writing.

He has written six novels, satires, political, psychological, philosophical thrillers and short stories. In 2007, he won the writing prize from the British Czech and Slovak Society for his short story 'Old Honza's Day Out'.

In addition to his books on English Language Teaching, many of his articles and papers on computer technology, language teaching, travel and philosophy have been published in a variety of magazines and journals.

He publishes an on-line literary magazine, *The Voice of Literature,* at **voxlit.co.uk**.

#

Death on the treadmill

Andreas Nudetzki was born in the beautiful city of Aachen (Aix-la-Chapelle, Aken) in Germany. He enjoys the arts, especially music (which he studied) and books. He now lives with his family (six children) in the Lower Rhine area of Germany. Andreas works as a teacher for children with behavioural and emotional needs.

After the discovery of being a nudist as a teenager, he started spending as much time as possible naked at home. After going to saunas and other nudist places, Andreas eventually joined a local nudist club and resort where he made lots of new friends. He is active online on Twitter and the Naturist Christians forum.

Inspired by conversations and observations at the resort, this story is his first publication.

#

Lovely Shade of Death

Jacob Drake has been writing for many years, but only published his first book, *Parallels*, in 2010. He is now the author of various Fantasy, Horror, and Science Fiction books, all available on Amazon.

His greatest problem in writing is not having enough time to write to completion all the stories he gets in his head. "If I wrote constantly until the day I died, I still would never be able to exhaust the imagination that is the source of these stories."

Oddly enough he doesn't like reading horror stories, but enjoys writing them. "Most of what I read in the horror genre doesn't match what I like in these types of stories, so I fulfill my sense of horror by writing my own."

#

Murder at Sunny Green Acres

Robert G. Longpré is a Canadian author who lives on the Canadian prairies. Robert is a retired educator with a background in mental-health counselling. He has been writing since the age of 17. He had his first poems and several essays published in a youth journal in 1967, a series of newspaper editorials in the early seventies, a social history book in 1977, a series of educational articles and chapters in the nineties, and finally his first novel in 2014.

Since that first novel, Robert has published three books of naturist poetry and three naturist novels, with a number of other naturist books in various stages of completion. His books can be found at his website:

https://rglongpre.ca/ and at **https://naturistfiction.org**

#

Murder in a Nudist Colony

Ted Bun. I was born in London and lived most of my life in the south of England. After a lifetime of not knowing what to do, I decided to do something new. I spent three summers running a naturist resort in Portugal. Mrs Bun decided this was our future. After spending two years searching, we found L'Olivette and started offering relaxing holidays in our gîte.

During the long evenings of the quiet season, a novella started to take shape, "The Uncovered Policeman." A light, cosy mystery with a cast of pleasant happy people, with quirky characters. This was my first book, the first in a series of over 12 novellas, and it was published in 2016.

Other titles followed - see the list at **tvhost.co.uk**

#

A Murder in Eden

Gregg B White was born in Napa, California, and as an "Army Brat" (soldier's son) lived all over the United States, moving every 3 years.

In High School in New York in the 1960's I lived an Urban Myth. My swim class was in fact nude. I have always been comfortable and happy to be nude, alone or in company.

The only professional writing I have done is computer code as the Director of R&D for a Los Angeles computer typesetting and printing company. Several years ago, I started a novel but quickly ran out of ideas. When this book's call for stories came out, I had a story idea. I was surprised how quickly I was able to flesh the story out. I have since gone back to my novel and am now over 200 pages. Whether it will ever be published or even good remains to be seen.

I am now retired and live with my wife in Big Bear, a lake and ski resort in the mountains behind San Bernardino, California.

#

What's Inside of People

Matthew McDermott is a technology consultant from Oakville, Ontario, Canada. He is a naturist advocate, member of multiple naturist organizations, and has been an active nudist for 15 years.

Matthew has published in many different genres, both in fiction and non-fiction. His first book on nudism, *How to Take Your Clothes Off*, is available in print and ebook formats. Visit his site **writenude.com** to find a copy, or to read his popular nudism-focused blog. You can follow him on twitter at @canudian1. He also works as a moderator for the highly active nudism subreddit, which you can join at **www.reddit.com/r/nudism**.

#

Murder in the Nudist Colony

Ana Jurić lives in Croatia with her husband and baby. Formerly Annette Wolfe, an American living in western New York, she has been a ballerina, a psychologist and counsellor, adjunct professor of psychology, and librarian. A vacation in Croatia allowed her to meet her future husband, Marko Jurić. (As she usually goes by Anna, she has adopted the Croatian spelling.) As a new naturism enthusiast, she took a chance writing about a murder in a nudist colony. Her other writing has been limited to scholarly articles and a dissertation on bipolar disorder in at-risk teens, but she has dabbled in erotica after hours. "Murder in the Nudist Colony" is her first fiction publication.

#

A deadly afternoon

Stan Muir is the pen name for a naturism-enthusiast French blogger. As such he is as much the figment of the author's imagination as the characters in the story.

Despite a busy professional schedule in the information technology world, Stan never misses an opportunity to write about nudism on his blog **nudeandhappy.com** or come up with a plot where naturism always holds a central or side role.

During the period of writing, he was enjoying all-day nakedness, residing very close to the action in the story. Like all fictitious characters that reach the end of the story alive, Stan reserves the right to reappear in the future in a time and place to be determined by the needs of a story!

#

Pest Control

Will Forest, a nude scribe, grew up in the Mid-Atlantic region of the US and currently lives in Oklahoma. He is the author of two naturist novels to date, with a third in progress. *Co-ed Naked Philosophy* tells the story of a college community who takes off their clothes to take on social conventions, and *Aglow* is a quest to uncover the ancient secrets of El Dorado that can only be understood when naked! He writes about naturism and related topics at **nudescribe.com**, where you can also find *The Nude Adventures of Doff de Chonez*, a serialized naturist adaptation of *Don Quixote*. Forest is one of the contributing writers to **naturistfiction.org**, and he is on Twitter @nudescribe.

#

Revenge for Stan

Hannah Steenbock is a German writer of Speculative Fiction. However, she mostly writes in English, as she loves its quirkiness and tends to think in that language when developing her tales.

She prefers stories with satisfying endings and generally refrains from slaying her characters. That's why she likes to call her tales "feel-good stories".

Sometimes, Hannah branches out into Science Fiction, paranormal or urban fantasy, as well as other genres, as you can see here.

You can read all about her books on her website: **www.hannah-steenbock.de**.

She also sends out a newsletter on every 13th of the month, as she considers that a lucky number. It contains writing news and an exclusive little adventure with her pet dragon Ember.

#

The Anniversary

Robert Payne. Born and raised in Texas where I still live, I am a child of the 50s. My days as an eager participant in the Hippy Culture shaped my personal views while the first true taste of The Arts happened at the same time in college. There I dabbled in renderings on canvas and capturing on film things that prompt me to compose in my mind accompanying stories.

I never thought of myself good enough to really share my drawings nor writings, but chance encounters a few years ago with two wonderful people, a local artist and a nudist author, convinced me to revisit The Arts. So, at the early age of 71, I took a leap of faith and submitted my first completed short story to this collection.

Thank you, Ted Bun, for helping me through edits and rewrites. Thank you to the group for accepting my work. I am honored to become a part of such a wonderful community of storytellers.

#

The Chase

Wallace (Wally) Greensage

Author of New Albion Naturist Books

After a lifetime of lecturing, I retired. Well, kind of semi-retired; I still kept my hand in with a few projects, mainly overseas.

I used this time to pen the first two books of the New Albion trilogy and discovered how much I enjoyed the newfound experience of writing about something I have been passionate about all my adult life.

And then suddenly, I wasn't retired! My new career on my overseas projects took off! Book 3 of the trilogy took forever! It is published now, happily.

I have plenty more naturist tales to impart: short stories, novellas and novels. All I need to do is semi-retire again!

Enjoy naturist fiction! It's easy!

Printed in Great Britain
by Amazon

49362749R00139